ALSO BY

HISTORICAL, BIOGRAPHICAL FICTION

- *The Secret Journals of Adolf Hitler*

  The Anointed - Volume 1

  The Struggle - Volume 2

- Stalin's Sniper: *The War Diary of Roza Shanina*

NONFICTION:

- *Love on Triple W: A Heartbreaking True Story About Love, Betrayal, and Survival*
- *Humorous History: An Illustrated Collection of Wit and Irony from the Past*
- *Tragic History: A Collection of Some of the Most Catastrophic Events in Human History*

DAUGHTER OF PARIS

THE DIARY OF MARIE DUPLESSIS, FRANCE'S MOST CELEBRATED COURTESAN

A. G. MOGAN

WITH ANNOTATIONS BY HER CLOSEST FRIEND, ROMAIN VIENNE

CONTENTS

DISCLAIMER

Marie Duplessis did not keep a diary. Except for that, this story is based on actual events. All characters have existed in real life. The majority of the events in this book are described as closely as possible to the real life events, but some incidents and timelines have been changed for dramatic purposes.

To my sister

"I lie to keep my teeth white."

— MARIE DUPLESSIS

FOREWORD

It would be a grave injustice to judge the conduct of Marie Duplessis—born Alphonsine Plessis—with the inexorable logic of cold and ruthless reason, without considering facts beyond her control, facts of revolting brutality, of which she was the victim. Publishing her diary is not meant to take the form of an excuse for the life she led, nor is it a justification of her choices, but rather a simple clarification of both. Her forgiveness through confessing, if you may.

I had been there, by her side, almost the entirety of her life. When I hadn't, because of reasons beyond my control, she willingly filled in the gaps with sad or joyful disclosure. I knew her better than anyone she ever met, being the only person who knew everything about her anguished childhood, one which can only be described as an unbelievable contest of deplorable circumstances.

An implacable fatality weighed on Marie from the day of her birth. The evil done to her was irreparable. In vain she tried, without proper direction and effective protection, to fight against her destiny. In vain she exhausted her strength and courage fighting the dizzying power of the temptations that finally crushed her will.

But, alas! You, my friends, be the judges.

The Marie I knew and loved was not the Marie who seduced and beguiled. To me, as her friend, Marie Duplessis was no less than the very incarnation of the poet's words:

> *Flowers on the forehead*
> *Mud on the feet*
> *Hate in the heart*

Romain Vienne
Normandy, January 1870

THE DIARY OF MARIE DUPLESSIS

I have loved sincerely, but no one ever returned my love. That is the real horror of my life.

— FEBRUARY 25TH, 1845

CHAPTER 1

LA TROUILLÈRE, FRANCE, NOVEMBER 1827

*J*am afraid. So very afraid. From the moment I heard Marie-Françoise say this morning, "The evil sorcerer is coming again today. If only the earth would swallow him on his way here." my heart has trembled within my small body. I know, of course, who the evil sorcerer is. My father. The brute of all brutes.

Marie-Françoise is Mother's aunt. Together with her husband Louis, they took us in, my eight-year-old sister, Delphine and I, when Mother abandoned us to go into hiding—from the brute.

I do not remember Mother at all, as I was only eleven months old when she left us with her relatives in La Trouillère, a hamlet a few miles north of Nonant—my place of birth—in the Normandy region of northwestern France. I was just a bundle of coos and happiness, like any other infant, with eyes always opened wide to receive the wonders of the new and fascinating world she had entered. I am almost four now and still waiting for those wonders to occur.

This isn't to say that I have lived as a battered child. Not by far. I am as happy as a child who knew so little can be. And if not for these frightening visits by Father, I would have no worries at all upon my little shoulders.

But today is one of those days I dread.

I hide behind the curtain cutting our large earthen-floored room in two. On one side is the kitchen and on the other, the family bedroom. My young unspoiled heart continues to throb at a maddening speed. And when the sound of my father's boots hitting the earthen-floored gets louder and louder and closer and closer, I struggle not to fall to the floor unconscious.

"Got you!" he barks, sweeping the curtain aside. A small scream escapes my lips as I pull back, now exposed to him. He goes down in one knee and pinches my cheek with all the force his calloused peasant hand can muster.

"Aren't you going to give your father a kiss?" he asks, tapping his cheek with his forefinger.

I make no answer.

"Alphonsine, Alphonsine..." he continues, shaking his head in disparagement. "A mucky little girl, aren't you? You smell like a pig. Have you been playing in the stables again?" His questions tumble out of his mouth in waves of disgust, each more frightening than the last.

I open my mouth, but no sound comes out. All I can do is remain stationary and endure the pain he continues to inflict on my cheek.

He goes on, seething. "I gather you're not only filthy, but simple, too. Standing there with that marble face of yours... just like your mother. A stupid whore, who gave vent to two useless daughters. That wasn't what I signed up for!"

I suddenly feel guilty. Of what, I am not sure.

He screws his face into a scowl and jumps to his feet. I look up to see his nostrils flaring from the evil mood possessing him. He rakes his thick dark hair with stiffened fingers, then reaches into a pocket.

"Here," he says, throwing a coin at my feet, "go wash yourself, birdbrain. Off with you!"

I snatch up the coin and run from the room as fast as my trembling legs allow. The more distance I put between me and my father, the less the clawing feeling in my stomach bothers me. It's like the most terrible earthquake has passed and I can finally breathe again.

I run to the stables, where I know Father would never come. Dropping onto a great sheaf of straw, I inspect both sides of the golden coin. One side shows the King's head, thrown into bold relief. Gliding my fingertip over it, a sigh escapes my lips. *The same coin he gave me the last time he came, which can't really buy anything.* I throw it to the muddy dirt floor.

As my heart settles to a normal speed, I gather the courage to think of him. Except for his terrifying words and gaze, and the pain he inflicts on my cheek every time he comes to visit, he's never beat me the way he has my sister. Maybe my crude age is what saves me. Or maybe it's our physical resemblance. I like to think that despite his aggressive attitude he still has a soft spot for me in his heart. After all, I was born on his birthday, and nothing in this world works better to bring people together than a shared event.

But Delphine, unlike me, had been thrashed by him for most of her life. Well, at least until Mother took us away from him, and placed us with her relatives. I once heard Marie-Françoise say, a few years ago, that a roofer passing by my parents' house heard a child screaming and looked through the window. He saw Father beating his terrified little girl. *The scene was taken out of a nightmare,* the roofer had said, when he reported Father to his landlord.

Apparently, the sensitive landlord wanted nothing of that, so they were all kicked out of the house. Who knows what devilry my sister had done to bring about Father's wrath?

ROMAIN VIENNE

Poor little Alphonsine... She's always searched for reasons to justify her father's bedeviled actions. It is as if in finding them, she could have put her mind at ease and felt less guilty about loving her father. But who's to judge a poor wretched little soul who'd cling to anything, good or bad, just to give herself, if only imaginarily, a sense of belonging?

The story Alphonsine heard, about her father Marin Plessis beating his little daughter, is correct. What is not correct, of course, is her reasoning. Her father didn't need any justifiable impulses from outside of himself to behave like that, because he was a brute when he came out of his mother's womb. The entire village was terrified of him, even more than they were of the police or the king. A common belief was also held that nothing could touch him as long as he was hand in glove with the Devil. By this token, his nickname was born: *The Evil Sorcerer*.

He beat his wife on their wedding day and almost every day since then. And one would rarely see him sober. On the day his wife gave birth to Alphonsine's elder sister Delphine, he thrashed her unconscious for failing to give him a son, then left her.

The poor young wife took her infant in her arms and went about the village to beg for food. The brute returned soon enough, and after a short, sweet reconciliation, the wife found herself pregnant again. Nine months later, on a cold January day, she brought Alphonsine into the world. A healthy beautiful baby, with skin as white as milk and eyes as dark as the night sky. Her only fault? She was a girl. The brute packed his bags once more and again abandoned his family.

Several months later, less than two weeks before Alphonsine's first birthday, he returned. He wasn't laden with gifts for his youngest's birthday, as one might expect, but rather was brimming with anger and stinking of alcohol. On that very day, he set the house on fire and dragged his wife toward the flaming hearth. Only God and His love for her saved the poor wife from certain death by sending a messenger, a young strong lad, to their door. On hearing the poor woman's soul-cringing cries, he flung open the door and grabbed the brute with a grip that almost pulverized his bones. Thus, she was saved.

MARIE DUPLESSIS

Only when I see dusk settling on the roof of our house do I get the courage to come out of the barn. Almost at the same moment, I hear Marie-Françoise calling my name as she usually does when our dinner is ready. I eat my galettes and drink my milk in silence, my thoughts still lingering on Father's frightening visit. My aunt is also silent and barely touches her food.

However, Delphine greedily munches her galettes, licks her fingers, then asks for more. Though older than I, she always seems disconnected, oblivious to what goes on in our house.

After dinner, Marie-Françoise tucks us in our beds, but no matter how hard I try to keep my eyelids shut, sleep does not come to me. Quitting my iron-frame bed, I tiptoe to my aunt's bed and swiftly slip under the linens.

"Alphonsine! What are you doing? Go back to bed!" my aunt chides. "It's almost eleven."

"Pray, tell me again about her. Tell me more about my

mother!" I beg, stretching to caress her face. She lets out a deep, prolonged sigh, then takes me in her arms. With yet another sigh, she begins.

"Your mother was the most beautiful girl in our hamlet. It was hard for the people not to turn their heads for a second look when she passed by. She was also intelligent ... and very loved. She grew up in the care of a countess, Madame du Hays, in their castle in Saint-Germain-de-Clairefeuille, not far from here."

"I know the castle, Aunty!" I boast.

"I know you do, butter cheeks. But there is a secret you *don't* know."

"What secret?" I prop up on one elbow, lest I miss some important detail.

"Well, such beauty your mother had, with such soulful eyes and plaintive expression, that people began to think she was a saint. They said she bore the likeness of the Virgin Mary. Some still say that the church in Saint-Germain has a stained-glass window in her image. A soulful-eyed Virgin modeled on your mother."

My heart throbbed at the thought of seeing her. I could run to the church one day, just to look at her.

"So, little one, if you ever find yourself in need to see your mother, go to Saint-Germain's little church," she says, as if hearing my thoughts. She sighs again, but this time her sigh comes from a different place. A clouded place.

"Then, she fell in love. ... with handsome Marin Plessis," she says, as if speaking to herself or castigating Mother's destiny. "It was the darkest hour of her life. In barely three years she became unrecognizable. I am still haunted by her image as she stood in the doorway, holding you with one hand and your sister with the other. I will never be quite able to forget her grief-stricken face and the sorrow in her voice as she kissed you goodbye." A warm tear fell from her eyes onto my face.

"Then what happened to her?"

"Well, then she went into hiding. You father threatened to kill her; if ever he discovered her hideaway. For weeks she hid in a neighboring barn, mingling with chickens and their manure. But she was soon spotted by a local gossip and had to leave – or else. She then hid at a farm, like a common criminal on the run. Thank the heavens her benefactress came to her aid, finding employment for your mother with a rich Englishwoman. So, in less than a week your mother was carried by stagecoach to Paris to become a lady's maid. She has been there ever since."

"Paris?" I ask, my ears pricking up.

"Yes, butter cheeks."

"Do tell me more about Paris!" With the thought of the capital entering my little head, a sudden euphoric sensation possesses me, and I begin fidgeting. "Pray, do tell!" I insist, nudging Marie-Françoise in the ribs.

"Had I been there even once, I would have known how to satisfy your endearing curiosity, my little one. But I have never set foot outside La Trouillère. All I know is dirt and chickens and harvesting buckwheat."

"Please, Marie-Françoise! You must have heard something!"

"Well, I know but one thing of that place, so you should probably know it as well. It is the incarnation of both good and evil, with the latter measuring far greater."

It is my turn to sigh, which makes Marie-Françoise titter. "Now, go to your bed. Time to sleep. We shall talk more about this tomorrow."

But there shall be no more talks about enthralling and equally frightening Paris. In the morning, my sister's ragged sobs startle me awake. I rub my sleepy eyes vigorously, so as to determine what had thrown my sister into such a distressing fit.

"They're separating us!" she cries upon seeing me awake.

"What?"

"He'll take you away from here! He just came! For you!" she shouts.

"What are you saying, Delphine? Who's here?" I ask, cowering at the head of the bed.

But I can no longer hear her answers. Whether that is because her hysterical cry prevents me from comprehending her words or because the image of Father just entered my head, I do not know. My eyes are suddenly wide open. My heart begins to pace again at an uncomfortable speed. I look at my little palms and see beads of sweat rolling down onto the sheets. I think I am about to faint. Or die!

Muffled noises coming from beyond the curtain steal my attention from the frightening feeling spreading rapidly through my chest.

"Is she awake?" I hear an unfamiliar masculine voice. Almost instantly, an equally unfamiliar face shows itself from behind the curtain. A tall man with peasant-like features, sun-burned skin and candid eyes, smiles at us. That causes my sister to cease sobbing, but increases my terror.

"My poor little thing!" I hear Marie-Françoise saying as she rushes from behind the stranger to my bed. "Don't cry, my angel," she begs, throwing her arms about my neck. "Please forgive me. I can no longer...we can no longer afford to keep you," she whispers in my ear. "My cousin here will take you into his family." She points at the stranger still standing and smiling in front of my bed.

"No!" I shout.

"You saw this coming, haven't you?" she says, nodding her head as if to make me believe I should understand all of this. But I don't understand. "You saw our empty dinner table, haven't you? And you saw my husband can no longer—"

"No!" I shout again, and jumping from my bed, I run toward the door. But the stranger grabs me by my waist and with a swift movement raises me in his arms. I kick and hit him in the face with my little fists. Moaning, I struggle to release myself from his grasp, but to no avail.

The stranger bows to Marie-Françoise and with me in his arms, turns on his heels and exits our house.

"My wife will take good care of you, you shall see," he tells me.

"Nooo! I hate you! Let me go! Let go of me!" I howl, as he carries me further and further away from the house. Now I am struggling with a force I never knew existed in me. It is as if my tortured spirit grew wings big enough to reach the Heavens. I hit his face harder and harder and bite his upper arms until my teeth hurt. He moans and for an instant loosens his grip. I fall onto the ground and begin running on all fours toward my sister, who's now sitting in the doorway. She extends her arms forward to receive me with sudden hope in her eyes, mingled with her tears. The sight breaks my soul in a million little pieces. The man grabs my ankles and again begins dragging me further and further away from her.

"Please!" I scream. "Don't let me go! Don't send me away! I beg of you!"

"Forgive us, child!" shouts Marie-Françoise.

"I shall be good! I shall not ask for food! Don't leave me! Don't let him take me! Delphine!" I continue screaming, as bitter tears wet my burning cheeks. My sister's hands are still outstretched to receive me, but I know I will never reach them. The man continues to drag me, causing dust to raise and obstruct my view.

"Delphine! Delphine?"

The man raises me in his arms, clamping me again in his suffocating embrace. As he carries me off, my sister's voice becomes less and less audible. And if that weren't enough, the tall barn, which served many times as my hiding place, now suddenly stands between me and my sister.

"I can't see her! I can't see her! Let go of me!"

The barn becomes smaller and smaller. It seems to float, then change shapes, elongating then contracting, and finally flowing like liquid on the ground toward me. All becomes dark and quiet around me, and I unwillingly relinquish my strength to the arms of the stranger who's taking me away forever.

CHAPTER 2

LA CORBETTE, FRANCE, JULY 1830

The trauma my fragile soul felt when separated from Delphine and Marie-Françoise still lingers. It matters not that almost three years have passed since that horrible day. It still feels as if it happened yesterday. That Marie-Françoise was only a distant relative does not matter either, for she was the only mother I ever knew.

The new home I was taken to on that day is in La Corbette—only a short mile from the place I was constrained to desert. A short walking distance that my sister and I would take turns walking almost every day to be together. So, the split shouldn't have been felt too deeply, but it was and still is. Every now and then my dreams are haunted by that terrible vision of my sister's outstretched arms, the hope I saw in her eyes, which said that maybe, in a stroke of divine indulgence, we would be permitted to remain together. That maybe our combined tears would soften the hearts of the adults who were committing such a horrible injustice.

But tears do not work like that in this world. This was my first adult realization. The second was that no child should meet their adulthood in such terrible a manner. That day, I left half of me behind with my sister. Since that day, gradually and almost imperceptibly at first, a predisposition toward brooding and melancholy started to grow inside me. It matters not how many kind people surround me—my soul still feels lonely.

And kind people are always around me...

Jean-François Boisard, the man with sun-burned skin, who took me into his house, is very kind. His features seem always to be smiling, and his tender, fatherly embraces are soothing to the core. By day he works as a clogmaker and roadsman and in evenings, he turns into a most marvelous storyteller, filling my and his son's little heads with stories about his wooden shoes, and the people who buy them. He isn't always successful in his trade and that often reflects on our dinner table. Now and then, there come evenings where his stories must make up for our grumbling stomachs. With Jean-François, I feel for the first time in my life how strangely pleasant it is to have a father. A present, joyful father.

And if Jean-François is kind, his wife Agathe is the milk of human kindness. With her plump cheeks and stocky arms, one couldn't even imagine her otherwise. Is it just my crude imagination or is there always an association between chubby people and kindness? It must be so; my short experience stands as witness. In contrast, Father, though handsome, resembles a bean stalk, and his well-earned nickname describes his personality perfectly.

And then there is their son, seven-year-old Roch, my own age exactly and a protective brother who steps between me and Father, whenever the latter visits.

Yes, Father visits me here, but merely to inflict pain in my checks and heart. He always promises money to Agathe to assist her with my raising, but except for the useless coins he throws at my feet, his promises amount to nothing.

About this time I notice a new frightening thing in him. It is a mischievous, wicked look he fastens on me for a long moment. I don't yet know how to describe it, but it is very unsettling.

THIS DAY IN LATE JULY, however, is affected by things seemingly far more meaningful and troublesome than my own little worries. And it only seems so due to the general unrest in our hamlet, as well as Agathe's prayers, intensifying.

"It's chaos! All around chaos! Paris is swallowed by revolution! May God protect our King!" cries Agathe upon my inquiries. "Pray, daughter! Pray!" she demands, pulling me down to my knees and motioning for me to join her in her prayers. I obey and bringing my hands together I begin to pray—for the king and for Paris.

But to me it doesn't really mean anything.

Or it means as much as it would for any other seven-year-old who merely absorbs the fears of the adults, without really knowing what they fear. The fact that the Revolution overthrows our king, Charles X, and places Louis-Philippe d'Orléans on the throne doesn't mean much either. However, it does grab and hold my fancy to such a degree that the memory of it stays close to my heart for the rest of my days.

The dethroned king is ordered into exile.

A week later on August 7, His Majesty, followed by his retinue, enters our little hamlet for a night's stay on his way to Great Britain.

The morning after the King's arrival, I jerk awake earlier than usual. Jumping out of bed and into my clogs, I run to the main street to watch the departure of our former king and his court. Roch follows behind, dragging his sleepy body and mumbling unintelligible things.

When we reach the main road, a double row of people already flanks it. I recognize only few, so the rest must have come from neighboring hamlets. Some watch with eyes wide and mouths open, while others cheer, whistle, and wave. Young mothers, holding their infants at their breasts, arrive in stagecoaches or on foot, some wearing no shoes. Men of all ages accompany them and I am struck by the discrepancy in their attire. It seems that everyone, poor or rich, wants to catch a glimpse of the spectacle taking place on this otherwise uneventful day, to be part of what seems to be a historically meaningful occasion.

I elbow my way through the people to get closer to the road. When I finally reach it, the pageantry unfolding before my eyes strikes me with the force of a thousand thunderstorms. I experience one of those moments in which you can neither speak nor move, yet you know at once that something inside you moves, changing you forever.

My gaze falls first on the King's coach. Eight majestic horses draw it toward where I stand. Four are black and four are white with light brown manes. They shake their heads; neighing, snorting, and flaring their large nostrils. Their great hooves strike the road, raising clouds of dust. As they pass by, I look up at them in awe, as if they've just descended from the heavens or charged out from the fairy tales Marie-Françoise used to tell to me before bed time.

I then shift my gaze from the horses to the king's coach. Its gold facing sparkles in the rising midsummer sun, making it appear enchanted. Paintings of chubby little angels decorate the doors, while large golden statues of angels blowing trumpets adorn the rooftop. Except for the glass windows, everything is sculpted and embroidered in gold. It was as if God himself decided to take a ride through our poor little hamlet.

Through those spotless glass windows, I see the king. His eyes are fastened on the people watching him, but he seems to be looking through us, into a faraway distance. I glimpse sadness on his face just before he is beyond view, sitting inside his gilded cage that carries him into exile.

Several carriages follow the king's coach carrying children, noble women and men, servants, escorting guards, and policemen. Of them all, the ladies in their smart sumptuous dresses and tall wigs, bedecked in jewelry, are the most spellbinding. Tears gather in my eyes, and I instinctively look down at my wooden shoes. Even though they made me the happiest girl alive when gifted to me by the kind, generous Jean-François, I suddenly hate them. For an instant, I truly hate them like the plague.

As the cortege procession ends with the wagons loaded with luggage, furniture and silver, I start to run behind it. Several other children follow suit, running alongside me. They are cheering and clapping as they try to climb on the bales of hay that serve as fodder for those magnificent horses.

I am the only one sobbing.

The rising dust and my own panting suddenly make a stand against me and I stop. Sitting on the ground I continue to gaze at the cortege until it becomes a dwindling dot swallowed by the horizon.

So, this is Paris!

I make an effort to cast away my wistful feelings.

Gold, and wigs laden with flowers, huge crinolines, and spellbinding jewelry! Marie-Françoise was wrong saying it's more evil than good! So very wrong! Maybe Mother could take me, make me her daughter again! A Paris daughter! And I could watch carriages driving by every day or learn how to ride horses and make my own dresses of silk and lace and velvet! White! I should like to wear white! We never wear white in the countryside. It gets dirty too quickly. Ah! White! What a marvelous contrast with my long dark hair!

I suddenly see myself riding magnificent horses and trying on the most splendid outfits, like those worn by the ladies in the carriages. If this comes from a place in my highly impressionable imagination or is simply my newest, most ardent dream, I do not know. What I do know is that, for a moment, when blinded by the sun reflecting from that gilded coach, I wasn't the poor clog-wearing peasant girl. And like a magic wand, today's procession had transported and transformed me irrevocably and forever.

In the following month comes the Saint-Mathieu fair, with its air of festivity engaging every soul in our hamlet. Having little money, all I can do is watch young girls buying dainty little bonnets, ribbons, shawls, and colored fabrics for their new dresses. The only thing the coins Father gave me, long saved in a jar, can purchase is getting my ears pierced. And even though the pain is terrible and I must bite my fingers to keep from screaming, this is the last happy memory of my childhood.

After covering my earlobes as best as I can to avoid Agathe's scolding, I return home with Roch and we are greeted by an uncomfortable silence. Roch gives me a puzzled, worried look as muffled words and sobs are heard coming from our bedroom. We run toward it and fling the door open. A heavy air of sadness hits us in the face, but it's nothing compared to the haunting, teary eyes of my sister.

"Delphine!" I exclaim, and run to embrace her. She lets go of Agathe and extends her arms to me, bringing back painful memories.

"Oh, Alphonsine!" she moans, shaking her head as if to shake off the thoughts tormenting her. "Oh, my little sister!"

"What is the matter?" Her strange behavior and torment start grasping at me and the unsettling fear I know too well makes its way into my chest. "Tell me! What is the matter?" I demand again, shaking her arms.

"Our mother!" She sobs freely now and wrenches her hands from my grasp to cover her face. Her crying verges on hysteria now and I shift my gaze to Agathe, who sits quietly next to my sister.

"I am so sorry, daughter...she...she passed away...a few days ago...from—"

I no longer hear her voice. My mind takes me to a most desolate place where, to my shame, my first thought is as selfish as those female cuckoos placing their eggs in the nests of other birds, and then abandoning them. In the midst of tragedy, my first thought is that of disappointment. *Who will take me to Paris now? How will I ever be able to do all those marvelous things?*

"I am with you both. And I will never abandon you," Agathe says.

"How did you find out? About Mother?" I ask, still hopeful that it is a mistake, a prank played by an evil mind. Maybe, Father's mind.

"Madame du Hays, the countess who raised her, told your sister. She ran to her with the terrible news as soon as she heard word of it. Oh, how beautiful she was!" laments Agathe, rubbing my sister's back and swaying back and forth.

"So, it is really true then? My beautiful mother is dead?"

"What say you? This isn't a matter for joking around," she replies, a hint of scold in her voice. Then, she casts her gaze into an unknown distance. "Our beautiful Marie! You know...she attended a special mass in the presence of the royal family! And the king had eyes only for her...only for her! And now this! Ah, the poor creature! What a tragic existence!"

Agathe's sorrowful words and my sister's sobs finally penetrate my heart, and I begin to weep for the mother I never knew. I cry for my sister's loss and for my own little soul that suddenly feels lonelier than ever.

Gathering us to her chest, Agathe promises again she will never abandon us. Her words feel like a safe haven that Mother's death and Father's harrowing visits could never destroy.

YET, little do I know that I would see Mother at one point. Not as flesh and blood, as God had made her, but rather as an angelic being in the dainty little church in Saint-Germain. She cast a rainbow over my pretty head from her high place on the church wall.

I am twelve then, and after attending the small girls' school in Saint-Germain-de-Clairefeuille, I am taken to the town's church for my First Communion. A priest asks for my sins, and then serves me a spoon of red wine and a small piece of bread. "The blood and body of Christ," he says, and then gives me a small prayer book along with his command to read it every morning and night.

As I exit the church, I turn to look at the stained-glass window adorned with mother's angelic figure. She is smiling at me and her slender, delicate hands seem to be calling me to her embrace.

"I will never abandon you, my dear child," I hear, as if in a daydream. A beam of sun reflects from the window where she hovers, which sends little colored lights to dance over my dress.

However, it seems Life decides to make a mockery of

me. And so, only a few days later, I learn that Mother's words are empty. Just as children's tears leave no mark on the hearts of adults, adults' promises turn out to be as vain and deceptive as those who articulate them.

With the arrival of a baby daughter to complete the household of the Boisards there is no place left for me. With tears in her eyes, Agathe informs me that, from now on, I will have to fend for myself. She can still offer me a bed at night, she says, but the days belong to me alone to shift for my own survival.

Deserted by Mother, passed on by Marie-Françoise and abandoned by Agathe, I am left to the mercy of hamlet strangers to feed my stomach and my starving heart.

CHAPTER 3

The end of October 1836 is very rainy. For many days now, the salty water from above has fallen upon my bare head. If it continues, my dark locks will soon turn white for good. Already my skin is paler and I am not sure if it's due to the absence of the sun or the lack of food.

The Saint-Mathieu fair has just ended. While it lasted, I joined the stray dogs in begging for food from the tens of merchants. It was...well, if not a downright happy time, at least a plentiful one. The rainy days wrought havoc on any hopes for bountiful visitors to the fair, which allowed for a largess of scraps for me to fill my grumbling stomach and share with the dogs. But now the plentiful days are gone and I must again rely on villagers or farmers to help me survive.

I gather my dress in my hands to squeeze the water from it. I also gather all the courage I can muster to knock on a distant neighbors door. With luck, they may not know me, which will save me from the shame and embarrassment that come with begging. Though I am not the only child in our hamlet who begs for food, I am certainly the most embarrassed one.

On my third knock, an elderly man wearing a funny white cap pops his head out from behind the tall wooden door.

"What do you want?" he asks peevishly.

I clear my throat. "Most esteemed gentleman, could you please spare a bowl of soup or a slice of bread? I shall forever be in your debt."

"You soiled tramps!" he bellows. "Always knocking on my door! How many of you are there? Coming here with that lice-infested hair! God knows what other diseases you carry on you!"

"The only disease I carry on my person, dear sir, is my constant hunger. Please, spare—"

"Off with you, you dirty vagabond!" he shouts, shuffling toward me, brandishing his fist in the air. I spin away, keeping my eyes on his nearing fist. "Come again and I shall break your legs from the knees!"

I sprint away, running until my legs hurt. My heart hurts too, for it cannot quite grasp the coldness of such grown-ups. Surely, their hearts must be frozen. *Is it age that does that to people?* I ponder the question as I sit on a rock near a chicken farm to rest my sore legs. *I should hate to turn out like them. No. Never. No matter how many children will knock on my door, I vow that I will feed them all.*

My thoughts pause as I look down on my clogs. They are now huge and misshapen due to the recent rains. I am sad to see this drastic change and sadder still that they no longer fit me. I must do without them from now on.

"Marcel..." A voice pushes into the moment, followed by a tap on my shoulder that startles me and I jump to my feet.

A sinewy lad about my age, red in the cheeks and smelling of chicken manure, smiles at me. I frown in return.

"That's my name ... Marcel. What's yours?"

"Ah, you—you gave me such a turn!"

He chuckles. "Well? What is it?"

"None of your concern," I say, still possessed by the jolt of his intrusion. However, his candid smile and messy blonde hair tell me I shouldn't be afraid. Nobody has spoken to me in days. The idea of him being pleased with my company is more startling than his intrusion.

"I am a farmhand here." He points at the huge farmhouse behind us. "I feed the chickens and collect their eggs every morning."

'That explains your smell," I say, then immediately regret it. I search his eyes for a telltale sign of hurt, but only find light and sympathy in them.

"You're a tough one, aren't you?" His tone is teasing, but not cruel.

"I don't know."

"Tough but pretty," he adds and we both go red in the cheeks. "Where do you live?"

"Here and there and...everywhere..."

"Secretive, too?"

"More hungry than secretive."

"So then, you're an orphan?"

"You could say that."

His expression turns clouded and he kneads his chin.

"Can you wait here?"

"I could ... but for how long?" My question goes unanswered as he's already sprinting toward the farmhouse. I sit on the rock and look again at my clogs. It hurts to part with them, but with swift kicks, I send them flying in the air. Ah, the joy! The freedom! I sink my sore feet in a puddle, smiling at the wave of relief it brings. It is my first moment of rest in weeks and the first moment I am thankful for the rain.

Heavy panting interrupts my small bliss and I turn to see Marcel hurrying toward me. He is loaded down with food: bread and boiled eggs. A bottle of beer peeks from under one arm.

"Here!" he says in one final, panting breath. He shoves the goods in the pockets of my dress, and then nearly shouts, "Run – before they catch us!"

I stare at him, mute and unmoving, only my grateful look and my tears do justice to this lad's generosity.

"Run, I say!" He's shouting now, pushing my shoulders.

I do as he says and take off running. Still within a hearing distance, I stop and turn.

"Alphonsine!" I shout. "My name is Alphonsine!"

He bows low as I race away.

WITH THE FOOD handsome Marcel has stolen for me, I go sans souci for almost a week. Not to say that I fall asleep at night with a full stomach. A beggar knows how to portion food to last as long as possible. One boiled egg today, another tomorrow and yet another the next day. Not thriving but not dying either.

As for sleep, once the rain passes, I prefer to spend my nights under the starry sky.

Returning to Agathe's home to sleep is my last solution, as sadness grips my heart each time I go there. Seeing her doting on her little daughter with all the love of a besotted mother makes me painfully aware of the absence of my own. I experience the loss of her protection and love all over again, along with the surety that I will always be denied the warm feeling of love from others, a home of my own or even a proper bed. I must also struggle with my hate of the little one, a hate so intense that it scares the wits out of me.

But here, under the starry sky, I can dream. I dream of the world beyond this little hamlet. I dream of splendid dinners served to me by kind affectionate people. And, I dream of Marcel. His tousled blond locks and bright blue eyes have entered my head more than once. And even though the image of his beautiful smile makes me blush, even in pitch black darkness, I relish the thoughts of him and fall asleep oblivious to the cold, damp earth beneath me or the bugs and rats roaming nearby.

With my food stash quickly diminishing, my only choice is to resume my begging practice. And about this time, I start making friends. Older friends, mind you, who covet being in my presence. They are the land workers and farmhands who, by day, inhabit the same fields that I do. This coveting is enough to make a person—any person, regardless of one's look or character—agreeable to me, so I allow them things that would otherwise make me balk and run away. But a beggar has no luxury in choosing friends. A beggar accepts whichever characters are willing to show them some kindness and attention, and of course, a warm meal now and then. A beggar is chosen rather than doing the choosing.

So, I begin to follow my new friends like the stray, loyal dog that I am.

In such company, my beautiful dream of Paris, with its riches, splendor and gaiety, begins to fade. I am more and more accustomed to my ripped clothes, bare feet, and empty stomach. Soon there are songs, always bawdy and explicit, that introduce me to a world I never knew existed, nor ever wanted to experience, including the uncomfortable stares and improper touches of my new friends. But, as the saying goes, we become our surroundings.

This formative period of my life was so baleful to my sensitive nature I wish it could be erased from my memory. I should also like to let others pass the blame and judgement, if ever those two would be sought.

There comes a moment though, when even a beggar can no longer close her eyes to what is going on.

At the end of November, I set my eyes—or should I say, stomach—on a harvester carrying a big bag made from rabbit skins.

"Is it bread you carry in that hefty bag?" I dare to ask as he approaches me.

The stranger halts mid-step. "What's it to you?"

"I am hungry, Monsieur."

He measures me up from head to toe, his gaze pausing on places I know it shouldn't, the same wicked, unsettling stare I received from my worker friends. The same gaze I received from Father, the last time he visited me.

"Are you now?" He raises his already arched eyebrow.

"Very much so."

"Well, I might carry bread, or I might not. That depends..." he says, showing his ivories, which are not ivory at all, but crooked, rotten, brown teeth.

"On what?" I ask half-puzzled, half-aware.

"Come here," he demands, as he squats. I hesitate, then move a step nearer. "Closer, closer." He urges me forward with effusive gestures, then says, "Depends on whether you are willing to pay for it or not."

"I have no money."

"That's quite alright. You can pay me with something else."

"I don't have any possessions, Monsieur."

"Yes, you do..." His grin turns to a leer as the back of his hand travels up my inner thigh. I now fully understand what he wants and take a step back, but the lout grabs my dress with one hand and pinches my private part with the other.

"You can pay me with this!" he sneers.

I begin screaming as loud as my lungs allow me. Struggling to wrench myself free of his hold, I bite his hands and fingers until I taste warm sour blood in my mouth. The ogre groans and hits me across the face with his heavy palm. That throws me to the ground, face down.

"Bloody cunt!" he seethes and readies to grab me again. But I am already on my feet running as if there's no tomorrow. Behind me, he gives full vent to an assortment of words I would never attempt to reproduce.

The fright and misery I felt after this terrible encounter forces me to make use of my last resolution and return to Agathe's home.

All that night, turbulent thoughts gather about me like dark threatening clouds.

So, there are other ways to acquire food besides using money or begging. Has a girl other options at her disposal?

There's no one still awake to provide an answer; however, I do sense answers within me. I also sense something else, a feeling as frightful and devastating as the encounter with the ogre. Hope. I sense hope. And it feels warm. After many months of rain soaking my feet, hope feels warm. My crude mind and immature nature is blissfully unaware of the dangers hope brings along with it.

Romain Vienne

Alphonsine was only twelve years old when the

encounter with the ogre happened and it was not by any means an isolated incident. Child abuse in the countryside was rampant in those days and for some hypocritical reason, girls Alphonsine's age weren't regarded as children. In an age that deemed a twenty-year-old young woman a spinster, it's not surprising that this was an accepted perception. Consider that in this year alone almost one thousand children were abandoned in our region and it becomes easy to imagine what was happening to those unfortunate little wretches. Poor Alphonsine...her association with those drunken brutes, and their uncontrolled cravings, truly proved to be her undoing. She had understood. She had seen. Her education in vice had begun.

MARIE DUPLESSIS

In the morning, before setting out for my usual day, I make a mistake. I recount everything to Agathe. Every detail about my whereabouts, about Marcel, my friends, and the ogre. I even sing a lewd song that my friends have taught me, upon her request.

At once, she grabs my hand and drags me to and along the street.

Our destination? Saint-Germain-de-Clairefeuille. Father's lodgings.

I suddenly realize my mistake. And just as suddenly, I come to a new realization. Not only can adults not be influenced by tears, but they also cannot be trusted. I must think twice before opening my mouth.

As Agathe's knocks furiously on the door to Father's lodgings, I make a silent vow to be as silent as a grave and as cold as a stone.

Father opens the door to let us in. There is but one room, I notice, containing his bed, a table, and some chairs.

"She's fallen! Prey!" Agathe's voice echoes along Father's empty walls. "To the perverts! To the charlatans! To her own budding desires! She'll end up in a pit!"

Father nears his table near the window and sits, seemingly pondering Agathe's words, his fingers ruffling his unwashed hair. I am happy he does not look at me. I use this rare moment of invisibility to analyze him, analyze his lodgings. My immediate impression is that this space looks like him, or perhaps it is that he looks like this space. Either way, both are soiled, unkempt and smelling of alcohol and urine. I pinch my nose closed.

"Is this true?" Father asks, his eyes suddenly on me. Malevolence shines in them, and that wicked flicker I was never quite able to grasp.

"No! I don't know!" I blurt, as my entire body starts to shake.

"I cannot look after her," says Agathe, stealing Father's gaze from me. "I simply cannot. I have an infant girl I must look after; not to mention managing a household and catering to a husband's needs. Be a man for once! Be a father for once!" Agathe's words tumble out unrestrained, making me fear my trembling legs will give out. Surely, no one has ever dared speak to Father like this. *He'll strike her now, I know it. He'll strike us both.* I clench my fists in defense, but to my astonishment, he does not even flinch.

"What would you have me do?" he asks, staring at the table.

"She's almost thirteen. She can work. Delphine is already working as a laundress. You must find her a job. And fast. Really fast."

With these last words, she grabs my arm and we exit Father's house. As I look at her, I notice the strangest thing: her face is white as paper. *So, she was afraid, too. Very afraid. But, dear me, what a courageous woman!*

The next evening, as if struck by a shaft of divine benevolence, Father arrives at the Boisard's home to announce that he has found a job for me. I am to work as a laundress, just like my sister, with Madame Toutain from Nonant as my new laundry mistress.

~

MADAME TOUTAIN IS a sturdy woman of unyielding character, a warm heart and a pleasant smile. The ten francs a month she pays me stands as witness to her graciousness and fairness. For a girl like me, this is more than my humble heart ever dared expect or deserve.

Not that I get to enjoy my earnings, though. Every Sunday, with a rigor stricter than even the church imposes, I must visit Father at his lodgings to hand over to him my weekly lucre. In turn, he rewards me with a glass of milk and a couple of hard, yeast-smelling cookies. To me they truly taste like heaven; if I manage to hold my breath until I swallow.

But I'm as happy as I've ever been. Learning a new métier is a deeply satisfying accomplishment, and coupled with my gratitude for having being off the streets, life truly feels like a blessing upon the head of an undeserving girl. No longer must I follow people. I now have a purpose, a meaning, a sense of belonging.

But this isn't all.

My new trade, no matter how hard the work from morning until night, opens a world so new and beautiful I can hardly believe my luck. A world of silky soft fabrics and colorful bonnets, silk shawls and cashmere stoles, taffeta dresses, summer gloves of delicate lace and winter gloves of velvet, silk stockings and crinoline petticoats.

And they all smell of Paris! Everything around me now

smells of Paris! And if Madame Toutain's attention wanders, I also smell of Paris when I try on all those beautiful marvels. I even look like a Parisian, dressed in such wonderous garb, and act like one in front of the mirror.

"Good gracious, Madame Plessis! But you look ravishing! May I take you on a stroll to the park?" I ask my reflection, in a voice meant to impersonate some nobleman and with a flourishing mimic of him doffing his high crown top hat and bowing low.

"Why, thank you, Monsieur!" I respond ... to myself. "But I am desperately needed elsewhere. My poodle is plagued with the most terrible indigestion. Any day now, Monsieur! Any day now! Au revoir!" I wave the lace gloves in the air and turn to one side, then the other, pouting my lips and giggling.

And then, like a lighting strike from a clear sky, Marcel's perfect smile pops unexpectedly into my head. His soulful eyes and gentle heart haunt me still. They make me toss and turn in bed at night, then proceed to haunt me in my sleep.

What if I should see him now? Does he still remember me? Does he also think of me in the way I think of him? The questions swirl in my head. *I must see him. I must see him now.*

Goaded by the sudden rush of feeling now possessing me, I quickly think up a plan to sneak from work without Madame Toutain noticing. There is only one exit to the outside and that is constantly used by customers. But not to fret. My natural traits, impetuosity and capriciousness, are ever ready to solve any dilemma.

Gathering up the expensive skirts in my little arms, I climb the window ledge and clumsily jump out.

As I start running, it dawns on me that I am not the smartest girl around. Simply disappearing isn't a great plan, in fact, it isn't a plan at all. *I might stand accused of stealing and end up in jail. Or in an orphanage!*

My thoughts make me burst into laughter, as I realize those are the least of all things that could ever frighten me. As a child who's worried without respite for many months about if there will be a next meal, *orphanage* sounds like a never-ending vacation in a luxurious seaside hotel.

I am almost out of breath when I reach Marcel's farmhouse. I gasp a couple of times, then place my fingers in my mouth and give a short shrill whistle. Lewd songs are not the only things my friends taught me. I now know how to whistle, burp like a man, and even win a spitting competition.

"Is that really you?" comes the voice I know so well. I turn to face a wide-eyed Marcel. My cheeks are already flushed, betraying my emotion. His are as tanned as ever and the beauty of his blue eyes still sparkles.

"Indeed, it is," I answer coquettishly. "Don't you like my new dress?"

"No."

"What? Why?"

"Because it is a thousand times bigger than your size. And because it is stolen." My eyes widen. *So, he is not just plain beautiful but smart, too.* I flush again.

"I ran here. To see you."

"Any particular reason for that impetuous action?"

"Umm..." I quickly ponder an answer in my head; a good one that would advance my plan.

"Well?"

"Well...I've been missing you." My cheeks burn from all that blood raised to them.

"You've been what?" His mouth opens wide along with his eyes. *So, he is going to make it difficult for me.* No matter. I am used to difficult.

"Missing you. I dared hope you might have felt the same way, all this time we were apart."

He does not reply. His only response is closing his mouth. I step nearer to him, using courage I didn't know existed in me. But apparently love or whatever this feeling is, once in your breast, makes you behave strangely. And if love nestles in my breast, my breasts now nestle against his chest.

He pulls back in horror at the touch, as if hell just opened, spewing burning hot tar in his face.

"What are you doing?" he asks, half-astonished, half-frightened. His reluctant reaction creates another strange feeling unknown to me. It is something that mingles courage with coquettishness.

"Kissing you," I reply, and before he can escape, I press my lips to his.

The feeling this first kiss rises in me is startling and it's my turn to pull back. Those lewd stories taught me what kissing was, and so much more, but I never suspected such pleasure to be hidden in a kiss.

"Are you a virgin?" I ask.

"Yes."

"And, are you frightened?"

"Yes."

"Me, too. But come along..." I grab his hand, drawing reluctant Marcel toward the nearby hedge. "It'll be easy. You'll play Alfred and I'll play Josephine."

And right there, under the thick shading of a double hornbeam hedge in the middle of the vast fields, I become, as every daughter of Eve eventually does, a woman. The experience is neither unforgettable nor as pleasurable as I imagine, but at last, I am a woman.

It feels as if the skies finally have given me the long due freedom and happiness I deserve.

Little do I know that this newly-found exhilaration will be as brief as a clear sky during winter.

Only a week short of my thirteenth birthday, Father also decides I am a woman, and grabbing my arm as lightheartedly as I grabbed Marcel's, he drags me toward my second experience reserved solely to women.

CHAPTER 4

*I*t takes Father only a few days to get bored of his little woman.

On the noon of 15 January 1837, a Sunday, as well as my thirteenth birthday, he grabs my arm again. Forcing me to get into my best dress, he then drags me out of his home. I know him well enough by now to suspect this isn't going to be a pleasant, harmless Sunday stroll along the main road. The sunlight reflected on his face enhances the wickedness of his expression and further strengthens my suspicion.

"I want to go back to Madame Toutain," I say, as an insufferable trepidation closes in on me.

"You are there six days a week. On Sundays you are mine."

"But she needs me."

"I don't care what that wench needs!"

"But it's my birthday."

"And?"

"Shouldn't you allow me to choose how to spend my birthday?" My question seems to have crossed the line, as I feel Father tightening his grip on my arm.

"*Should?*" he echoes angrily, halting mid-step. He then squats so his eyes are at the same level with mine. "Never are you to use that word in my presence, do you understand? No one ever tells me what I should or shouldn't do. Some learned it the hard way. You're being the lucky one for being warned. Do we understand each other?" He shakes me by my arms.

"Yes, Father!" I answer quickly, if only to escape the shaking and his burning glare.

He truly is a sorcerer; I now know for certain. As if by magic, everything he does or says to me transforms some part of me. If it is his glare, my heart freezes like water during winter. If it is his voice, all my senses suddenly sharpen, as a soldier ready to throw himself into battle. If it is his touch...his touches are the worst. They change things in me I know not how to describe. And in the other cases whatever was altered soon regains its natural state, while the things his caresses transformed will never be the same again.

"And I know it is your birthday," he says next. "That is why I am taking you to dinner."

I just nod, afraid of uttering another word. *Father, taking me to dinner? Could that be? Might he be a kind man, after all?* Maybe everyone judges him too harshly. Perhaps his caresses are only his way of showing me the depth of his love. After all, he's never beaten me, as he has my mother and sister.

We resume walking in awkward silence; broken only by Father's panting and cursing. After walking for over an hour, leaving behind all the taverns in our hamlet and the next one, the hope of a delicious dinner dissipates like dew drops in the morning sun.

I count my steps silently, but soon lose track of the number as minutes pass like hours and hours pass like days.

When we finally reach our destination, the hill town of

Exmes, it is pitch-black night. Gas-lamps here and there light our way. One illuminates the house where Father says we're invited for dinner.

Situated at the end of an alley, with nothing but the wind beyond it, the house looks like a monster's hideout. Goosebumps crawl over my skin as I am reminded of a fairy tale Mare-Françoise would recount, *The History of Jack and the Bean Stalk,* and the rhyme spoken by the giant monster:

> *I smell the blood of an Englishman,*
> *Be he alive or be he dead,*
> *I'll grind his bones to make my bread.*

The verse menacingly replays in my head and I shrink back, but Father tightens his grip on my arm and drags me to the door. On his second knock, the door opens, revealing an old man with a hideous hump on his back who leans upon an equally gnarled wooden stick.

So, there is a monster hiding in here!

"Ah! I've been expecting you," he says and appears to bow before us. However, I soon realize that is his natural posture.

"Good evening, Plantier," Father says, as he drags me inside. "This is my daughter. The one I've been telling you about." He nudges me in the ribs to close my open mouth.

"Good evening, Monsieur!" I blurt and make a little curtsy. "It's a pleasure to meet you."

The gentleman bends forward and I can see crinkling at the corners of his eyes as he squints to inspect me. He checks my skin, my mouth and eyes, then reaches to feel my hair.

"But your description simply doesn't do her justice, Plessis," he finally replies to Father, his eyes still on me.

The whiff of decay coming from his mouth is

horrendous, a stench of beer mixed with carrion. My bile rises in rebellion.

"I gather you are pleased," says Father.

"Indeed." He grins and lightly pinches my cheek. "What is your name, little one?"

"Alphonsine."

He grins wider and nods. "Now, should we dine?" He points to the dining room with his stick; then, not waiting for an answer, begins shuffling toward the table. We follow; though I pull at Father's pants to make him look at me. I must tell him that we should get out of here while we still can. But Father ignores me. Instead, he silently pushes me forward, forcing me to sit at the table.

Throughout the frugal dinner, consisting of oven-baked potatoes and watery soup, both men are silent. I follow suit, for I know better than to speak in Father's presence unless asked. But there's something that strikes me as strange. Even though not speaking aloud, they seem to be talking with their eyes. What's even more puzzling is that, after we finish eating, they retreat to a corner, sharing whispers and nods. The old man then hands Father what seems to be a small velvet purse. Father weighs it in his hand and I hear a metallic clink. Then he quickly shoves it in his pocket. With a last handshake he exits the house, leaving me to stare at the closed door.

For what seems an eternity, I look at that door, praying it will open again, that Father's silhouette will appear. But, like a dog that waits endlessly for his owner's arrival, I feel my heart sinking deeper and deeper. I can neither move nor breathe. My mind, however, races to rewind the last hour's events.

...*This is my daughter...the one I've been telling you about...I gather you are pleased...*

The old man leaning in, inspecting my skin, eyes, and hair. The conspiratorial glances over the dinner table.

The velvet purse. *What did it contain? Gold coins? To purchase what—or who?*

"Father!" I scream, as I run for the door. "Father! Don't leave me here! Father!" I throw myself upon the door, but the old goat grabs and locks me in his arms. Hateful memories from the day I was taken away from Delphine rush into my head. I wrestle to release myself, but to no avail. This man, as ancient as the earth, proves stronger than me. He grabs my hair with one hand and raises his gnarled stick in the other.

"Be still, tramp," he growls through gritted teeth, "or this shall meet your silky cheek."

I look up at him in horror and seem to be staring into the eyes of the evil god of the underworld, in the red eyes of the guardian of Hell. I know there is no escape. Bitter tears stream from my eyes and I go limp, sliding down his body to the floor.

"Father..." I cry, looking one last time at the door. "What have you done?"

There is, of course, no reply to my question, save from the voice in my head: *He sold you. That's what he's done.*

I make the sign of the cross, then let the satyr drag me away.

THE NIGHT that follows is a night of new discoveries. Brutal discoveries. I discover that monsters do not live in fairy tales, but rather are here, in our real world. Children are fools for being afraid of the monsters in such stories, as the ones living among us are far more dreadful. They are monsters that do not disappear at dawn, with the settling in of daylight. Monsters that do not grind and feed themselves with your bones, but with your spirit. Monsters who appear as fathers.

Later still, when the satyr orders me to lie upon his bed, I discover I am too numb to care whatever it is he will do to me. And he does many things. He orders me to undress so he could examine my naked body. As I do so, he glides his hungry gaze over my skin, then compliments its sheer beauty and milky white color. After several minutes, he sits on the bed next to me. Perhaps his ancient eyes cannot give him the connection he wants, but I don't wonder. I simply wait as he now glides his fingers all over my skin. Mumbled compliments follow, which only serve to intensify the surreal experience. My numbness is speedily quitting me, as a new series of discoveries begin. He reaches out with wrinkled, trembling hand to fondle my breasts and I discover disgust. When his fingers trail to my private parts, I almost throw up. His shaking fingers push into my being; long, dirty nails scratch and tear at my tender insides.

Thank God I gave it to you! Thank God, Marcel, that I gave it to you first! I squeeze my eyes shut to dream of him. To dream it *is* him. With much exertion, my imagination proves superior to reality. The serenity invading me, the newly-found solution to my ongoing torment, is hard to describe. What is certain though is my discovery of how to pretend. In my mind, at least.

The rotter proceeds to push other things into my privates and, fists clenched, I resolve to continue with my daydreaming.

It is not until he begins striking me with his twisted stick that I discover hate. Hate, loathing, pain—call it as you will. For the first time in my life, this dark feeling possesses me so viciously that I'm afraid I'm in danger of losing my soul. I clench my fists even tighter, lest I grab that stick myself and kill the satyr with it.

But I am no murderer. He is.

For the rest of the night, my little body, as well as my innocent soul, serve as nourishment for the monster. For the same amount of time, hate also feeds on me, biting and chewing, scarring my spirit. And though the monster will finally have enough, hate never will. Before I know it, this feeling that introduced itself to me ever so eagerly, warns me that it is here to stay. No kindness or forgiveness or struggle, indeed no religion or God in this world or another, will ever make it go away. Like a watchdog always on the lookout for intruders, hate vigilantly watches, snapping and drooling, with slobber pouring from its mouth.

And like a watchdog, I discover that I also now have an owner. And like any true daughter of Eve, my owner is as old as Adam. A man that is no man, but a sorcerer buying spoiled goods from another sorcerer. A lecher who's long lost his youth but has plenty of coins to now buy another's. A knave born with no soul who steals the souls of others. A clever beast who teaches me his greatest secret: coins can purchase any thing of this earth.

When I leave the satyr's house the next morning, I understand with every fiber in my being that I am no longer the same person. As I halt to look back at the haunted place, I realize that this house, which from the very start I thought of as being from another world, proved its wizardly magic. I entered it still a child and left it a broken grownup.

The fact that this change happened on my thirteenth birthday further strengthens my belief in the Devil. It is as if a wicked higher power decided this birthday should be the most important cornerstone of my life. I shall always, from now on, believe Evil truly exists. I have ceased to believe in goodness. My neighbors and relatives were right. There is no goodness in Father. There's only the Devil, nestling comfortably in his breast. There was no goodness in the ogre shoving his peasant hand under my dress or in those farmhands teaching me lewd songs and curse words. Nor is there any in *Monsieur* Plantier.

Isn't this what you've hoped for? My inner voice whispers in my head as I take the long road back to work. *Other means to acquire food, besides begging? Wasn't this the hope you saw after the encounter with the ogre? Didn't you see yourself as a seductress paying for food with your body?* Maybe. But that was before I was given a chance at a real life. That was before I had a meaning in the real world or food in my stomach. And, I had no idea what I was talking about.

The questions and answers unreeling before my mind's eye were painful, because this new mature person growing in me could now see the evils of the world with a clear mind. The evils of all those people she wanted nothing from, but love.

My eyes well up and I am surprised there are tears still left.

Man up! I look at the twenty-franc coin the satyr placed in my hand before he let me go. *If you cannot beat them, you might as well join them.*

I surprise myself by nodding at this proclamation.

As the warm sunlight reaches to caress my face, I recollect the discoveries made over the past night. My mind reviews each, but pauses on only one. It is my greatest discovery and, alas, my most fateful: men are willing to pay for their pleasures. And if coins can really buy anything, I might as well use men and their coins to buy my freedom.

. . .

Iᴛ ɪs Monday evening when I reach Madame Toutain's. I enter her place not as a fearful child, as she would expect, but as an indifferent woman. A mercenary woman, with a mercenary purpose.

"You! You! How dare you show your face in here at this hour?" she barks. "Do you know what time it is?"

I don't care to answer, just pull out the twenty-franc coin from my dress pocket and place it on her table.

"This will do for my absence, will it not? It's worth two months' lucre."

Her eyes open like river clams on a full moon, then narrow in a suspicious gaze. "Who gave you this?"

"My father."

"Did he now?" Her gaze turns even more distrustful. "Well, I don't believe you."

I sigh and yawn. "Madame Toutain, I am tired. I am going to bed."

And to bed I go, without her objecting. From now on each time I am tired, I rest or go out, sometimes right in the middle of the day. Each time I am hungry, I drop my work and make myself a sumptuous meal, then rest some more. It is as if *I* am the mistress now, with girls working for me. Time and again, I am reminded of what coins can buy. Freedom. Slowly but surely, I begin to revel in my new discovery and soon enough, almost without me knowing it, it becomes part of my nature.

As I embrace this new feeling, my impetuous disposition decides that such a discovery must be imparted. And as I watch the other girls sweaty and flushed near the boiling water tanks, rubbing and scrubbing and squeezing the heavy vestments with their little hands, I decide they, too, should become aware of other means. Why shouldn't they feel like mistresses? Why shouldn't they feel free?

Soon, I begin teaching the girls everything I have been

taught. Lewd songs, indelicate language, words they should use to seduce a man, feelings they should expect when having sex for love or money. And, of course, I drill my new favorite maxim into their heads: *coins can purchase anything.* They blush and giggle, and I become the mistress of their hearts as well.

In my spare time, I return to Monsieur Plantier, each time willingly. I learn that consent goes a long way in providing not only a sense of empowerment, but a sense of having fun as well. The long weekends spent with Monsieur Plantier are no longer dreadful but a means to an end. And that end materializes each time with a ten or twenty-franc coin. I begin to think less about my honest work and more on my future as a rich seductress.

THE NEXT TIME I am late for work, a rainy Tuesday evening, Madame Toutain pushes me into a corner to lay down the law.

"Mademoiselle, I won't have this behavior overlooked anymore," she says. "You're sluggish and unruly. A bad example for the other girls."

I smirk. *If only you knew.*

"Where have you been these past days?" she asks.

"With Monsieur Plantier." I pull out the ten-franc coin and brandish it before her eyes.

She grabs my hand. "Who gave you this?"

"Monsieur Plantier."

"Who is that?"

"My father's friend."

"Why did he give you the money? What do you do there?"

"He plays with me and I play with him."

"I'm going to tell your father!"

"You won't be telling him anything he doesn't already know. He's the one who's sent me there."

She lets go of my hand and exits the room.

Ah, the horror! The horror in her eyes! I burst out laughing. I know that horror only too well. But what good did it get me? What good did tears and horror and supplicating get me? Nothing. So, I might as well laugh at it.

Unfortunately, my unwise confession pushes Madame Toutain into action. She sends her husband to Exmes to make inquiries. Before long, they are both acquainted with the nature of my association with the old debaucher. And if that wasn't enough, word reaches her about the lessons I teach her other girls. Fearing scandal, Madame Toutain resolves to let me go.

Left without any other engagements that could procure the necessity of food, I must move in with Monsieur Plantier. We become a sort of man and wife, with him catering to my every whim and I closing my eyes to his age, tastes, and smell.

For the next few months, I temper my impetuous and restless nature with all the patience I can muster. No child of nature can long acquiesce being kept indoors, with nothing but oldness and its consequences to keep her company. With the arrival of summer, the boredom that has long since creeped into my soul makes a final stand and I begin thinking of ways to escape my self-imposed prison.

But it is not until an event as natural as my owner's senility comes over me that I make my final escape. At thirteen and a half years of age, I become a true woman, not only in my silly impressionable mind, but also physically. The sight of blood flowing down my legs gives rise to such primitive savage terror that I literally flee from the house.

The old satyr's long dirty nails infected me! I shall die

any moment now on the side of the road, like a wretched stray dog!

Goaded by this primal terror, I begin running to escape not so much the nefarious house but my doomed miserable existence.

Upon reaching the main road, I fall to the ground.

Any moment now I shall be introduced to my maker.

My exhaustion, rapid breathing, combine with the sight of my bloodstained dress and prove stronger than my will. With what seems like my final effort to cling to life, I crawl toward a nearby inn. The pain of my head hitting the inn's front steps is my last feeling before plunging into complete darkness.

THE NEXT TIME I open my eyes I see, as if in a daydream, a kind beautiful face hovering above me. For a moment, I think it is Mother, who has come to accompany me to my final judgment. But alas, there is no mother and no final judgement. The face belongs to Madame Denis, the owner of the inn on whose steps I had collapsed. She found me there, she says, more dead than alive, clutching my belly, and covered in blood.

The beautiful young Madame Denis becomes my next mother figure. With as patient and sweet a countenance as could possibly be, she explains everything a young woman should know. My fear of defilement feels foolish now and we share laughter about it. As I recover overall, I begin helping her with daily cleaning chores at the inn, for which she decides to pay me sixty francs a year. It's half the sum I was earning as laundress, but once again I discover the ever-coveted sense of belonging.

I will not be allowed, however, to receive a year's income, for at the end of October Father appears at the Inn's door. It took him less than two months to find me. Now I know I will never be free of him. It seems only death, mine or his, will save me from the sorcerer.

With a new pair of clogs in his hands, he announces that we must leave at once.

"Where to?" I ask, with no hope in my heart or head.

"To Paris."

CHAPTER 5

I jump into my new clogs without further ado. *He's come to take me to Paris! He was riddled with remorse, surely! And now he wants to make it up to me! He wants to be a real father and please me, for once!*

I hastily say my goodbyes to Madame Denis.

The mere allusion to that wonderful word—Paris—makes me forget and forgive in less than an instant everything he's ever done to me. Yes, he's treated Mother and Delphine poorly, and caused the former to abandon me. Yes, he's frightened me on purpose on his dreadful visits and never given me a damn franc. And yes, he's used, then sold me like cattle, to an old smelly satyr without giving a second thought as to the consequences to me.

But everybody deserves a second chance, don't they?

Well, maybe Father requires more than just a second chance, but if I feel I can forgive him, then why shouldn't I? After all, he's taking me to Paris! And that carries more weight than a useless apology.

We start out for Paris at once. I ask Father if we must

walk as far as we did to Monsieur Plantier's house. He just smirks and nods.

"I could walk for triple that distance in a single day! After all, it's Paris!" I gush, looking up at him with complete adoration. A childish demeanor possesses me once again and I find it's a great weight off my heart. My enthusiasm does not match Father's though, and several hours into the journey we break into a stable for a night's rest.

The next morning, before dawn, we resume our walk, travelling in stages, stopping only to eat or rest, or sometimes, to rub Father's sore feet. By dusk, as we enter the forest of Saint-Evroult, Father stops again. I lay face-up on the damp earth and thank God for the forest's shade, the soothing chirping of carefree birds, and for changing my father's heart.

Miracles do happen, came my next thought, as I sit up, propped in my elbows, searching the growing darkness for Father.

About twenty meters to my right, I see him. He is talking to a short, scruffy man with dark skin and long unkempt hair. More men like him surround them, and women, too, with hands propped on their hips and looking curiously at Father.

Gypsies! Yes, they must be gypsies! But why is Father talking to gypsies? He must be asking for directions, surely. Or maybe he wants them to rent us a tent for the night, now that darkness is approaching. Yes, that must be it.

I see father hand a hand-made envelope to the oldest of the women.

And then comes the nods and conspiratorial smiles, and Father weighing a purse made of animal skin in his hand as the small sound of coins clinking rings out clearly. And I instantly know that God hasn't changed Father's heart. That monsters will be monsters to their graves.

I jump to my feet. But not to wave Father *goodbye* as I see him departing and leaving me behind, not to cry or scream his name and beg him to come back, not to ask him why he's again sold me—but to meet my fate. To meet the beginning of a new struggle. The struggle of fending for myself against strangers with corroded hearts. For this must be what God really has in store for me for eternity: following strangers and fending against them.

I stand up straight to meet my new owners.

ROMAIN VIENNE

I was destined to hear these stories some years later, from Alphonsine's own lips. They made me bawl and shriek in emotional pain. How all these atrocities could happen to such a sweet, kind, unaffected child and pass unnoticed is something beyond my comprehension. And by whose hand? The evil hand of her own father, her own flesh and blood.

As I read her words again, so delicately committed to paper by her own small white hand, tears invade my eyes once more. For no one knew her as well as I and no one understood her pain, so deeply and unmercifully ingrained into her tender soul, better than I. The memory of her tears while recounting her story to me, brought back such a devastating wretchedness that I was totally desultory for days.

Marin Plessis came back to Nonant alone and I remember my mother, as well as other neighbors, asking why he had not brought Alphonsine with him. His reply, according to my mother, was something I shall never be able to forget. "What do you expect?" the Sorcerer had said. "Paris is so big that I lost her. In that devil of a town, there's no drum you can beat to find stray objects."

I was so happy when the entire hamlet—myself included—got together to teach The Sorcerer a lesson. The pity we felt in our hearts for his poor little daughter made us forget the fear we'd had of that devil for years. We threw out all his belongings and furniture and vowed never to offer him shelter again.

But despite our efforts to punish the devil, Marin found some goodness in the proprietor of a house in Ginai who offered him a place to sleep in an outbuilding used for sheltering animals. In a sense, that's where he belonged. With the animals. For a beast he was and should have never been allowed to live decently like a normal human being.

I remember one day I chanced to see him dragging his body toward the tavern of Ginai—a filthy, railing drunkard clad in rags, a mere shadow of his former smart physique and haughty demeanor—and almost felt sorry for him. My brother-in-law, the hamlet's doctor, was treating him for leprous sores and other ailments, as by now, perhaps even God had had enough. But only to God are these scourges of humanity forgivable, and this one received another three full years of life, until at last, the great gates of hell opened up to receive him.

It was a chilly early February day in 1841 when his decaying body was discovered by neighbors in the animal shelter he'd used as residence. Marie never saw her father again.

Marie Duplessis

The first owner who approaches is the older gypsy woman to whom Father handed the hand-made envelope. She is short and sturdy with dark skin and charcoal black eyes. She wears her long raven hair in two braids dangling on each side of her face. Gold coins and small strange trinkets are fastened in her braids, making a melodious sound as she moves. More tinkling sound comes from bangles that cover her arms to the elbows. Her brightly colored skirts sweep the ground and the dry leaves covering it.

"I am Zora, Queen of our Romani clan. And that is Ferka, King and my husband." She points at the man who paid Father. "What is your name, daughter?"

"Alphonsine."

"Do you know who we are?" she asks with a huge smile that reveals a mouth full of brown teeth.

"Yes."

"Did you consent to this, then?"

"No."

"But you are very poised. Too poised, I should say."

"That's because I got used to being sold."

Her eyes narrow in a soulful gaze, which she fastens on me for the longest time. Finally, she smiles again, and taking a bangle off her arm, hands it to me. "Do you like it?"

I look at the gold bangle sparkling in the setting sun. "Is it of real gold?" I ask, confounded.

"The purest of all."

"I never had such a valuable possession before. Thank you!" I say and smile back at the sturdy woman. *The queen.* I never thought I would be in the company of royalty so soon.

"We'll give you much more than this. And we'll teach you how to dress and behave."

I look at her with mouth half-open, not knowing what to reply to that. For what purpose would gypsies buy children and give them things and teach them things? For an instant, I dare dream that a great fortune just descended upon me. Father never gave me anything and here are strangers who will give me things any girl could only dream of.

And yet the feeling of uneasiness continues to tease me like the cold forest wind before a storm.

"And why should you do all those things?" I ask.

The woman furrows her brows. "You said you've been sold before."

"I was."

"And what did your owner do with you?"

"He used my body every time it suited him."

"Then you know what we'll do with you. But you must be trained first. Then, we can sell you to the highest bidder."

"Bidder?"

"A very rich man who's in need of a young, beautiful body."

"Now, now, let's see our money's worth..." A masculine voice interrupts our exchange and the other gypsies approach, all staring at me with curious eyes. "Not bad for two hundred francs. Not bad at all," the woman's husband continues.

"And look at this marvelous treasure!" a younger woman exclaims, as she pulls my hair. "If not for that milky white face of yours, you could pass for one of us. A beautiful gypsy!"

They all laugh and come nearer, some pulling my hair, while others pinch my cheeks and arms and bottom.

"She's so tall!" says one.

"And so skinny!" cries yet another.

"On my blood, she's so beautiful!" says a third, and then spits on the ground as if to break some real or imaginary curse.

It is as if a flock of crows suddenly attacked me and are thrusting their merciless beaks into my flesh. I cover my face with my palms and begin to cry.

And crying is all I do, almost uninterruptedly for the next several days. I cry when I must share a tent every night with a dozen smelly gypsies who snore and pass gas and sleep holding daggers. I cry when those men bring freshly killed forest animals and order me to pluck and cook them. I cry upon seeing the women's jealous glares and the men's covetous gazes. I cry when I remember my parents and acknowledge their lack of presence or love or their monstrous deeds. And I cry when the old woman lectures me on the manners I must adopt to fit into the high society of rich men. She does it while we walk through forests and meadows toward Paris. But I never learn. I never want to learn. I just stare at my clogs and rewind in my mind the pleasant and hurtful memories left behind. The woman nags and scolds me for my lack of attention and interest, then spits on the ground and swears at me in a strange language I understand only intuitively.

As we reach the hills on the outskirts of Paris, we stop again for a final night's rest. As the males put up the tents, I walk a few steps to the edge of the hill and sit on the grass.

"So, this is Paris!" I exclaim in wonder. The immensity revealing itself to my eager eyes is breathtaking. A sea of lit gas lamps baptize the city in a magnificent golden light. Their flickering flames make it look alive, as if it were a pulsating, breathing enchanted creature from another world. A happier world.

I ask Zora for permission to sleep at this spot and she agrees. Sleeping under the stars is as common to gypsies as it is to an orphan. More so to the gypsies, I should say. For while to an orphan, not having a roof over his or her head is a constant source of wretchedness, to a gypsy it's a way of life, a predilection.

I fall asleep only when the pulsating gas-lamps finally manage to tire my eyes beyond performance. But the peace found in my sleep lasts only a minute. Violent jolts jerk me awake, as a hand covers my mouth.

"Shh, don't scream," Zora whispers. "You have to run away at once! I told my husband you were not making any progress towards our goal. I told him you are as stubborn as a mule. And now he's changed his mind. He no longer wants to sell you but make you a beggar. *As long as she makes me money, I don't care what she does. Tomorrow. We will cut off one of her arms. She'll be more productive that way.* This is what he said and now I'm telling it to you. So, run! Run as fast as your legs allow you!"

By now I am fully awake, with my heart racing at a maddening speed. "Why are you being so kind to me, Zora?"

"Don't get soft on me now. I am as mercenary as is my husband. I would have sold you to an old rich man without the slightest remorse. But now he wants to butcher you. He did it before, to a little boy. To Fonso there," she says, pointing with her chin at one of the tents. I knew Fonso, the lad without an arm.

"Mon Dieu!" I whisper.

"I cannot again hear those nerve-wrenching screams. You are too young. Take this and go." She hands me the hand-made envelope Father had given her.

"What is it?"

"A letter your father asked me to give to you when we've sold you."

"What does it say?"

"Do I look like I know how to read? Go, stupid girl! Waste not one minute! Or else he'll catch you up on the morrow." She smacks the back of my head, and then scurries to her tent.

Frightened by her last words, I begin running. The darkness still lingers, and it feels as if I am running with my eyes closed. Weeds cling to my clogs and tree branches to my dress and skin. I squeeze Father's letter even tighter in my hand and push through the obstacles in a near frenzy.

When dawn finally breaks through the tree crowns to reach me, I pause. Letting myself fall freely onto the damp earth, I greedily breathe in the fresh forest air. As my panting gradually subsides, I gather the courage to open Father's letter. Thanks to my short attendance at the small girls' school in Saint-Germain-de-Clairefeuille and to Sister Huzet's insistence on teaching me how to read and write, Father's words come to life from his almost unintelligible writing.

"If one day you will try to escape the plentiful life I envisioned for you, go to my cousins, the Vitals, on the rue des Deux-Ecus, in the old quarter of Les Halles."

And that is all. No apologies, no remorse. Just a written statement of his overbearingness.

A few days ago, I would have thought his intention was a kindly, fatherly one. I would have thought: *Look, he wants me to be safe. He wants me to run away and is providing me a safe harbor.* But now, at long last, I know better. Now I think: *He doesn't want me to be safe. He merely wants to know where to find me if ever I escaped.* There will always be another satyr or gypsy willing to buy his daughter.

With this heartbreaking realization materializing through bitter tears, I enter Paris.

CHAPTER 6

My first stop in Paris is the Pont-Neuf bridge that crosses the river Seine, which cuts the city in half. Because following people seems to have become a habit, I followed people here, too. It seems that this place is the belly of Paris, sucking in the city's inhabitants from all its quarters. From the cobblestone bank, the bridge looks like a giant concrete monster. Hideous stone masks decorate each side of it and seem to be snarling at me. None look the same and there must be hundreds, yet all remind me of Monsieur Plantier.

The bridge itself seems to be the incarnation of both Parisian joy and devilry. Acrobats, jugglers, fire-eaters, and musicians, all perform to the enchanted gazes of the passers-by, reminding me of the Saint-Mathieu fair. Other people sell tickets to some upcoming show or ball, while still others make a living pulling failed teeth or putting them back in, making crystal eyes or wooden legs to repair the violence of bombs. Then there are those who claim they can cure incurable illnesses or have discovered the virtues of some powdered stones to beautify the face or remove wrinkles from the forehead and eyes, and even make the old young again.

Students and working girls can be seen among the crowd, as well as ladies and gentlemen of the court—ladies in resplendent dresses wearing tall wigs and bedecked in jewelry walk on this very bridge.

I have found my place in this world.

Booths for the sale of various items or foods line the sides of the bridge. The smell coming from them is out of this world. As I approach the booth selling fried potatoes, tears fill my eyes. They are tears of yearning, for I have eaten naught in two days, except an apple I stole from one of the booths. They are also tears of anger, for this is one of those moments where I realize no creature on earth must spend a life of constant hunger—hunger that is never quenched. Tears of dismay, for nothing seems to get better for me, and all my yearnings and hopes and dreams are ever trampled upon by a renewed struggle. The struggle for survival. And when you struggle to survive, there is no place left for dreaming and hoping, only yearning.

As my desolate thoughts play with my feelings in a vertiginous rollercoaster, I notice, from the corner of my eye, a figure standing beside me, watching me.

"You look hungry, my dear," says the man who seems unable to take his eyes off me. His suit is like those I used to clean while working for Madame Toutain in Nonant. It is made of the most expensive delicate fabric. He wears a top hat inclined over one ear and carries a cane.

"Do I?" I reply with a smirk. "Then, I must be."

The gentleman approaches the booth and orders the largest cornet of fried potatoes I have ever seen. He then hands it over to me. More tears fill my eyes as I begin devouring the hot brownish wonders. They are tears of gratitude.

"Thank you, Monsieur," I say, with my mouth full. "You just bought yourself a place in Heaven."

He bursts out laughing, tilting his head back. "You are pretty clever, aren't you?"

"I wouldn't know."

"Well, you are."

"Thank you, Sir. And you are quite kind."

"Well, my lady, it wasn't my kindness that bought you those potatoes, but your beauty."

I smile. "That works, too."

The gentleman laughs some more, then doffing his hat, he bids me goodnight. I make a curtsy, a low one, like servants make for royalty, and bid the gentleman goodnight as well.

ROMAIN VIENNE

What Marie didn't know was that the gentleman offering her the first meal in two days was Nestor Roqueplan, the French writer, journalist, and theatre director. He was the editor of *Le Figaro*, the most celebrated newspaper in France, and later the director of the very popular *Théâtre des Variétés*. A rich man, but also a dandy with an eye for working girls who could often be found on Pont-Neuf.

Another thing Marie did not know was that she would meet Monsieur Roqueplan again. Not as the waif as she was then but as one of the most beautiful budding courtesans of Paris. Her metamorphosis would produce a shock of delight in Monsieur Roqueplan, who never could forget Marie on her first day in Paris: "She was nibbling a green apple which she seemed to despise," he will recount later. "Fried potatoes were her dream. She dropped her apple core and devoured the chips in three minutes."

Alphonsine remembered his small gesture of kindness on her first day in Paris for the rest of her life.

MARIE DUPLESSIS

By day, I walk on the bridge back and forth, hoping to find the generosity of other rich people who might chance to see my hunger. By night, I must leave the bridge behind, as gangs of questionable individuals hid out in and around it, robbing and murdering people. And so, I wander about the streets of Paris, learning their names by heart, or sleep on a secluded park bench, with the Parisian sky as my beautiful vista.

But it soon becomes clear that gestures of kindness from smartly dressed gentlemen were indeed isolated incidents.

Another few days pass before I happen upon an announcement in the window of a clothing store in the Latin Quarter, which says: *Young, pretty girl needed. Inquiries inside.*

I can do this. I run my fingers through my hair to tame it, and taking a deep breath, I push open the entrance door to the luxurious clothing shop.

I get hired on the spot. The owner says I must sell dresses to rich women, as well as gloves and stockings and bonnets. He even allows me to sleep in a crammed den at the back of the store as part of my remuneration. That makes me ignore the fact that the pay is bad, very bad, even for a beggar or an orphan who would agree to *any* pay, as long as they are taken off the streets.

But by the end of the month, I realize the poor wage is not my biggest problem. The owner, a dark man with an insatiable belly and even more insatiable ego, forces me to spend my first month's lucre on new clothes and shoes from his shop. He says he can no longer allow a peasant-looking girl to present his merchandise as he might lose his esteemed customers, who are always richly dressed and clean and smelling of the finest Parisian perfumes.

I buy myself a modest silk dress and black leather ankle boots. To complete my attire, I also cover my head with a little pink, lace-trimmed bonnet. My new belongings force me to go again on empty stomach for several days. But neither this, nor the poor wage is what soon gives me truly serious cause for concern.

Late one evening, as I prepare to lock the door behind my last customer, I suddenly find myself dragged by the hair toward the back room.

"You filthy peasant," sneers my employer, while throwing me onto the floor. "How many times must I tell you: you are not to let any customer go out of my store with empty hands?" He then launches himself upon me, hitting my arms and thighs with his fists. "You worthless little filth! I'll teach you obedience!" he seethes while slapping my face. I struggle to wrench myself free while screaming as loud as my lungs allow me. But there is no one here to hear me. No one to save me. I cover my face with my hands as the brute continues to apply his unbearably savage blows to my fragile body.

As his anger subsides, he abruptly stands up and leaves. In my crammed den, I spend the night mending my wounds and blotting my tears. The next evening, the brute proceeds to repeat his evil doing, this time because I wasn't smart enough to cover the bruises on my face.

Why aren't you running away? I scream in my head. *And go where?* comes my reply.

And thus, convincing myself that there is no better fate for me out there, I continue to slave by day and get beaten by night.

But then comes those evenings when a thrashing is not

all he does. Evenings when the brute's malice and darkness make me remember Monsieur Plantier with fondness.

Inevitably however, there also comes the moment when I know that any sort of fate waiting for me beyond the clothing shop's doors is better than the one I have acquiesced to live. And I realize I am no longer afraid of Father. For anything Father would want to do to me next, as sure as the sun rises, it won't be worse than this.

So, packing my scarce belongings, and squeezing Father's letter in my hand, I escape into the night.

~

LOCATING Father's cousins proves to be child's play. After all, I am my father's daughter. Unlike him, though, I do not have to do too much detective work to find out where the Vitals live. I walk straight to the des Deux-Ecus street—a medieval alley, as it turns out—in the old quarter of Les Halles and ask a neighbor if he's heard of Madame Vital.

He points to the second floor of an old, yet distinguished-looking, building. I thank him, then gathering all my possible courage, I climb the stairs to the second floor.

The Vitals receive me well, after the astonishment of finding about my existence subsides. They say they haven't heard from Father in almost two decades and never knew he had a wife, let alone a daughter. I tell them about Mother and Delphine, and about how the evil doings of Father killed the former and severely damaged the latter.

But I uttered not one word about my own experiences. Why? I do not know. If it is because I am deeply ashamed of Father or myself, or because I am afraid I'd be looked upon with disbelief or even cast away, I simply do not know. What I do know, however, is that the Vitals—this kind, elegant, above average couple—became my new family.

Once again, I become a daughter. A Parisian daughter.

My new family leads a modest, yet comfortable life, thanks to the vegetable stall they own at the nearby market. I help them in any measure I can, unloading the horse-drawn carts of the vegetables they bring from the countryside, as well as washing and stacking the merchandise to be sold. Be that as it may, no matter how comfortable this small business makes our life, it is still too modest to allow me to live unperturbed by the urgency to provide for myself, as well as to assist the Vitals with the expenses a city as magnificent as Paris mercilessly plagues its inhabitants.

In less than a fortnight, my cousin gets me a job, as apprentice in a dress shop belonging to one of her friends near the Royal Palace. And as much as it saddens me to part with the Vitals in order to take up my lodgings at Mademoiselle Urbain's dress shop, the thought of again spending time surrounded by sumptuous crinolines, enticed by laces and caressed by velvets and silks, is beyond enthralling, and it considerably softens my sadness.

ROMAIN VIENNE

Alphonsine was quick to jump over a significant chapter in her life. She omitted recounting that before her cousin found her employment at her friend's shop near the Royal Palace, she helped to employ her as a maid in yet another one of her acquaintance's laundry business.

However, she worked there for only six days. Reveling in her newfound freedom and exuberance, she had accepted a young man's invitation for dinner on the last day of the week. And even though she hadn't mentioned to me how she'd met him, she did tell me her beau took her to a ball, and then to dinner. After dinner was served, he took her to

Bois de Boulogne, the famous and beautiful park of more than two thousand acres. She recounted with great amusement, and even disdain, how her admirer had caressed her on a footpath overhung with flowers and declared his everlasting love to her. However, an unpleasant surprise came about an hour later. As Alphonsine was walking at the hand of her escort, near the forest of Montmorency, she happened upon her new employer who was taking a stroll with her two daughters. Alarmed by the possibility of scandal, as well as fearing for her daughters' reputation being tarnished, she relieved Alphonsine from her duties at once. Only after this incident, did her cousin introduce her to Mademoiselle Urbain.

While the incident itself may not have been noteworthy, her visiting Bois de Boulogne was. For it was there in the Bois de Boulogne that she became aware, for the first time, of the tangent she would later willingly take. This was where prostitutes made their mark and courtesans drove in their dazzling carriages, displaying their magnificent attires to the eyes of the bewildered. It was in the Bois de Boulogne that fashions were introduced, where women and men alike competed and infamous affairs commenced. In the Bois de Boulogne, rich dandies swarmed to make acquaintance with the women ready to serve them, in exchange for material support that promised the continuation of their flamboyant, riotous, exceptional lives.

This was the place where rich men and poor women gasped and sighed and yearned. There is no doubt in my mind that Alphonsine was one of them. Perhaps she was even more awestruck by the *grandes dames* of Bois because she was as capricious as she was impressionable, and as beckoned by luxury as she was sensitive and generous.

And no matter how rich or glamorous she'd become; she never fully forgot her origins. From the standpoint of a poor girl from the countryside, the decadent spectacle of Bois de Boulogne couldn't have failed to seduce her. It couldn't have failed to produce an everlasting transformation. So, she couldn't have forgotten.

But, alas, women are and always have been a constant source of mystery to me.

MARIE DUPLESSIS

For six months, this new order of things makes me experience something I've never experienced before. Tranquility and happiness. It seems that my life has finally settled into a pleasant succession of joyful events and I can now enjoy the little pleasures of ordinary people. But it is not long before I realize that *ordinary* is not a word to describe my nature. Whether my nature, as it is, is something I was born with or whether it's been irreparably damaged by my childhood, I cannot say.

I am also not altogether cut off from my new family. Every Sunday I return to the Vitals' home to spend time with them. On my fifteenth birthday, in January 1839, they prepare the most extravagant dinner to celebrate the daughter they came to love as their own, and Mademoiselle Urbain allows me and my colleague, Ernestine, to be absent from work on the great day.

Ernestine and Hortense—the shop girl working in the boutique next to ours—have become my great friends. Ernestine is tall and a bit more attractive than Hortense. There are traits in her character that suit my own nature, like the pleasant mischievous demeanor always present on her face. That alone casts away my ever-lurking melancholic thoughts. I guess one could say she has a devilish side to her, but it seems that side of her is exactly what I need to forget about my past. And plan for my future.

Hortense is the shortest of the trio. If not for her long reddish locks and demure appearance, she would easily pass unnoticed. Her crooked nose and bushy eyebrows distract one's attention from her beautiful hair and pale skin. But her tender heart is in the right place and whenever I need to unload the weight in my own heavy heart, Hortense is the friend to go to.

As for myself? How would I come across if I started bragging about my own beauty? There is a certain embarrassment that comes with talking about oneself, and I am no exception. Madame Vital said once that I've become disturbingly pretty. She was afraid that a city like Paris might not be the safest place for a girl like me.

"Debauchers, charlatans and nobles alike swarm about this city uninterruptedly," she once said to me. "Every quarter has them, and every quarter, every single day, reports a catastrophe. And the catastrophe is always about a beautiful girl being raped or murdered or lured into the clutches of a rich man who ruins her reputation forever. Look at you, Alphonsine! Look at your splendid dark hair and eyes! Look at your marvelous white skin and your stature! You are the most beautiful creature the gods and mortals alike ever produced. The great goddesses of Olympus would cry with bitter envy and resentment if they could see you. How am I to protect you? How am I to save you from this treacherous city?"

I had tried to comfort her, saying that we should always put our lives in God's hands. That we must be vigilant, yet at the same time accept that there will always be things beyond our control. I then decided to confess to her what Father did to me, just to reinforce the idea that no matter how careful one is, fate will always have the last word. It was my second mistake. I forgot the vow I made long ago, that I should be as silent as a grave and keep my secrets to myself. She was inconsolable. And not being a religious person, everything I said afterword, was of no comfort to her. Yet my youthful exuberance made me scorn my cousin's advice and deciding I should not trouble my heart with her worries, I returned to my friends.

RIGHT AFTER MY BIRTHDAY, Hortense, Ernestine and I plan a trip outside Paris for the following Sunday. The weather, however, makes a stand against us and disperses dark threatening clouds. But mere bad weather could never dampen the enthusiasm of youthful spirits, and so we decide that window shopping in the Royal Palace is a wonderful alternative.

It takes six complete tours around the Royal Palace galleries to tire us and remind us that even youths must eat. As we enter one of the restaurants flanking the galleries, I realize how strangely pleasant it is to be admired. All eyes are on us, measuring our bodies from head to toes. If that is because three young beautiful giggling girls could never pass unnoticed or simply because our modest clothes make us seem totally unfit for the luxurious environment we've just entered, is a matter of guesswork. My guess goes for the latter and I instinctively touch the brim of my modest straw hat.

But when a bottle of old Burgundy arrives at our table accompanied by the owner's compliments, I know I was wrong.

The good Monsieur Nollet, a middle-age man with sparkling eyes, offers us not only his fine wine but his splendid food as well. My cheeks begin to burn. On the one hand this is because the wine has already reached my head and on the other because the embarrassment of again feeling like a beggar is spreading through my blood faster than the wine. Yet the wine proves stronger, and I become chatty. I confess to M. Nollet our disappointment at having had our excursion to Saint-Cloud cancelled, and then I curse the weather. He offers a hefty laugh, as well as an invitation to Saint-Cloud on the next Sunday. We all agree.

THE WEATHER at the end of the following week proves kinder, sending sunshine to warm our shivering bodies as well as our foolish heads. M. Nollet also proves the kindest of men, taking us to the Saint-Cloud fair in his splendid carriage. Treating us to an equally splendid lunch in a popular restaurant, he then proceeds to buy us everything our hearts might happen to desire from the animated fair. His generosity extends to the three of us in equal measure, but his sparkling, yearning gaze is reserved solely to me.

In less than a month, my fate, as well as my reputation as an innocent girl, changes forever.

"Would you come and see a little furnished apartment I have found for you in the rue de l'Arcade?" M. Nollet asks me several days later. Leaving my as well as others' principles behind me, I go at once.

"Will you allow me to offer it to you?" he asks again. "I will rent it in your name and when you move in, you will find in this drawer three thousand francs for your initial needs."

Taking M. Nollet's hands in mine, I find myself struggling with renewed scruples and embarrassment. How am I to accept? I will never have the chance to again call myself a respectable woman. I will trade my innocent dreams for the luxuries of the material world. What would Mademoiselle Urbain say? And my cousins? Will they love me still, or am I trading their love for a lace-trimmed hat? But then, like lightning crackling across a clear sky, the image of Father suddenly enters my head; and after that, of the ogre forcing his hand under my dress and Monsieur Plantier raising his gnarled wooden stick above my head.

Still squeezing M. Nollet's hands in mine, I look up at him:

"Nothing else would make me happier."

CHAPTER 7

Settling down in my new plentiful extravagant life proves easier than I have previously suspected. With every new hat, dress or cashmere shawl, another recent guilty feeling that plagued me melts like a snowflake in the warmth of a March sun.

Yet my embarrassment still lingers, and it is a full week after I move into my new, small-but-fancy, apartment near the Tuilleries gardens, that I summon the courage to visit Mademoiselle Urbain's dress shop.

"Mon Dieu!" exclaims Ernestine, as she runs to embrace me. "I almost did not recognize you!"

"Ah, this?" I say, touching my white silk dress.

"Yes, that! And that! And that!" Ernestine giggles while pointing at my white lace gloves and hat. She rests her gaze on the hat, inspecting it curiously, as if it were a strange animal at the museum.

"I've never seen a hat like this," she says. "Tilted to the front, decorated with ribbons, and flowers, and lace..." Her eyes well up. Startled, I drag her to a corner and place a twenty-franc coin in her hand.

"Guess what, my lovely Ernestine! I have more hats like this at my apartment, and it just dawned on me that I should like you to have one. What do you say? Will you come visit me soon?" She throws her arm about my neck, suffocating me in her embrace.

"How is he?" she whispers in my ear, then pulls back to look me in the eyes. "Monsieur Nollet? How is he?"

"Kind, generous, and...absent. He comes only once a week to ask about my needs and...fulfill his."

"Ay, ay!" She chuckles.

"I know! And he has this strange thing for my underarm...he likes to run his tongue over it every time he—"

"No! That's disgusting!"

We both break into a fit of laughter that ceases when Mademoiselle Urbain enters the shop.

"Mademoiselle Urbain!" I exclaim and run to her.

"Alphonsine?"

I nod.

"Look at you! How you've changed!"

"Only on the outside, Mademoiselle."

"I was mad at you. Not showing up for work in more than a week. But no need for scolding any longer, is there?" My cheeks glow bright red and I search her eyes for a sign of approval. There is none, but there is also no malice or smugness either.

"Mademoiselle Urbain..." I say, as tears fill my eyes. "I cannot thank you enough for your kindness. You extended your hand toward me when I most needed it. I shall never forget you."

We hug, and I realize that it is relief that dominates my heart more than gratefulness. Relief at not being judged by her. We part as better friends than ever.

But there is one more visit I must make, a visit I cannot

bring myself to schedule.

If visiting Mademoiselle Urbain turned out to be a good idea, I am not equally sure about visiting my cousins. I rehearse in my head the story to tell Madame Vital, then proceed to forget it, realizing that no embellishment could fool my cousin's agile mind. Alas, after a torturous week of deciding and undeciding, I resolve to write them a letter. Madam Vital's reply reaches me in less than two days. A single sentence, laid down on plain white paper, confirms what I have already suspected.

"If ever you set foot in my house again, I will chase you away like the vermin you are."

A single tear glides down my cheek and onto the paper. I am an orphan again. This vast city is my home now, my mother and father. I have become a true daughter of Paris.

THE SUDDEN ABUNDANCE of material things I can now afford acts like a magical substance playing with my senses, vanity and capriciousness. I feel possessed by a mood never before experienced, a mood that goads me to spend all my waking hours shopping. In less than a month, I become acquainted with all the high-end clothing shops in Paris. Thus, it is no wonder that an entire month proves too long a time for the three thousand francs M. Nollet has given me.

On the last week of March, I confess to my patron the insufferable misery that is now possessing me after parting with my last dime. He wipes my tears with his fingers and places another two thousand francs on the corner of my bed.

But if one month was too long for his first handout, how long am I to live with his second? I now must abstain from entering the enticing shops of Paris. After all, I did acquire a magnificent wardrobe, fully equipped with white and pale pink crepe garnished with lace and velvet, silk stockings, cashmere and taffeta shawls, and lace gloves.

Yet, I must think of an alternative that would succeed in keeping a bored girl of fifteen from ruining herself.

I continue to acquaint myself with the wonders of Paris, although this time I choose to do it with the city's cafes and restaurants. Soon enough, I begin to discriminate which of them offer the best drinks and food, and wealthy men. But it is not until I enter Jardin Mabille, near the Champs-Elysées, that a welcoming thought springs in my head: *I shall never go hungry again.*

The owner, a certain Monsieur Mabille — a dance instructor, I find out later — introduces himself to me, then proceeds to tell me he's never seen me before. But I can barely hear what he says, so enraptured am I with the enchanted garden, magnificent sand paths, lawns, trees and shrubs, galleries and the grotto. About three thousand very modern gas lamps illuminate the spellbinding place after dark, so people can dance long hours into the morning. Colored-glass globes illuminate the areas under trees and strings of lights and chandeliers are suspended between them. In a distant spot, there is an area with a roof for protection from rain, while opposite it is an enchanting Chinese pavilion, artificial palm trees, and a carousel. Everything seems to glisten in gold, silver and precious stones. And everything smells of money.

I leave Monsieur Mabille behind and begin to inspect the people crowding the magnificent place. There seems to be only a single type of man here, and a single type of woman. The former being wealthy, young and old, who allow their manners, language, and attire to speak in their stead. The latter are grissettes, lorettes, and courtesans. In lesser words: the romantic frauds. Prostitutes.

The grissette is the delightfully immoral working-class

girl, forever striving to attain the status of a lorette, who has replaced her straw bonnet for a lace hat, her cotton dress for one of silk, and her small shawl for a cashmere. I was a grisette—a year ago. Today, I am a lorette.

And then, there are those whom both grissettes and lorettes look at in wonder and veneration, and not infrequently, with plain jealousy: the courtesans.

The courtesan is more than a mere prostitute. She's no longer the beggar, the orphan being chosen. She chooses her protectors. Her wealth of rich lovers is directly proportional with the wealth of her purse. She is spectacular in appearance and often an influential figure in high society. The perfection of her art can often lead her to acquire a much-coveted title, like that of duchess or countess, for when she sells her love, she does it with genius.

I SIT ON A BENCH, continuing my inspection, when the sudden feeling of wretched yearning crosses my heart. Is it jealousy? Envy? I struggle to push it away, as I take in everything the spectacle in front of me has to offer. I analyze the courtesan's gesturing, manner, and posture. I learn when she laughs and when she chides; when she advances and when she retreats; when she entertains with her brains and when she draws attention to her cleavage. On and on, until bit by bit, my envy is replaced by the overwhelming feeling possessing all those men the courtesan entertains: fascination.

With my eyes wandering over the people in the gardens, my gaze happens to pause on a familiar stack of golden curls. *Is that...? No...that's impossible!* I stand up at once and making my way through the people, I halt behind her. And if her golden stack of hair might have been misleading, her voice and laughter never could.

"Ernestine?" I hear myself whisper. Her long curls brush against my face as she turns about to face me.

"Alphonsine! I...I..." The vibrant, animated Ernestine of seconds ago switches places with a deeply embarrassed, shocked one. But of us two, I am the most shocked, the most appalled.

She drags her voice and forces a smile upon her lips. "Alphonsine, this is Monsieur Vanier. A banker, and my friend," she says, introducing me to her companion.

I take my turn in forcing a smile upon my lips, and making a little curtsy, I extend my hand to the gentleman. "A pleasure to meet you, Monsieur Vanier."

He bows slightly and kisses my hand. "The pleasure is all mine, Mademoiselle. I am happy to finally meet one of Ernestine's friends."

"That makes two of us. Now, if you'll excuse us..." I retort, and the gentleman doffs his hat. Dragging Ernestine to and along the alleyway, I pinch her upper arm.

"Mon Dieu!" she cries. "What is the matter with you?"

"With *me*?" I burst. "What's the matter with *you*?" I push her toward a bench and order her to sit. She immediately becomes remorseful and apologetic.

"Alphonsine... I am sorry. I should have told you. Many times I wanted to come and visit you...but then I was too embarrassed to face you..."

"Embarrassed, huh? *I* swallowed my embarrassment! *I* came to our shop, displaying my dresses, my hats and my... disrepute! *I* trampled on my pride and fear and came to see you! And *you* are the embarrassed one? Is this what I get in return for my loyalty? The most shocking discovery of Jardin Mabille?"

"I really am sorry...I should have come to see you... Please, forgive me," she cries.

"Yes, you should have! What is it? Two months since

last I saw you? The all-demure damsel dreaming of getting married and have a nursery full of babies! And look at you now! Your clothes are even more expensive than mine!"

My friend just nods at my every word, still looking apologetic. But there is a strange spark in her eyes, a spark of enthusiasm and eagerness mingled together. It is as if she waits patiently for me to shut up so she could unload her heart to me. I sigh and take her hands in mine.

"Alright. I forgive you," I say. "Embarrassment and shame are the two feelings I understand best. Go on then. Who is he? And don't spare me the details." As if by magic, Ernestine's expression turns animated again. She draws nearer, then squeezes and rubs my hand.

"A banker. A wealthy banker. He came into the shop with his wife. She was trying on our dresses and hats, asking her husband's opinion on colors and fabrics and the like. I was awfully amused and at one point couldn't hold myself and burst into giggles. It was then that he noticed me, and for the remaining time they spent in the shop his gaze never left mine. Upon leaving, he slipped a card in my hand. It took me an entire week to finally get the courage to use the information on that business card."

"An entire week of self-torment," I whisper.

"Quite right. It felt as if I was deciding my whole future life."

"That's exactly what you did. There is no turning back, my lovely Ernestine. In the society of today the once-fallen woman can never reform — however sincere her contrition might be. We lost girls will be eternally reproached. Every honest door is to us closed. It is in vain for us to invoke pity, as social conventions are without pity. Rehabilitation? Never! Pardon by men? Never! I've come to know them too well in that regard to still retain the smallest illusion."

"Ay, come on, Alfonsine! Not that faraway look again!"

she chides. "Look at us! We have everything we have ever wished for!"

"Except for one. Love."

"Pfff, love..." she scoffs. "I quit that idea the moment I decided to respond to Monsieur Vanier. And in the end, what have I really given up? Scraping by, scrubbing floors and male undergarments, and cleaning babies' bottoms? That's hardly an ideal life."

I just smile and let her comment pass unaddressed. "Where do you live now?" I ask.

"In the most splendid apartment on the rue Tronchet. You must come, Alphonsine!" she begs, folding my hands to her chest. "I also have a carriage, equipped with a coachman and groom and everything! We can drive together in the Bois de Boulogne! And you must attend my dinners! You cannot even imagine the men coming to my dinners! Politicians, writers, artists, men of letters! Please, swear to me you will come!"

Fascinated with my friend's exuberance, and even more so with her fulsome transformation, I smile and nod.

WITH THE IMAGE of the courtesans laughing and dancing at Jardin Mabille replaying in my head, along with that of Ernestine draped in the finest clothes teasing my envy, I run home to write to M. Nollet. The letter, couched in the most dramatic tones, succeeds in acquiring for me the much desired third handout. But the sum is pitiful, and I request a fourth.

It is my third mistake.

In less than a week, I discover that M. Nollet has already taken a new protégé, a grissette of thirteen, less demanding and capricious.

CHAPTER 8

After I recover from the shock at having been abandoned by a middle-aged man who seemed utterly infatuated with me, I resolve to look at my mistakes in a different light.

Every kick in the butt is a step forward becomes my new surviving precept. For how can I advance past my status of lorette if I am to mingle with men only half-rich, half-generous, and half-hearted? How indeed?

The kick I receive from M. Nollet must be regarded with gratitude. For it succeeded in making me realize I want so much more; deserve so much more. It also brought about another realization: a man's affection is shorter than a winter's day. This is a lesson I should have known since cradle. For what example could have been better than my own father's? What lessons regarding men and their conduct could have been more thorough than the ones already laid out by Father? And what existence could have taught me about priorities if not my mother's? What good had love brought her? None. Just loneliness, abandonment, and finally death.

I should know better from now on.

The week following M. Nollet's abandonment, on one of the most splendid spring days of 1839, I decide to visit Ernestine.

As soon as I enter her home, I realize her choice of a protector has been so much better than my own. Only the thought that I had not much to choose from softens my wounded pride. Double in size and with a magnificent staircase leading to her bedroom, her apartment is nothing short of spellbinding. And with the dining room set to receive its illustrious guests, her place indeed looks like one of the most popular salons in Paris.

The mild envy that possessed me at Jardin Mabille grasps me again, but it is all too readily forgotten on the drive to the Bois de Boulogne's magnificent park.

I look out the carriage window at the spectators gathered to watch women like us. Women who flaunt their dresses and carriages and services. I remember the day — not too long ago it seems — when I, a poor peasant girl from Nonant countryside, watched the king and his court with eyes full of tears. The memory of running behind his retinue in my wooden clogs, drowning in dust and in my own sorrow is almost beyond bearable. My feelings of long ago seem to be my feelings of today.

"I shall introduce you to a man after your romantic heart," Ernestine says, patting my hand. She's certainly noticed my wet eyes, and now I've made a fool of myself. I continue to stare through the little window as the horses push through Bois de Boulogne and into Neuilly-sur-Seine.

"Don't be embarrassed, my darling. We might have sold our bodies, but not our hearts. This is our secret to keep," she continues, patting my hand some more.

In the evening, that marvelous dining room of hers becomes animated with the most interesting chatter. I have never seen so many distinguished men gathered in one place. Well, perhaps only at Jardin Mabille, but there they were surrounded by the most splendid courtesans, who made them look unattainable. Here, however, they are ours only. And their eyes are all riveted on me.

All my blood seems to have raised to my cheeks. I flutter my hand-fan close to my face with rapid strokes, when a light tap on my shoulder startles me. I turn around.

For what seems like an eternity, a big pair of brown eyes stares inquisitively into mine. I recognize those eyes, and yet I don't.

"Little Alphonsine? I'll be damned! Is that really you?" asks the possessor of those magnificent eyes.

"Um, yes. It is," I mumble, as I make a little curtsy. "How have you been, Monsieur?"

He bursts out laughing. "You don't recognize me, do you?"

I blush again, this time even more violently than before. "I...I am not sure..."

"Well, let me give you a hint. Are fried potatoes still your favorite dish?"

The image of the man in expensive delicate suit and top hat inclined over one ear offering me my first meal in Paris lights up in my head. Forgetting all about etiquette and the inquisitive eyes around me, I throw my arms about his neck.

"Monsieur Pont-Neuf!" I burst in his ear.

"Let me look at you!" he says, and grabbing my waist in his hands, he gently pushes me away from him. "Aren't you a sight? To be quite frank, I never expected to find you here, little Alphonsine."

"And I never expected to see you again. I never expected you'd remember my name! You've been in my thoughts so often, that the mere thought I would never be offered the chance to thank you was a misery to me. I am so happy fate decided otherwise, Monsieur—"

"Roqueplan. But do call me Nestor, dear one."

"Nestor," I whisper, as I fight back the tears invading my eyes. "You have no idea what your kindness meant to me. Or your fried potatoes."

He laughs again, his head falling back with the effort. "Well, my lady, I am happy to have been of service. And beyond happy to see you are now doing better."

"I see you've already met Monsieur Roqueplan," Ernestine's voice pushes into the moment.

"You have no idea," I say, exchanging complicit glances with my earliest benefactor.

"Your food is exquisite, Madame," Nestor says to Ernestine, bending forward to lightly kiss her cheek. "As usual."

"Only the best for the best," she replies.

"Please visit me at Café de Paris, little one," he says, again looking at me. "I hold a table there every night. And will introduce you to the worthy."

"I certainly will."

"It's settled then. I now must catch up with the gentlemen," he says, bowing slightly. "If you'll excuse me..."

As he shifts off, I find myself plagued by desolate memories. Regardless of how pleasant re-encountering Monsieur Pont-Neuf proved to be, it still brought the anguish of yesterday.

"In our profession, knowing Monsieur Roqueplan is enough to be set for life," says Ernestine, winking at me. "Now come. I have a promise to fulfill." She drags me about the room, introducing me to her guests, each one more remarkable than the next. Writers, poets and journalists mingle and chat together, debating the most important events of the day. I make a mental note to read more often.

Well, to read. Knowing the works of these men should prove to be yet another weapon in conquering them.

"You've already met my dear Monsieur Vanier," I hear Ernestine say, stealing my attention from the crowd.

"It's a pleasure to meet you again," says her protector, bowing slightly forward. I follow suit and lower my head.

"And this is Monsieur Valory," says Ernestine, smiling at the man standing on Monsieur Vanier's left. His youth alone is enough to make my blood raise to my cheeks. "Monsieur Valory, this is my friend, Alphon—"

"Marie," I say, as I extend my hand. He bends and kisses it. I catch Ernestine's confused gaze. "Alphonsine is the past, Marie is the future," I whisper in her ear. With this evening placing me at a crossroad, I feel I should somehow make a new choice. Looking in Monsieur Pont-Neuf's eyes, I saw my past. And looking now in those of Monsieur Valory, I can see my future.

"Marie...what a wonderful name," Valory says. "Like The Virgin's..."

"Well, Monsieur," I say, "I should think The Virgin would be relieved to be left out of this conversation." We all laugh.

Ernestine breaks the laugh first, telling us she must attend to her guests. As she retreats, dragging her protector after her, I find myself analyzing Valory with an uncommon interest. Within this crowd of grey hairs and physical flaws, he looks like an exotic bird. Standing alone, he resembles a Greek god—the Greek god of masculine beauty. His large blue eyes are the stuff of poems, while his light chestnut hair the inspiration of painters. A sudden urge to raise my hand and run my fingers through his hair makes me shudder.

"Marie, I have heard so many things about you," he says, pulling me out of my daydreaming.

"Have you?"

"But those words simply don't do you justice." He smiles, revealing his perfectly white teeth. I imagine throwing myself around his neck and running my tongue over them. *What in the heavens? Running your tongue over his teeth? What in God's name possesses you?* The question remains without an answer. Yet possessed I feel.

"Would you come visit me, Monsieur Valory?" I ask breathlessly, skipping the introductions. "I live not far from here, on rue de l'Arcade."

And visit me he does, on the following day. On this first visit, I discover that aside from his endearing youth and splendid beauty, my new acquaintance descends from a noble family. A very rich noble family who bestowed on him an annual income of a hundred thousand francs. On the second visit, I become his mistress.

For the next months, I am finally allowed to live in the Garden of Eden. It is as if God decided to allow me a respite from all the heartaches and worries of the past.

At night, a passion I never knew existed in me materializes itself in wild animalistic lovemaking. Neither Marcel nor Monsieur Nollet could have prepared me for this avalanche of feelings and impulses love conceived in me. For this must be love. This must be that feeling artists always rave about in their masterpieces. The feeling that contains the power to transform you until you no longer recognize yourself.

Soon enough, the world of vice and empty pleasures seems a faded memory. It is as if someone else had chosen it for me. Someone else discarded my ideals. Someone else derided love and bet instead on abundance.

And slowly, this new better version of myself, gloriously transformed by love, begins hating that someone else who seems to have misled me into embracing that world of emptiness. It is this better version of myself who kneels and bends and compromises; the better me who speaks in a language so strange and yet so enchanting; the real me who caresses and kisses and promises.

Thinking back to Mother and her tragic existence, I can hardly believe my luck. I wish she would have had the chance at experiencing at least one day in the arms of happiness. Or at least, be here to experience my own. And because I think of Mother so often lately, I also begin to think of myself as a simple woman, marrying for love. For my dearest Valory behaves like a married man, catering to his wife's every need and whim.

But in the end, even Valory proves to be just a man; a man like every other, abiding by the same general rule: *a man's affection is shorter than a winter's day.* And more than anything, it is probably this best version of myself that proves to be my undoing. This true me that made me forget about the vow I made not long ago: *to be as cold as a stone.* To be a mercenary woman with a mercenary purpose. For that is the woman Valory fell in love with; the woman he signed up for. My spiritual transformation never was in his plan. My kindness, romantic streak, my sweet words and new bending nature never were and never will be incentives for young rich men. After all, they do not meet us at church mass. And exotic birds can never be contained. They fly freely in their exotic surroundings.

Only three months am I allowed to live in the Garden of Eden. Three months that passed like three minutes — just enough to carve deep scars for an eternity. At the end, Valory leaves, never to return. And he doesn't leave empty-handed, but with my shattered soul under his arm.

~

I SHOULD NOT LIKE to longer dwell on the misery that became my constant companion after Valory's departure. Suffice to say that all my following actions and motivations are the product of his abandonment. For how can one's life be, when one is coerced to live it in the absence of one's soul?

ROMAIN VIENNE

There is no doubt that Marie fell deeply in love with Valory. But the young man, after having given her ten thousand francs in less than three months and having spent the same amount on parties, balls, and little presents, had made the judicious remark that if he continued to keep her as his mistress, she would devour his entire inheritance. As her passion for him was growing by the hour, his was extinguishing as quickly as the money in his wallet. So, he pretended a forced absence in Picardy. In vain, Marie waited for him. This abandonment was a very unpleasant shock for the poor girl. Oh! How she ranted when she recounted the story to me! How she said she vows, with bitter regrets, to revenge herself on every man she'll ever encounter!

MARIE DUPLESSIS

I resolve to lock this new better version of myself in an imaginary box and bury it under the thick veil of my wretchedness. Every man I meet becomes another sorcerer resembling Father and Monsieur Plantier, another Valory eager to steal my soul.

Then, more eager and determined than ever, I renew my vows.

I am Marie Duplessis. I am a new woman. Beware, dear

men, or else you shall burn in the greatest fires of Hell. For I shall be your Hell, and nothing will prevent me from ruining you.

My forlorn disposition prolongs well into the spring of 1840. The winter I spend cloistered in my apartment, away from both the prying eyes in the streets and the men willing to take on what Valory discarded.

It is not until the first sunrays of spring hit frozen Paris and my equally frozen heart that I decide to resume my old self and the visits to Hortense's salon. It is there that on the early days of May 1840, I meet Monsieur Viscount de Méril.

The gentleman's affable nature alone pulls me out of my misery. Kind-hearted and amusing, Monsieur Viscount de Méril, succeeds — where others have failed — in placing upon my lips the first smile since the day my soul was taken from me. A very handsome man, he bears with dignity a name dear to France, an illustrious name attached to the Minister of the Interior.

But none of the attributes of my new protector will ever be able to make me forget about the true nature of men: kind and generous today, thieves and deserters tomorrow. De Méril cannot be any different. So, instead of following my natural romantic impulses, I sharpen my potential in the direction of his wealth. As a result, in less than a month, I become the best dressed woman in Paris. I even hire a servant, Rose, to attend the household chores in my stead.

Another result of my newly discovered unscrupulous nature is a sudden craving for traveling. Following my consistent suggestions, de Méril has his doctor issue an ordinance prescribing the use of thermal waters and asks for a month's leave, which is granted him. We set for Germany at once, traveling to Baden Baden by stagecoach. The journey lasts for six days, a long, tiresome undertaking. But in the end, the excursion, full of unforeseen, new sensations and exuberance, proves a marvelous choice.

Baden Baden instantly becomes my favorite country town. It is like nothing I have seen before. But again, I have seen only Paris and the countryside of Normandy. In a sense, this town incarnates the spirit of both and that is probably why I fell for it at a first glance. Though resembling Paris in many ways—with its air of sophistication, with people speaking in French no matter their background, with the names of hotels, restaurants and their menus written in French—it still retains the rustic air of countryside, nature, and connection with one's roots.

Imposing mountains embrace the town from all around, seeming like a giant stone monster protecting a rare, invaluable jewel. On the outskirts are boundless fields overcrowded by pasturing cattle, which remind me of my native Nonant. The promenade of Lichtentaler Allee recalls the Saint-Mathieu fair with its booths of food and trinkets and fake jewels.

But nothing is fake in Baden Baden. This is the gathering place for the aristocracy of all of Europe. Only dandies and crinoline women crowd the alleys. No thieves, no beggars, no murderers hiding under bridges are to be seen in Baden Baden.

And then there is the casino.

Since the casinos in Paris were closed down by law, avid gamblers took the route to Baden Baden. One can honestly say that half the visitors to this country town are here for the thermal waters and their benefits, while the other half rush here in and out of season to part with their splendid fortunes.

What proves less than splendid is *my* newly discovered inclination toward gambling. I have gambled with cards before, but that didn't prepare me for the enthusiasm brought about by the spectacle of a real casino. The piles of gold and silver on the green baize, the ivory ball spinning into the bottom of the roulette wheel, the uniformed croupiers quickly moving their scoops—all act as a mysterious substance able to slow down my thinking, make me forget my sorrow, and cheerly throw Monsieur Viscount de Méril's coins on those alluring green or red or gold casino tables.

Soon enough, however, not even the sudden rush the casino gifts me with can keep me away from my lurking, deep-seated feelings of loneliness. If it is due to the green fields with cattle reminding me of my childhood home or simply due to my despondent nature, isn't clear.

What is clear though, is that once we return to Paris, I resolve to reconnect with my past.

In mid-January, on a downcast lonely day and my seventeenth birthday, I resolve to write to my great-uncle, the man who took Delphine under his roof, after Father sold me to the gypsies.

My dear Monsieur Mesnil,

You probably think me a most ungrateful great-niece for not writing to you sooner. Although I search not for excuses, it must have been my shyness which prevented me from doing so. My thoughts have run back to you and your family on numerous occasions, for I have never had the chance—or should I say the maturity—to thank you for your unremitting love and care you always showed for my sister, Delphine. Is she still working as a laundress? I do miss her dearly and I am asking you to send her my best wishes.

As for myself, I live in Paris now, and am taken care

of very well. My friend, Monsieur Viscount de Méril, is truly a godsend. I lack nothing and am filled with hope that I will now have the means to live as I please.

I beg you not to deprive me of your friendship, dear Monsieur Mesnil, and please write back at the address you shall find on the back of the envelope.

Your most loving great-niece,

Alphonsine Plessis

Having expedited the letter, my heart feels lighter now. But it isn't meant to last. At least not for long.

THE DARK CLOUDS of this unfriendly January seem to emerge more threatening than ever. They also seem to close in on me, gnawing, swishing, blowing their grey baleful murkiness in my face. I try to grab the curtains flanking my apartment's window, but it is just more air, just more murkiness. The sharp pain to my head is the last thing I feel before passing out.

When I regain my composure, I find myself in Monsieur de Méril's strong arms. He sits quietly on my bed with his arms about me and his nose plunged into my hair. Freshly-washed linens cover me, and I find their flowery smell nauseating. I raise my eyes to the unfamiliar gentleman standing smiling by the window.

"My compliments, Mademoiselle Plessis," he says. "You are with child."

As if all too eager to escape his surreal words, or my even more surreal condition, I close my eyes and let the spinning clouds take me back to the dark calming nothingness.

CHAPTER 9

child? A child! What am I to do with a child? I pace the living room, as soon as I recover from my transitory indisposition. *But no! This is no transitory indisposition! This is for life! And it grows and grows until it will transform me into a bloated mass resembling a gestating cow! It will expand in me until I will no longer be able to fool myself into believing this is just a stupid joke! And when it will finally exit my body, it will continue to stick around to remind me of my one mistake, for the rest of my life!*

For only one time did I do that mistake. Only one time did I allow my impetuous, careless nature to transport me in the land of forgetfulness, without any precaution. One time! But it proved enough. And with who? With Monsieur Viscount de Méril, a man double my age, with as bloated a stomach as mine will soon be, a man I do not love.

I continue pacing my bedroom, pulling at my hair and slapping my face in a desperate effort to wake myself up from this incredible nightmare.

But it wasn't his fault...that I didn't follow his advice...

For he did advise me, the poor viscount, as best as he

could. But how could I have listened to that ridiculous urging of his? He told me to hold my breath and contract my stomach muscles. He said he read it in some magazine that had a column dedicated solely to women. My first thought was why would the monsieur read such a column? The second was that older men assume odd habits. Then I laughed. So loudly and mockingly, that the poor man almost said goodbye to his erection.

But alas! It returned. And when the deed was done, he showed himself equally eager to impart to me some more feminine secrets. He said I should squat and push. "Push! Push! Push! Until it's all out!" he screamed, red in the face. I did squat and pushed, but his red serious face got the best of me, and I collapsed on the floor in a fit of laughter.

But, no one is laughing now. The gentleman behaves nicely, though, reassuring me he'll always be by my side.

"I will never abandon you, my dear. You have my word. I will take care of you and your child to the grave, and beyond."

A few days ago, I would have laughed at him. I would have told him what I *really* think of promises and of the people making them. Yes. I would have laughed in his face, and then would have spent a few thousand francs of his money at the casino, just to spite him.

But now, my condition prevents me from enjoying my newly acquired sense of mockery. It also prevents me from eating, and when I do manage to swallow some fruit or glazed grapes — the only food items I can stand seeing and smelling — I find myself following my protector's advice. So, I squat and push, this time through my mouth, everything that went in.

Another thing my condition prevents me from doing, is going out of the house. I become a prisoner in my own apartment, and of my own resolution. Gone are Ernestine's dinners and balls and adulatory gazes. The only gaze left for me is my own, reflected from the mirror. And it is far from adulatory. A girl like me cannot afford to be seen in such a state. A girl like me would lose her potential benefactors faster than she lost her reputation. And then I will be nothing but a fallen woman, this time both in morals *and* in prospects.

So, I keep to my rooms, cussing and fumigating, using all the swear words I was taught in my early childhood, for close to seven months. When the time of the great delivery draws near, the viscount moves me into the apartment he's rented for me outside Paris, at Versailles. He also employs a midwife, a tall, skinny, old lady, with wrinkled hands and foul breath. And it is there, away from the enchanted blinking lights of my adopted city, that in the early hours of the most wonderful and warm May day, the horror of horrors begins.

I AM oblivious to how much time has already passed since I was carried to the improvised delivery bed I now lay upon. All I remember is the sharp sudden pain ripping through my body, and my silly thought of being struck by a firebolt that came with the pain. Then all went dark around me, and I began spinning lower and lower as if I were taken to the core of the earth. I then saw the aged hands of Monsieur Plantier, with long fingernails scratching my thighs, pulling my legs open, reaching for something, grabbing, twisting, growling...

"Get away from me! Get away from me!" I roared, kicking the sorcerer with my legs. He stood up from between my legs, and calmly propped them up against the two wooden poles on each side of the bed. But in a flash of lucidity I realized there was no sorcerer, only the midwife, straining to help a lunatic, with weak, wrinkled, trembling hands. The pain returned then, another firebolt striking me almost senseless, and I began kicking and screaming and cursing, until the being trying to make its way out of me, relieved me at last.

I shall not be able to ever forget the day of 5 May 1841. It is the day that shakes both my body and mind to the core. The day I bring a healthy looking boy into this world of good and evil. The day the midwife places him in my arms then disappears into the night like a wandering ghost. And the day when, for the first time, I look in my son's little dark sparkling eyes and feel...nothing.

You're tired. I am desperate to get rid of the guilt. *No human being, and all the less a fragile woman like yourself, should go through that. You'll again be yourself tomorrow. Just wait and see.*

I do wait, for two nights and a day it seems, for this is how long my body decides to sleep. When I do finally wake, it is not the little dark sparkling eyes of my son that gaze into my sleepy ones, but those of the congratulatory doctor who gave me the news of my life, seven months prior.

"You are not well," he says upon seeing me awake. "Your temperature has dropped, but I'm afraid the delivery was deeply traumatic for your body."

"You don't say!" I scoff, struggling to sit up. The sight of those wooden poles at the side of the bed almost make me throw up. Pain returns at the simple memory of it, I realize.

"I suggest you remain in bed for another few days," the doctor continues, and I look at the woman standing next to him, who nods in agreement. She holds my son at her breast, and I deduce she must be the wet nurse. "Then at least three months of retirement in the countryside."

"I'm in no disposition for humor," I say, reverting my gaze to the doctor.

"Neither am I," he retorts. "And this is not negotiable. Either you'll recuperate in the country, or you'll be pushing up daisies before having had the chance to name your baby."

I look at the doctor with a straight face, having already decided to disregard his advice. What does *he* know, by the by? He might know that a woman like me can perish if she's seen with a bloated stomach. But does he know that she could perish just as quickly if not being seen at all? Three months in the country could prove my ultimate undoing. It could throw me back into my beggar clothes, and that is something my delicate psyche could never endure.

"I must return to Paris at once!" I proclaim, frightened by the thought of my demise entering my head. But as my hands push me off the bed, the firebolt returns, hitting me right in the head. The menacing pain reclaims my strength and I fall back upon the bed.

"Are you out of your mind, Madame?" the doctor blurts, rushing to my side.

"I might as well be…"

"You have a child to raise!"

Frightened by my grievous condition, as well as by the guilt arising from the doctor's outburst of castigating words, I mumble some sort of agreement. Resigned, I sigh and extend my arms toward the wet nurse. She approaches me and places my son in my arms. I caress his pinkish cheeks and he smiles. His little eyes look curiously into mine, while I curiously search into my heart. But there is nothing there. Still nothing there. All I can trace within me are painful memories of my past. A little girl abandoned by her mother; a little girl taken away from her sister; a sensitive heart thrown out into the street; a hungry little soul spurned by everyone she's ever loved; a starving waif humiliated by those who should have guided and protected her. An orphan always on the run from grown-ups.

Then, still looking into his little eyes, I think of his father. It startles me to think of his father only in connection with not thinking of his father. For not once has the viscount entered my head. Not once have I called for his help or screamed his name during those excruciating labor pains. Not once did I realize I already have a protector and should not be thinking of searching for another.

It's only pain you remind me of! Only misery and wanting! Bitter tears gather in my eyes. *There is no love for us in this world! There is no more love left in me, my little one...not even for you.*

Acknowledging my thoughts as well as my lack of feelings feels like self-created hell. For it is hell I have created and in hell I shall be living.

"What will Madame name him?" the voice of the wet nurse breaks through the silence.

"Name him..." I whisper. "His father shall name him."

And his father does name him, I suppose. For I demand never to be told his name. Or other things about him. For only when you know such things do you begin to feel for a creature. Only then does pain begin. Do we ever feel love for the meat on our plates? Do we ever feel sorry for the veal we've just eaten? Never. There is no single thought about the pain a creature went through to adorn our tables. No thought about the sacrifice.

I remember the rooster we had when I was but a child. He was my companion every time I would run to hide from Father in Agathe's barn. He wouldn't talk, of course, but he would stay there by my side and even let me pet him. For hours he would just nestle in my arms, listening to my silly stories of woe. I named him Roux, so fascinated was I with his ginger crest. Then, one day, he simply disappeared.

Vanished. In vain, I searched for him with eyes full of tears. In vain, I called his name, cajoled and clucked. But in the end, I did find him. Not in his vast surroundings wiggling his crest in the air, but on our plates. Both me and my sister refused to eat that stew. Even famished as we always were, we refused to eat my friend, and went on for days crying and castigating Agathe for her slaughter. Roux was a friend, for I had made him a friend.

Thus, I learned the difference then. And thus, I learned never again to make that mistake.

THE FOLLOWING WEEK, almost half-mad from so much repose, I demand to be taken back to Paris at once. Once in my old familiar apartment, I let myself fall freely onto an armchair. On the gold coffee table, I glimpse a letter. My maid, Rose, must have placed it there in my absence. As I rip open the envelope and read the content, my heart, once again, alerts me that there is no space left in it for love or compassion.

> *My dearest great-niece,*
>
> *There is so much to recuperate through both words and deeds, but for now, suffice to inform you that your father, Marin Plessis, has died of leprosy and was buried in Ginai. Upon his death, I have become your sole guardian. Should you wish to visit his grave anytime soon, I shall gladly accompany you. My condolences, dearest Alphonsine.*
>
> *You ever loving great-uncle,*
> *M. Mesnil*

"Rose!" I scream at the maid, who rushes into the room. "Yes, Madame!"

"Pack my hats and frocks. And yours, too. We're going to the country."

Tired of searching for answers to my inner questions, and even more tired to question the answers I discover, I resolve to do what others say, for once.

AT DAWN, following my doctor's advice, I climb into the stagecoach taking me to the country. With Father dead and buried, and since on his timely departure he had also taken with him my fear of him, the choice of destination is a breeze.

It's been only three short years since I left Normandy, but I am ready to rediscover the place of my birth.

FROM WHAT I REMEMBER, never did Normandy looked fresher and more beautiful than in summer. But now, in the summer of 1841, it looks beyond beautiful. Now, it looks magical. Every house, tree, and tavern we pass by evokes a wretched memory. But today, those memories are distant, as if from a different life—someone else's life.

As the stagecoach nears Nonant after a long tiresome journey, I find myself pondering on the differences in my perceptions. Returning here, I expected tears, as the clawing feeling in my stomach has not relented. But tears do not come. Instead, all that comes is the realization that Normandy has always been as it is today. The difference is my perception of it.

Another realization washes over me and I now understand that while Father was alive, everything was dark and gloomy. But Father is no more, and by token, tears are no more. No wonder Normandy seems magical, for only through magic will I ever forget and forgive my past.

I instruct the coachman to stop at the Hôtel de La Poste. Having been on the road for four days, I resolve to spend a night or two in the comfort of the hotel before continuing to my final destination—my sister's home. As I sit in front of the hotel, strange but pleasant feelings take hold of me.

"It's good to be back," I whisper and make my way inside.

ROMAIN VIENNE

On that first day she spent at our hotel, I met Alphonsine. At the time she arrived in Nonant, I was twenty-five years old and still living at my parents' house. They owned the post office and the Hôtel de La Poste, a vast establishment of the first order with numerous employees, a hundred horses in the stables, and thirty foals and mares in the grasslands.

A young lady, accompanied by a maid of sixteen or seventeen, fresh and pink-skinned, took a seat at the hotel's table and asked for the finest room. The former was tall and slender, with an elegant appearance and wearing a simple but tasteful toilette, and a little bonnet adorned with lace. She had the pale, almost sickly face of a convalescent. And although she said nothing, we were all persuaded that she was not unknown to us. However, there was no address on her luggage; only a name on the driver's sheet: Marie Duplessis.

At five o'clock in the evening, after a restful sleep, she came downstairs, approached my mother and said, "Good evening, Madame Vienne. You do not recognize me, yet you know me well. I am the little Plessis girl."

"Ah! Certainly, my poor girl. I would not have

recognized you," replied my astonished mother. "Are you staying here tonight?"

"Oh! Yes, madam, today and tomorrow. I feel so good in this pretty room and good bed that I will stay two days at your house to rest. I will notify my sister of my arrival tomorrow evening. Would you kindly allow me and my maid to take our meals at the same table as you?"

"Certainly, I do not mind, since it pleases you."

Then, Marie held out her hand to me.

"Hello, Monsieur Romain," she said, with a large smile.

Not having seen her in five years, I did not remember any of her features, so just stood there with her little hand in mine, awestruck by her gentle manner and terrifying beauty.

Marie Duplessis

Invigorated by a two-hour sleep in one of the hotel's rooms, I find myself famished. Going downstairs, I meet the hotel's owner, a lovely woman I remember well. I also meet her son, Romain, whom I also remember, though he doesn't seem to remember me. His flushed cheeks and uneasiness while kissing my hand enliven me and I instantly take a liking to him.

I ask permission to dine with them, so eager am I for news of my relatives and acquaintances.

"You did not recognize me, did you?" I ask Romain, while taking our seats at the table.

His cheeks redden again. "Um, I'm afraid not, Mademoiselle Alphonsine. My mother told me—"

"Call me, Marie."

"Marie..." He nods, and I smile.

"But I do remember your mother," he says next.

My heart is not entirely dead it seems, for him merely alluding to my mother stirs it profusely.

"How lucky you are...to remember her," I say. "I was very little when she left us to go into hiding. How was she, Romain?"

He drops his shoulders. "Very beautiful. But it was a sad beauty. She had grief stricken eyes the last day I saw her. She was at the market and my mother stopped to greet her. She was very polite, but I could never forget the harrowing sadness in her eyes. It wasn't long thereafter that we learned that she'd fled."

Tears are glistening in my eyes now, and he stops.

"Yes, from my father," I add.

"I know. I know everything about it. And even though I did not recognize you at first, I know many stories about your childhood. People here still talk about you. *The poor little Plessis girl* is what they call you."

"The poor little Plessis girl," I echo, looking through the window into an unknown distance. "I do have something left from my mother, though. Something I can use to always remind me of her."

"What is that?"

"Her name. A tragic beauty with a tragic name." I sigh.

"I do hope, Mademoiselle Marie, that you are more fortunate than your mother."

"I am. Not so poor these days."

"And your heart?"

The food arrives and I thank God for this distraction that allows me to ignore his question.

After the meal, I ask Romain to show me around the garden.

"Tell me, Romain, what do you do in life?" I ask while greedily breathing in the fresh Normandy air.

"I help my parents with the hotel now. But I lived in

Paris, too. I studied medicine and law there for several years."

"You don't say. What made you return here? It's hard to leave Paris, isn't it?"

"It wasn't. But it was Normandy that brought me back. My roots, I suppose. This very air."

"This air brought me back, too. But I am not here to stay."

"Only recuperating?" he asks, avoiding my look, while bending to pick a bunch of cornflowers.

"Is it that obvious? Well yes, you are right. I told everything to your mother. I gave birth to a handsome boy and have come to restore my health in the country."

Romain extends his arms full of flowers and I gladly accept them, while searching his eyes for signs of disapproval. But there is none, nor judgement either. The rest of the night I confess everything to him. About Paris, about my decadent life and lovers, about my lack of feelings for my son. He gives me his shoulder to cry upon and in return I share with him my unadulterated soul.

SEEING my sister after three years fills me with exhilaration, but also with sadness. She is twenty now, a pretty brunette with great potential. But her manners are those of a peasant —brusque and callous. No more hands extended to receive me; just a cold, indifferent gaze.

The sudden idea that I could change her perspective enters my head and I begin promoting my Parisian life with unusual vigor. To advance this plan, I also write to Ernestine, instructing her to describe Paris in the most favorable terms in her reply.

In less than a week, the letter arrives and I take my sister to the post office. I read Ernestine's letter aloud, emphasizing each word I feel could trigger my sister's enthusiasm.

But her reaction is far from what I expected and hoped for. Not only she does not appreciate my effort to change her miserable circumstances, but she proceeds to call me a fallen woman who's given birth to a bastard, who's lost her way and only the church could now save her soul from certain damnation. Hurt, humiliated and scorned, I resolve to take my belongings and my lonely damnable soul and move to stay with our great uncle, de Mesnil, for the rest of my imposed convalescence.

And as if my sister's insults and rejection of my good intentions were not enough, the good providence decides to deride me again.

At the end of September, I receive a letter from my protector. It is not the usual one containing the hundred francs he sends every week, but one containing words I would give anything to erase from memory.

Marie,

I pondered for a long time on whether I should write to you or not, especially now that you're in such a weak condition. But after a long conflict with my own conscience I have decided in favor of the former.

There are no appropriate words one could use to pass on such dreadful news. So, I am telling it straightly. Our son contracted pneumonia a fortnight after your departure and has died. I have buried him in consecrated ground even though he hadn't been baptized.

Marie, my heart is too shattered to ever be disposed to see you again. I also have asked for a transfer to Burgundy and am now leaving my sorrow behind to embrace a new beginning.

Farewell, my dearest Marie. I hope that one day you
will find it in your heart to forgive me.
My condolences,
V. De Méril

It takes a mighty tragedy to realize that I do have a feeling heart. Only in the face of uncompromising death do I realize what I have lost: the only soul who could have truly loved me.

"No!" I howl, shortly before succumbing to the vast spaces of nothingness.

CHAPTER 10

One can suffer only so much before one realizes that continuing to nourish a feeling heart is the worst possible resolution. It seems that my life is a continuous succession of discoveries meant to turn me into a marble statue, with nothing but dead stone inside. And though I acknowledge most of these discoveries as baleful, I can't fail to also notice the good I must learn from them. The more of them I witness and experience, the faster I seem able to plumb the depths of my pain. Maybe God wants me to stop feeling. Perhaps my life is one mysterious journey where I learn that as long as I will let myself be guided by emotions, my doom will always be near. Or maybe life should be nothing but a stage where you execute your finest skills— and my finest skill is that of merchandising love.

But merchandising love, upon my return to Paris, seems to be the last thing in store for me. On account of my prolonged absence, as well as de Méril's abandonment, I find myself not only displaced from high society but also molested by my finances. In other words, I am stone broke.

And because keeping an extravagant house, a

demanding maid, and the status of *best-dressed woman in Paris* requires immediate action, my last resolution is to return to work. Not in Ernestine's salon, where it would take me weeks to find another worthy protector, but in Mademoiselle Urbain's new clothing shop.

The humiliation is felt deeply. Only three months ago, I was Mademoiselle Urbain's most proficient customer, leaving hundreds of francs on her counter with each one of my visits. Alas, today, if I am not to return on the streets again, I must make do with the pittance I receive from her.

But as the saying goes, there is always something good in everything bad, and I realize that it is much easier to tolerate my wounded pride while at the arm of a friend. Lili, my new colleague, is a fragile eighteen-year-old girl with a luxurious stack of golden curls. She becomes my new protégée. And though we are about the same age, the girl's unfortunate condition arouses an urge to mother and protect her. If this urge is because I remember my own unfortunate past too well, or because I try to redress the deed of abandoning my son to the clutches of death, I do not really know. But what I do know is the sorrow of a girl who's been abandoned. And just like me, Lili was seduced and discarded like a mongrel dog by the man she'd fallen in love with, a man who left her behind—without means for survival—to gather the pieces of her shattered soul. Deeply ashamed, she abhorred the idea of returning to her rich parents, who surely could have provided for her. But no.

Just as it was with me, being goaded by shame and hunger had brought her to work for Maidmoselle Urbain's pittance.

Once again, men's repugnant hypocrisy hits me, and at these times I work myself into shouting, pounding my frustrations into poor Lili's head.

"They did nothing but subdue us! For centuries! They

force us into an inferior position since the cradle! Starting with our fathers!" I rant, as I slalom through the racks of dresses, throwing my arms about.

Lili just smiles and nods.

"They allowed us no significant role outside of kitchens and barns! Disallowed us basic rights they themselves take for granted on an hourly basis! God forbid we should read, for then we'll get bizarre ideas! But that wasn't good either, for they loathed seeing us turn out stupid and uneducated! They hated our simplicity and reproached us for not being able to stimulate them! Not intellectually, and not in bed! And all the while forgetting that we were *their* creation! *Their* own blasted doing!"

"How right you are, Marie..." Lili says, shaking her head remorsefully. "Gustave said I was but a spoiled girl from a rich family, with no notion of reality. 'Too demanding for nothing', he said."

But I can barely hear her, so engulfed am I in my harangue.

"Then, we in turn become displeased for having displeased them! And no sooner did we start thrusting our heads out in search of some education, distinctiveness, and independence, than they began calling us harlots and wantons and defilers of their good morals and high breeding. Damning us once again to a life of eternal shame and disrepute! Us! *Their* creation!"

"Who's that?" Lili asks, putting an abrupt end to my passionate tirade.

"What? Who?" I ask, half-dazed, half-curious.

"That gentleman standing outside. Do you know him?"

I look through the shop windows to see a tall, blond, young man staring sharply into my eyes.

"Ah. Him." I smirk. "He passes by the shop twice a

week and always pauses to look at me for several minutes. I don't know him."

"A secret admirer!" she bursts, clasping her face between her palms. "Isn't it the most romantic thing in the whole wide world?"

"Yeah, well. Need I remind you what happened to you the last time you were in a romantic frame of mind?"

My question goes unanswered, as Lili has already darted outside and is speaking with the gentleman. Enervated by her audacity, I resume my trot between the racks. Five dreadfully long minutes pass before she returns. The gentleman still lingers beyond the windows, looking like a fanatical stalker.

"What in the world possessed you?" I snap at Lili. "Running out, addressing yourself to a total stranger? He could be a criminal or a—"

"Oh, my sweet lord Jesus! He is totally besotted with you!"

"What?"

"He said he knows you. That he'd seen you at the house of some Madame Ernestine, but you only had eyes for another gentleman and never noticed him."

Hearing his confession from Lili's mouth embarrasses me. I raise my eyes to his again and see he's still staring in my direction. That makes me even more uncomfortable and, grabbing Lili's arm, I drag us both out of his sight.

"Why is he still there? What does he want?" I ask.

Lili smiles the most warm, loving smile I have ever seen.

"He's asked me to introduce him to you. He begged me to curb his misery, for misery is the only thing hovering about him since he's seen you looking in another's eyes as he should have wanted you to look into his. These are his very words!"

I am quiet for a while, trying to process Lili's words. She, on the other hand, sways from foot to foot.

"He said he knows me, you say?"

"Yes!"

"What is his name, then?"

"That, I don't know."

"Foolish girl! You ought to be more caref—"

"But I'll ask." She's disappeared again only to reappear a few seconds later with an even brighter smile upon her lips.

"Well?" I ask, impatiently.

"Brace yourself, for you're about to get the break of your life! He's a duke! Duke Agénor de Guiche! Oh, mon Dieu, his peers are royalty! Oh, Lord...A romantic hero! A romantic hero utterly infatuated with you!"

I smile at Lili's innocence. If only she knew ... the history of the person standing in front of her. If only she would suspect that her "romantic hero" is nothing but a man in heat, who knew my real profession all along. The romantic hero who passes by the store to buy not expensive clothes for a beautiful young bride, but for my very expensive sexual services.

"Very well then. You can tell the gentleman he can call on me on Saturday at ten o'clock. Not one minute earlier or later. Saturday, ten o'clock sharp. Here's where he should come." I grab a piece of paper to write down my home address.

"How cold," Lili whispers, while reluctantly taking the note from my hand.

"Come again?"

"Cold. You are very cold. Merciless. The gentleman is so...and you...you have no heart."

I burst out laughing. "I do have a heart, rest assured. Now, go give the duke what he asked for. Off with you."

As she trails off, I find myself envying the simplicity of

her heart and mind. A simplicity I have long lost and never will be able to reclaim.

On Saturday morning at ten o'clock sharp, there is a knock on my door. I instruct Rose to receive the visitor in my drawing room. Then, for half an hour, I prepare myself: dressing up, styling my hair and applying red tint to my cheeks and lips. I also perfume my wrists, the back of the ears, and my décolleté.

Prior to this visit, I made sure to enquire about the young duke. Having a trick up your sleeve is better than none when meeting a potential protector.

Upon entering my drawing room, I see Monsieur de Guiche sitting lazily in an armchair, his expression unnerved. I clear my throat; and he jumps to his feet. The image amuses me terribly and I make every effort to contain my laugh. He is unusually tall, with bright blue eyes, and dressed as if going to a royal ball.

"Mademoiselle Duplessis! What an honor to be received by you," he says as he nears me, hand outstretched.

"I thought I mentioned ten o'clock sharp," I say, as he kisses my hand.

"But, Mademoiselle, I have knocked on your door precisely at the time you instructed! I arrived earlier and waited in the street!"

I cannot contain myself any longer and burst into a hefty laughter.

"Ay! Silly me!" he says. "You're especially mischievous this morning, Mademoiselle. I am happy to find you in such delightful mood."

"Forgive me, Monsieur. You must allow a young girl her foibles, mustn't you?" With a gesture of my hand, I indicate that he sit next to me. "What could bring a gentleman like yourself to my humble home?"

As he sits next to me, seemingly pondering his answer, I again think of the hypocrisy of high society. Of course I know why he's come. Of course he knows I know why he's come. And certainly we both know what we both know; we're just secretly hoping the one does not know the other's thoughts; hence, we're pretending. One would not like being called a skirt chaser and the other would loathe being told she's sought only for sex. And never mind being asked about how the payments should be made. This is high society. High society members have manners. Hypocrisy, in my view, but still manners.

"Mademoiselle, I will confess everything to you at once," he says, taking my hands in his. "I am hopelessly in love with you. I cannot go on another day without having the certainty that you will receive me often to keep your company. As a friend, or as anything you would like me to be. For I have lost my sleep since first I saw you."

Have you now? Mon Dieu, you're quite good at this game, aren't you?

"Monsieur, you make me blush!" I say, fluttering my hand fan close to my face. "I must tell you a little secret. You are the first man to have that power over me. No one has ever had it."

He throws himself to his knees and brings his hands together as if in prayer, then looks into my eyes with the most hopeful and plaintive of gazes. "So, there is hope then?"

I purse my lips for a few moments, then grab his face between my palms.

"Well, my darling Agénor, there could be hope, but..."

"But?" His eyes are welling up, and I am laughing gleefully on the inside.

Ah! High society!

"But...there are certain conditions I impose on those who suddenly find themselves enamored with me."

"I am all ears, Marie. May I call you Marie?"

"You may. After all, we've just past the moment of... uncertainty—if I can call it that."

I wink and he throws back a furtive smile.

"So. For one, my angel, you must love me above all others. You must be neither possessive of me, nor jealous of those who might also happen to be loving me."

Head down, Monsieur Agénor de Guiche, the great lion of Paris, nods at my every word.

"But most importantly, you must, in your pure heart, think about my future. Should you like to be seen and admired escorting at your arm the best-dressed woman in Paris, then you must think there is always a price that comes with that status."

"Of course."

"You are young, so very young. But I've heard about you. A ladies' man who doesn't waste time on love. That's the talk spreading about town. Is it true?"

"I only give my heart to the worthy. And my heart is yours, Marie."

"Ah, my angel, you're making me flush again. Barely a stroke of the clock since you came and you already have so much power over me."

He takes my hands in his again. "When shall I come and see you, then?"

"How about tomorrow evening?"

He eagerly agrees and we part.

THE TALK about town goes further than my dear Agénor's preference of disposable ladies. It says that my duke could hardly be much grander. The son of Duke and Duchess de Gramont, his family is one of the most influential at court, his father having been no less than the First Gentleman to the heir to the throne of France. But as much as his family's position inspire reverence, the talk goes that it is by no means as rich as it once used to be. In fact, they are quite poor, as only recently the Duchess has had to sell her diamond and emerald jewels. This says much about my young lion. For one, it says that it is his position and influence I should go after, as it might prove even more advantageous than his money. For another, it allows me to take other protectors, if the one with the heavy title fails to look after my expenses in a manner that pleases me.

And by my side, he does look proud, as he said he would. Conversely, at his arm, I am introduced into a new world, the world I always dreamed of. A world of abundance inhabited by the most worthy of France; frock-coated nobles who all bow to me as if I were their equal. A new world with new habits I must acquire and assume as my own. A sharply defining world that teaches me the poise, walk, and movement of the arrogant wives of those frock-coated noblemen—women who fear and despise me and will never allow me to forget my humble background or my current, disgraceful profession.

I like to think it is fear rather than hate that goads the society women to act against me on the occasions I attend public performances. Having a private box at the Opera is out of my financial reach, so I must mingle with the rest of the opera goers in the stalls.

On one such occasion, barely having sat for a few minutes, I am approached by an angry-looking bailiff who, in very rude language, asks me to leave the premises. My efforts to escape his determination to throw me out, by showing him my ticket and hinting at the law, are in vain.

But, it isn't the bailiff's rude language that's the worst, rather it's the smug glares and judgmental nods coming from the ladies in the audience. It is my young duke offering me his arm and escorting me elsewhere that saves me.

But this is only one occasion. On others, even if I am allowed to retain my seat in the stalls, I feel like a human target roped to a forest tree.

And there is yet another world into which Agénor de Guiche introduces me. A more private world dedicated to the art of lovemaking and to Art itself. He teaches me a great deal of novelty and I follow his instructions like a dutiful student. His strong hands guide mine across his naked skin, teaching me where and when I should touch; when to be gentle and when not; how to use my stare to seduce, subdue, and control; when to submit and when to lead; when to caress, kiss, lick and suck, and what parts of my body are especially enjoyable to men. I learn that, in bed, using my mouth in other ways than uttering words or tasting food has the power to make a man go down on his knees literally and figuratively.

Using my other orifice, however, the one destined solely as exit for the food I hinted at earlier, proves particularly unpleasant for me on these first days of training. But guided by my young duke's patience and gentleness, I discover a new world of pleasure I can now impart to both my lovers and myself.

And finally, my experienced gentleman teaches me how to use the art of dirty language, of powerful expressions whispered behind closed doors to arouse men's appetites. Expressions that if whispered outside bedrooms would cause a commotion of fainting ladies and visits to the priest for an imposed exorcism.

After his lessons end and we both fall sweating onto our backs, Agénor reads to me. He resolves to take it upon himself to make a respectable woman out of me—but only outside the bedroom—by teaching me to love to read. The characters of classic and contemporary novels come to life through his sometimes candid, sometimes raspy voice, and he transports me, yet again, into another world. A world of endless possibilities, of lives lived without restrictions, of both passionate love and harrowing suffering; in fewer words, a world of magic.

In less than a fortnight, I build my own indoor library, a magnificent piece of carved oak, as equipped and comprehensive as that of all society's intellectuals. For I want to know the refinements and pleasure of artistic taste, the joy of living in elegant and cultivated society. More than two hundred books grace the shelves. Among them are the great classics, Rabelais, Marivaux, Byron, Cervantes, and Molière. The works of Lamartine and Victor Hugo are kept on a special shelf, for these are the men one could meet at Mabille or the Maison d'Or. I have seen them, though only from afar; but these are the men with whom I want to keep company.

While Agénor likes to read aloud from the classics, I, in turn, like to read to him the missives I receive from my other protectors. These are our best moments, which always put us in the best of humor, laughing at an old gentlemen's gaucherie with words, the pathetic pleas and comical requests.

One such missive I read to Agénor went like this:

Ma chérie,

My heart is still pounding at a maddening speed as a result of what my poor eyes have seen the other day while I was walking in Bois de Boulogne.

There I was, engulfed in a lively conversation about you with The General, when I suddenly saw the carriage I have gifted you last week furiously speeding past us, almost knocking us off our feet.

My heart almost leapt out of my chest, thinking that your coachman had lost his grip over your horses, and you, ma chérie, were now heading toward certain destruction. But looking closer, I saw the coachman being fully in control, and...lo and behold, he wasn't even your coachman but Monsieur de Guiche! That young lion was driving you through the park while you were laughing like a madwoman!

And what's more, M. de Guiche was holding the black spaniel I also gifted you along with the carriage, on the high-bench next to him!

Madame, you leave me no choice but to provoke M. de Guiche to a duel, or in the best of cases, and guided by your suggestion, to have a witty word with the duke.

I am most displeased with your conduct, Madame, and expect a believable explanation from your part.

Count F. de Montguyon

Monsieur de Montguyon's words, apart from being hypocritical, are utterly comical. For the count freely admits that he was *"engulfed in a lively conversation about you with The General"*, the latter being one of my protectors and the former couldn't have not known this. Their conversation might easily have been about The General surprising de Guiche in my bed on an impromptu visit, or about him complaining that I do not receive him as often as I used.

Ah, men!

There is no duel and no exchange of witty words between de Montguyon and de Guiche. What is more, the gentleman expedites another letter to me in which he apologizes for his *"impudent transgression"*.

But my laughter doesn't last long. Word of my lover's

infatuation reaches the ears of my young lion's mighty parents and he is ordered to leave the country at once.

At the beginning of July, Agénor sets sail for London, abandoning me just like all the other men that ever met me before him.

CHAPTER 11

*W*ith my favorite lover gone, I have no choice but to accept the unwavering attentions of Monsieur de Montguyon who buys me another dog and resolves to get rid of my current one.

"He's been tainted," he says. "But not to worry. I have found the perfect companion for him," he continues, gently squeezing my arm.

"Another Marie?" I ask mockingly.

A satisfied smile beams from his face. Poor Montguyon...he fancies me jealous and him quite the dandy.

Two weeks seem like a lifetime spent in total confinement, and at their end I am looking for a way out, or else. I could either visit my lover in England or go to Baden Baden, where the glitz and buzz of the casino could keep me entertained until his return. I write a letter to Agénor to sound out his intentions. His reply makes it plain that I am not wanted there.

Although my pride is wounded, I have come to terms with where I am welcome and where not. Except for the men's soirées or the various Parisian cafes, there are very few places that welcome me. Nonetheless, I must keep the duke on my side or he might suddenly find himself enamored with someone else.

My dear Agénor,

Although you have not been gone for long, I have some things to tell you. First, my angel, I am very sad, and very bored because I can't see you. I do not know yet when I will leave for Baden Baden, but I would like it to be soon, because I am being bothered by The General, who insists that I receive him and continue to be with him as before. He has no intention of changing his conduct toward me...The journey must be done if only to serve in guarding my fidelity to you, my dear Agénor. Sadly enough, my angel, I have been obliged to borrow forty thousand francs for my journey and must think up a way to repay them on my return.

But let's talk of the present, my poor angel—and not regret the past... I would like to ask your advice: whether or not I should travel with Mme. Weller. I am very bothered because I hardly understand this woman, who at times is excessively nice to me and at others changes her manner completely. So, I am waiting to get your response as a friend.

Write me a long letter soon—tell me everything you're thinking, and what you're doing—tell me also that you love me—I need to know this, and it will be a consolation for your absence, my good angel. I am very sad, but I love you more tenderly than ever. I embrace you a thousand times on your mouth and everywhere else. Adieu my darling angel, don't forget me too much, and think sometimes of she who loves you so much.

Marie Duplessis

As soon as I finish writing the letter, I tell old Mme. Weller—the fickle servant—and my maid, Rose, to pack my bags. On Friday, the 22nd of July 1842, we arrive in the resplendent Baden Baden.

My choice of lodging is of course, the Hôtel de l'Europe. And my room, the best in the hotel, is facing the river and the Conversation House, where a ball takes place three times a week.

The first few days I give myself over to resting. My strength, although not as glorious as it used to be, still allows me long walks on the Lichtentaler Allee, Baden Baden's own Bois de Boulogne. The tall fir trees above my head remind me of a long-lost world; a world in which nature and simplicity were enough for mankind; a world in which neither the brilliance of one's attire nor the refulgence of one's finery mattered. I yearn for that world and yet wonder if I could live in it. For nowadays simplicity sounds to me so much worse than luxury.

Such are my thoughts when my eyes gaze upon an old distinguished gentleman sitting on a shaded bench. I had seen him yesterday, and the day before that sitting on the same bench with his teary eyes fastened on me.

If I were in a different place, I would have been scared. But not here. Scary things don't happen in Germany, I heard. At the least, not in Baden Baden.

Yesterday he even stood up and walked behind me at a safe distance. I could feel those teary eyes burning my back. I even got the urge to approach him and offer my assistance, lest he perish from that heartrending wretchedness nestled in his breast.

"Mademoiselle?" A low, shaky voice pushes into the moment. I turn around to see that the distinguished gentleman has finally gathered the courage to speak to me.

"Oui?"

"Mademoiselle, may I be granted the pleasure of walking with you?" he says, as he doffs his high hat.

"Well..." I hesitate.

"Do not fear, Mademoiselle, that I am trying to woo you," he says with a candid smile. "It would suit neither my age, nor my taste. You are very beautiful, but you will understand the kind of feelings your beauty inspires in me when I tell you that I have recently lost a daughter whom you resemble like a sister...more than a sister."

"Very well then," I say and smile in return, offering him my arm. "I have seen your eyes, Monsieur—" I say, as we resume walking on the cobblestones.

"Count Gustav von Stackelberg."

"I am Marie, Monsieur von Stackelberg. Marie Duplessis."

"I know your name. My daughter who you resemble so much was also called Marie. Can you imagine my delight at finding that out?" I smile at the old man whose enthusiasm rather matches that of a boy. "And please, call me Gustav," he resumes. "I might be an old relic, but I certainly don't like to think of myself as one."

"Very well, Gustav. I was saying that I have seen your eyes and they grieved me. But not for a moment have I thought such ordeal to be the reason behind your sadness."

For a moment the gentleman closes his eyes as if to conceal the real depth of his pain. Fighting back tears he says, "Mademoiselle, I have a favor to ask you. I would like to see you often to remind me of my daughter. It is not unusual to commission artists to paint portraits of those one has lost, and you would be the living portrait of my child."

By now, his begging eyes, the white eyebrows sheltering eyes holding an unspeakable sorrow, his very shattered voice give rise in me an array of conflicting feelings. It is mostly reverence in the face of a father's anguish at losing his daughter, but there is also shame; for the gentleman stands in front of a woman who had abandoned her child; in front of a heartless mother who spared no tears when her child joined the land of the departed. My shame and embarrassment make me hesitate again. It is as if I am not worthy to listen to his anguish, not worthy to be thus worshiped.

But then, the count speaks again, and my shame is replaced with relief.

"The purity of your features reveals a soul at odds with your conduct," he says. My eyes widen, my mouth opens. Yet no word comes out.

"Forgive me, Marie...but my interest in you is complete. Ever since I saw you the other day— the day I thought my angel daughter had returned to me—I made inquiries about you. I wanted to know everything about you."

"And is the gentleman disappointed with his findings?" I ask, taken aback. I suddenly realize that the shame hasn't gone anywhere.

"So, you do not deny it then?"

I give a scoffing little laugh. "Monsieur, I might spend a lot of time in a horizontal position, but in my spare time I am quite a vertical woman. A woman who will always own her deeds and choices. There is nothing to deny, for I am the creation of my own will." My throat contracts with tears.

"Please, forgive me," he rushes to add, stopping me in mid-step. He takes my face in his hands. "I am sorry. I had no intention to offend you. I just found it hard to believe what I was hearing about the angel crossing my path. I am a very wealthy man, Marie. Will you renounce the existence you lead? You can name the figure of income I will undertake to provide. Accept the offer I am making you, Marie. Help me to accomplish a doubly pious act—that of

honoring the memory of the deceased and of bringing honor
to the living."

I find myself at a loss for words to explain how deeply
his proposition moves me. It is the first time that anyone has
spoken to me in this way. I stare at the old man who is
willing to give a lost girl the charity of comparing her to a
child untouched by vice. I remain silent and dab at my eyes.
The gentleman takes my action to be my assent.

"Thank you, Marie, from the bottom of my heart. I
promise you will not regret it. I am a man of his word. You
will believe this when I tell you that I have been a diplomat
my entire life. I have also been one of Catherine the Great's
favorites, and it was in Russia that I spent most of my
adulthood."

We resume our walk. "I am most proud to be in such
company, Gustav. Thank you for—" But he doesn't seem to
hear me, so I resolve to let the octogenarian pour his
heart out.

"I have served my country well, culminating with my
receiving Russia's most prestigious award: the Order of St.
Andrew. Also, my surroundings proved instrumental in
helping me choose a wife to my pretentious taste. I was very
young when I met the Austrian ambassador's daughter,
Countess Caroline von Ludolf. We were married in a
fortnight. She blessed our family with twelve children over
a period of three decades. And when my retirement arrived,
we decided to move to Paris, my wife's favorite city in the
entire world."

"Mine, too!" I interrupt. "There is no place quite like
Paris!"

He smiles at me candidly and sighs deeply.

"To me, it is the place I will always associate with the
most dreadful news of my life. It was there, two years ago,

that we learned our two daughters, Marie and Elizavetta, had died in Turin."

Silence swallows us both. What am I to tell this poor man to comfort him, when I myself proved shameful in the face of death? I continue to be at a loss for words.

However, the week isn't yet over when the grieving father turns into a lion and begins courting me with the conceit of a young hero.

Men shall be men to their graves.

By August 2nd, we both move out of our hotels to reunite at the Hotel de Hollande. There, on the quiet premises of that secluded Baden Baden hotel, I again remember how to find pleasure in grey hairs and physical flaws.

UNDER THE PROTECTION of my octogenarian count, bitter want becomes an unpleasant, distant memory. My other protectors' material attentions seem like brightly lit torches risen toward a resplendent sun. Even I, as equipped as I lately became with the greed of an orphan who has known so little, feel embarrassed to ask for more. But the beauty is that I needn't ask. The more I spend, the more content the Count seems. And I realize that the more he gives me, the surer he becomes in his complete possession of me. If Monsieur Plantier's money bought him my youthful body, that of Count von Stackelberg buys him peace. My old dictum proves truer and stronger than ever: *coins can truly purchase anything.*

M. Mayor, the clothing supplier to the Queen and the Court, the Empress of Russia and the Ladies Grandes-Duchesses, becomes my own supplier; while from the perfumer to the Duchess de Nemours, I make a habit of acquiring the most expensive Portuguese soaps, lotions, and perfumes.

The Count also commissions the greatest and most expensive living painter, Olivier, and I sit down for my first ever portrait. The outcome is so delightful that I fall in love with myself. As does The Count.

However, the next time he is absent for more than a few days, I take the portrait down, with the help of my coachman, and drive to my dear Agénor's house, where I corrupt his butler with a heavy purse and hang my portrait on his bedroom wall. He must not forget me. I must be the first woman he sees upon his return.

And then, there are the horses. Ever since that fateful day I gazed spellbound at our former king being drawn into his exile by those magnificent thoroughbreds, the dream of having some of my own never quite left me.

So, I proceed to search the entire country for my equine nobles. Having at last found them, I commission for them attire as magnificent as their master's: buckskin culottes, coronets of embossed polished leather, and chain-mail breastplates that steal the sun's rays and project them all around us. As we ride, people gather in stampedes to watch us, mouths half-open, eyes teary. Children run behind the speeding carriage, riotous with joy and glee. My thoughts return to that fateful day, the day the horizon swallowed my king and his thoroughbreds into eternity, leaving me to stare, with teary eyes and a shattered soul, at my wooden clogs.

I have come a long way.

Romain Vienne

And she has gone a long way, not only figuratively but literally as well, for when I presented myself at her address in Rue de l'Arcade, there was only the wind and a pile of discarded furniture to greet me. I was now living in Paris, having been there for quite some time, after quitting my job at my parents' hotel for the more prestigious one as a journalist. Being in touch with Marie's friends, it was Hortense who informed me of her friend's whereabouts and invited me to join them for dinner on the following weekend.

Marie Duplessis

Even though I may be in danger of sounding hypocritical, I still must record that running around the entire city in search of the best of everything is downright boring and tiring. But finally being finished with decorating my new home, locating new horses, and establishing my new, reputable self, I proceed to throw a party for my closest friends in honor of these new beginnings.

Shock engulfs my dining room the moment Romain — my dear friend from Nonant — enters. Both our faces display it. On my part, the shock is produced by seeing a friend I haven't seen or talked with in ages entering my house. And knowing he couldn't have had the address. On his part, the shock is even more obvious by his slightly opened mouth.

"My dear friend! How very good to see you! How in the world did you find me?" I exclaim, while hurrying to embrace him.

"Hortense gave me your address. I trust she hasn't committed an impudence," he says, sidestepping my embrace to stare wide-eyed at my new possessions.

"Mon Dieu, no! She did what I should have done, and for that, I must apologize to you. Will you forgive me, dearest Romain?" But my friend doesn't seem to hear my plea.

"You've done well, little Alphonsine," he says after a long minute. His back is still to me. Odd thing.

"Are you avoiding looking at me?" I ask, half amused, half enervated. But this time, too, my friend is saved from answering by the bell to my door.

ROMAIN VIENNE

I never knew she'd noticed right then. Never knew she knew, right in that instant, that I became besotted. So much so that looking at her for more than a glimpse would have made me blush like a young bride. On that Saturday, a glorious October evening with reddish sky and a soft warm breeze, little Alphonsine succeeded in enslaving my soul, too.

And how could she not?

Tall, slender, fresh as a spring flower, the richness of her forms without which perfection does not exist, had enslaved many a gentleman. I was but an ordinary youth trying to make his way up in elusive Paris. But she ... she was deliciously pretty. Her long, thick black hair was mesmerizing, and she combed it with inimitable art. Her face, oval and regular, slightly pale and melancholy, usually in a state of calm and repose, would suddenly come to life at the sound of a friendly voice, and offer warm and sincere words.

She had a child's features. Her mouth, cute and sensual, framed teeth of dazzling whiteness. Her feet and hands were so thin they made you regard her fingers as almost too long. The expression of her large, long-lashed, black eyes was deeply penetrating — almost too penetrating for my safety.

And the sweetness of her countenance could make one dream. Even her voice had changed, acquiring a melodious tone. She was an apparition. There was nothing more graceful and elegant than the appearance of that open and luminous countenance, with kind smiles and seductive eyes.

And while her beauty aroused admiration, the affability of her manners gave rise to an unmistakable disposition toward friendship, which was all she would allow me. If thoughts of confessing my burning ardor to her entered my head, they were immediately destroyed by her own words, whispered carelessly, but with undeniable intent: "Our lovers often bore us, our protectors always do, our friends never. I was happy, dear Romain, when I was certain that you were not going to try to be my lover. If it had been otherwise, our splendid, uncomplicated relationship could have never existed."

As a consolation, she gave me a superb carnation, with white and red petals, which she pinned to my chest. She loved flowers. Oh, how she loved them all! There was no room in her resplendent home lacking them. Japanese azalea, imperial roses, heathers, Dutch hyacinth flowers, and camellias. Only later, with the onset of the disease that was to kill her, did she prefer camellias to the rest. For camellias don't smell. And smells, any smell, would gravely disturb poor Alphonsine's lungs.

Marie Duplessis

Rose, the maid, opens the door to let Ernestine and Hortense in.

"Marie!" they both exclaim in chorus, approaching me for a group embrace. As we hug, I look at Romain who's finally looking me in the eyes.

"Still using 'Marie'?" he asks, furrowing his brows. I let go of my friends and invite everyone to sit at the dining table with effusive gesturing. As the fickle servant pours food on our plates, I hear Romain again.

"Marie?"

"Yes, still," says Hortense. "Marie Duplessis. And close your mouth."

We all laugh, but mine is more of an escape from embarrassment. If it stems from the fact that Romain knows me from the time I could barely speak or because I bared my heart to him, one thing is certain, in his presence I feel like a fraud. My theatrics sound and look foolish and rehearsed. With him around, I can only be myself, the self I left behind in Nonant—*the poor little Plessis girl*. No wonder his eyebrows furrow on hearing my aggrandized nom de plume.

"Yes, my dear friend," I finally say, waving my hand fan in a near frenzy. "It is my mother's name and also the name of the Virgin."

He smiles. "There's an original idea! Do you intend to add Magdalene?"

We all laugh again, and I relax a little. My friend is no prude, I gather.

"But why add *du* to your beautiful last name?" he asks. "We all know there's not one drop of noble blood in your veins."

"You're a journalist..." Ernestine jumps to my rescue. "... find out for yourself."

"Well, my dearest," I say, "call it a project, a fantasy— whatever you wish—but if it comes up for sale, I intend to buy the beautiful chateau of Plessis in Nonant—which *you* know better than anyone." Leaning slightly toward him, I whisper, "You alone, dearest Romain, in my entourage, know everything about my life that I kept hidden from the world. Please, keep my biggest secret to yourself." He nods and I smile in gratitude. Hortense and Ernestine do not know about me having given birth to a boy who later died.

I try to keep my spirits high throughout the dinner, but the damage has already been done. All that returns to my mind's eye, coming and going in flashes of guilt and unbearable sorrow, are images of the poor baby boy with no name, a little body swallowed by fevers, finally laid in a terrible cold casket.

By the time dessert is served, the bitter melancholy forces me to look for an escape from the walls of my home, which now suddenly seem to be closing in on me. I embrace my friends and, mounting my carriage, ask the coachman to drive me to the Opera.

CHAPTER 12

*P*erhaps the most endearing acquisition Count von Stackelberg's money affords me is my own private box at the opera. The magnificent Théâtre des Variétés becomes my second home.

IT IS on a frosty December evening in 1842 that I reclaim my dignity. A dignity every human being should be able to retain regardless of one's background or choice of profession. Now, it is I who looks down from my private box at the distinguished women in the stalls. But while their eyes are even more afire with the wrath of consternation, there is no malice or superiority or even resentment in mine. Maybe just a bit of sadness for their lost souls. I raise my bouquet of small flowers at them in salute, which sends the ladies' glares elsewhere. God forbid they should be associated with me.

On this same frosty December evening, my favorite actress, Madame Judith is performing. Her role, that of Manon Lescaut, the young courtesan with an uncurbed greed for luxury, is touching me to the core. For two hours straight I make every possible effort to fight back my tears. I even ask the men coming to my box to pay their compliments to leave me to myself and shield my face with a hand fan. I shall not produce another moment of satisfaction for the ladies in the stalls.

The last act feels particularly painful. Manon, in the last stages of weakness, looks at her lover, who is beside himself with despair. He finds a resting place for her and goes off to look for water. Manon, thinking he has forsaken her entirely, feels there is now no hope for her.

"Only the tomb," she cries, "can release me from my burden!"

Her lover returns in time to be present for her last moments, and she dies declaring her love for him, who then falls senseless on her body.

Forgetting about my tears or pride or the women downstairs, I jump to my feet and begin clapping vigorously.

"Bravo!" I shout. "Bravo!" I scream yet again, throwing my bouquet near to where Madame Judith lies with her fellow actor upon her. Tens of similar bouquets land noisily all around her. But she does not rise to her feet to collect them as she usually does, and seems to be prolonging her final collapse for far too long. *Such a marvelous actress!* I think as the red curtain descends to steal the actors from our view.

As I wonder at her motive for prolonging her collapse, the curtain ascends again. I see a woman rushing from behind it making effusive gestures at the two men stepping onstage. They carry a handbarrow and I realize Madame Judith's collapse was not an act.

"Cerebral fever, my little one," says Monsieur Pont-Neuf upon my inquiry. As the theatre's director, Nestor

Roqueplan is the first person I run to upon hearing the news.

"Good Grief!" I say, kneading my hands and pacing his large office. "Will she recover soon?"

"Very possible. They released her from the hospital and took her home. Why not send her a letter to show your concern?" he says with a glint of mischief.

"Truly? I am afraid she'll be appalled at my audacity. I am who I am."

"Well, you'll never know until you try."

I nod, and blowing Monsieur Pont-Neuf a gentle kiss, leave him to his business.

I DO NOT WRITE Madame Judith a letter, but instead go to her home and leave with her maid a small bouquet of flowers along with my kind wishes. For more than a week, I repeat my action daily. At its end, Madame Judith's maid hands me a note from her mistress.

> *You've shown more kindness than anyone I know but failed to do a most basic thing: disclose your name.*

My hand as well as my heart shiver as I scribble the reply on Madame Judith's note.

> *Your devoted and unworthy admirer, Marie Duplessis. I feared that if you had known my identity you would refuse my flowers. And I am afraid that in learning it today you will regret having received them.*

The next day she invites me to see her. Embarrassed and laden with flowers, I enter Madame Judith's bedroom. She sits at the top of her bed, massaging her temples.

"Come. Come," she says, lightly patting the side of the bed. Her hair is disheveled and messy, but she looks more beautiful than ever I've seen her.

"It's an honor to finally meet you, Madame," I say as I approach her and place the flowers on the small table near her bed.

"Sit..." She motions again. "Let me put that name on a face."

"On a flushed face..." I say, feeling my entire blood raising up my cheeks.

"You are beautiful," she says as I sit next to her. "Very beautiful. But I wanted to convince myself of your self-abasement. Your note was full of it, and I thought you either were a masterful writer or were trying to steal my profession."

My hand goes to my face. "It isn't an act. I truly am most honored you've given me the chance to meet you in person. Especially after—"

"After?"

I pause for a long time. "I know your opinion of women like me. After the incident with your other admirer, Madame—"

"Céleste Mogador!" she interrupts. "She's no *madame* but a dancer and lesbian! Her daily flowers went straight into the rubbish!" she booms, as her hands gesticulate angrily, mimicking invisible flowers being thrown into the garbage. Her eyes and facial expression are angry, too, full of disgust.

I turn my face away lest she see all my shame and blood raised to it. It is always the others, the other people, who can make us feel so unworthy and pitiless, regardless of how much we're actually enjoying our lives, and thriving in what we're doing.

"And yet here you are, receiving me," I say. "Why?"

"You proved yourself worthy. It was your modesty, Marie, that spoke in your stead. Now! Tell me everything about yourself!" She pats the edge of her bed again. "Let me know all about this marvelous sinner who is the talk of Paris."

For the next two hours, I pour my heart out to my new friend. I tell her about Father and his monstrous deeds, about the ogre and the king, and the initiation of Monsieur Plantier. I tell her about the gypsies and my first day in Paris, about the sadness an orphan feels and of a woman who's been deserted by the one she loved most. Her eyes widen with every one of my words. And each time there is another emotion they let out.

Then I tell her about my profession, both good and bad, about my protectors—many of them mutual acquaintances —and how the good old Count first tried to save me, then became the most staunch supporter of my profession by deciding he should also taste my youthful body. And about the vow he snatched out of me.

"For some time, I lived without lovers," I say standing up to pace the room. "I had hoped to reform, believing it possible to accept the life which he offered me. The days were reserved for sleep; evenings and nights devoted to shows, parties, supper dinners, unforeseen events. I tried to enjoy the present, without worrying about the next day. Every day new toilets, a senseless luxury, an orgy of mad spending. But I found I was dying of boredom.

"I then imagined that the Count would allow me the freedom to love a young man, while still supporting my expenses. I thought I might perhaps find such a young man who would understand my remorse and make me his companion, but the only ones to appear were adventurers drawn by my money. The young men who might have attracted me mocked my ideas of marriage, questioned my self-restraint, and constantly threw my past at me."

Sweat invades my forehead as I recount my story, and I try to cool myself with quick flicks of my hand fan.

"My new, beautiful friend," Madame Judith whispers tilting her head to one side and eyeing me in a strange way. "You are a wonderful storyteller, and any actress would revel in such a good story. But, I have one question for you."

"Oh?"

"What is the point of listening to the depths of the human heart that manifests its impressions, but does not reveal its secrets?"

I pause. "I am afraid I do not know what to answer, for I do not understand your question."

"You are a smart woman, Marie. But I am, too. I understand the roles people play in real life just as much as I understand those I play on stage. I can sense when something is being kept hidden. You speak like a tragedian, yet your actions, your manner, and even the clothes and the luxury emanating from your person speak another story."

I stop in my track and avert my face again. I wasn't even aware I was playing a role before the words of Madame Judith escaped her lips. I must be a marvelous actress if I had been able to fool even myself.

"Madame, forgive me!" I say as I pat the sweat on my neck with a silk handkerchief. "Everything I told you about my unhappiness is to make myself more interesting, isn't it? Maybe even to arouse your sympathy and pity! To make sure you will accept me as your friend. I act well, don't I? Almost as good as you!"

She smiles. "People lying about themselves, especially to themselves, are a constant source of fascination to me. I act, you see... but in my spare time I like to know myself for who I truly am. I like to bring to light my deepest desires to fulfil and share with others. I am brutally honest—not a characteristic today's society appreciates."

"Then what say you about my profession? It has all the characteristics our society condemns."

"It is true. Maybe that is why learning to lie becomes a necessity. That is why playing roles outside the stage must become our second nature."

"Well, I lie to keep my teeth white," I say, going for a bit of humor that would maybe succeed in dispelling my embarrassment.

"Your teeth are perfectly white. Now, tell me your truth," she demands. "I promise I will not change my favorable opinion of you."

Madame Judith has conquered me. My pacing has tired me. I sit in an armchair and continue to fan myself.

"I don't feel I am blessed with virtue sufficient to become a hermit. I have been, for too long, accustomed to the pleasures of my era to consider attempting to deprive myself of them... to break off, without transition, without hope to return, the past habits of the flesh, of the blood, of the character to which I am enslaved. An enslavement I no longer know to be either my real nature or a disposition welded out of the treatment I received since early childhood. Alas, it is too hard. All I feel is revulsion against such self-exile."

"I believe you now. This is your real truth. A truth that must reveal other truths, of which I am eagerly expectant. Go on! Keep me entertained! An actress fastened to her bed without a good story in her ears is as devastated as a sailor forced to remain on land."

I sigh deeply, rise, and resume my pacing around Madame Judith's furniture.

"As I was saying... For some time after I gave my word to the Count, I lived without lovers, hoping to reform, and filling my time on sprees of mad spending. The Count always insisted that I should increase my standards of luxury, so that is what I did. I would spend thousands of francs in a single day. I would saturate myself with items even the richest of the ladies of the court wouldn't have dared to spend on. But none of those succeeded in keeping my melancholy at bay. Nothing that I was doing succeeded in silencing the voice of my true nature trying to make itself heard."

"What have I told you? That voice can never be silenced. At least, not for too long. So, we might as well stop trying."

I nod.

"And then?" she asks.

"Then, my dear angel returned. My dear Agénor de Guiche returned from his imposed exile in England. It was the moment I knew it was I who forced myself into a self-imposed exile—an emotional self-imposed exile. I who shun my true capricious nature. All my feelings—be they the longing for the pleasure of the stimulating conversation I had in the company of so many learned men or simply that of the flesh—surfaced with a force I never knew existed in them."

"And you broke the vow you made to the old count."

"It was a fortnight ago. I was in my dressing room preparing myself for the opera. I had put on my dress and stockings and was powdering my face at the mirror when I noticed a shadow moving in it. A little scream escaped my lips as I turned in my chair to see who it was."

"Agénor de Guiche!" Madame Judith exclaims.

I nod and smile. "For some reason I had not heard the bell to my door and Rose, the maid, let the gentleman in. She was very accustomed with the ones I wanted to see no matter the time of day or my personal disposition. So, there he was, standing in front of me looking as if he had just bathed in the sun. The same dashing beauty but better, the same ardor in his eyes but livelier, the same protective arms but stronger. He uttered only a few words, '*I just returned and saw your portrait on my bedroom wall. I had to come to make love to the one I missed so dearly...*' then threw himself at me, plunging his sweet tongue through my opened lips and into my mouth gasping for breath... then he removed my dress but kept my stockings which he kissed and smelled and pulled with his teeth... he had me right there, on my dressing table, between my crystal bottles of scents and lotions, brushes and combs, bows and ribbons..."

"Thus, breaking your vow..."

I remove myself from Madame Judith's view and approach her window. Small snowflakes hit the ground silently and effortlessly. The calm and naturalness of their journey to earth force me to ponder my own inner guilt.

"I didn't think of that then. The naturalness of what was happening made me act without thinking much. And when I did think about it, I could not see the harm I was doing to another, but what I was doing to myself. I thought it was long overdue that I should break my self-imposed exile that had done me nothing but harm."

"But you are not a merciless soul. So, of course, the guilt came too, eventually," Madame Judith says, shaking her head in slow motion, as if understanding all the ills of the world.

"Agénor and I remained indoor for two days, remembering the past in deeds of the present. We made love passionately and almost uninterruptedly, taking sparse breaks only for some frugal dinner, or so he could read to me from the classics. But then it happened. For the stupidity of some people knows no limits."

"Rose?"

I nod. "She let Count von Stackelberg in. She knew he could come and go whenever it pleased him, for he was my sole protector for so many months. But she couldn't reason further. A dog! Like a dog, doing only what it has been trained to do!" I blurt, feeling my hands starting to shake.

"Heavens above! Who would have thought?"

"I should have! I should have thought! For there the Count was, standing erect and motionless in my bedroom, looking straight into the eyes of his protégé's lover lying naked in her bed, reading to her as she fed him big white grapes purchased with the Count's money! Herself naked!"

A burst of laughter, coming from my friend in ripples, stops my harangue.

"I can only imagine the Count's face, trying to grasp it all," she says.

"Oh, he grasped it fast, all right. He bent slightly forward and said: *'If the lady will excuse me'*, then turned on his heels and was gone. I haven't heard from him since. I should have fired my stupid maid, but in the end, it was all my fault. I also should have broken up with the Count before he saw the extent of my vileness. Good grief, he saw me as his daughter! I tainted his daughter's memory!"

"Good grief, you are very simple, aren't you?" my friend says, with a wry smile.

"Oh?"

"All your good old count did was take advantage of his daughter's misfortune. All he did was use an extraordinary pick up line to play on your sympathy and use your pity as fuel for his ardent passion. And there he had it—the youngest, most beautiful girl in Paris, the best-dressed woman in France walking at his arm. It was his money that kept you, but his wicked wits that seized you in the first place. For no amount of money in this world or another could have erased the image of his wrinkled, saggy skin from the eyes of a young girl. He had one chance only. And he took it. Old crook!"

It is my turn to laugh, not only at Madame Judith's twisted humor, but also because her words bring my much sought after relief from my tormenting guilt. It is as if I breathe for the first time, walk erect for the first time. I embrace my new friend with the most sincere gratitude and thank her for giving me back my peace.

It will not last long, though. In less than a fortnight, I discover that my dear Agénor took not one but two society ladies as his companions, and curtailed me not only in his affections but with his handouts, too. The shock is felt deeply, though I am aware it springs from the effects of my own doings.

CHAPTER 13

I have rarely let myself be protected by one man only. It was either a few at the same time or none at all. Count von Stackelberg was the only exception to this general rule, and that only because his overflowing purse was able to supplant all my needs—real or imaginary—and with less work and feigning from my part.

I am a whore. A luxurious whore. Yet, even as promiscuous and mercenary as my profession requires me to be, the abandonment of those I hold dear is felt deeply. A woman will never be able to part with her tender, impressionable nature, no matter her profession or material interests. It's how Nature created her. What she becomes and the many masks she chooses to wear throughout her life is the product of the society in which she lives, and which will always be at odds with her true nature.

Behind the Count's abandonment I am left with a suppressed guilt and much poorer. But after Agénor's desertion, I am left with that much less. It is always the young, beautiful, witty protectors that conquer not only our bodies but our minds, and sometimes, our hearts. When these benefactors leave us, our life becomes poorer not only in material things, but of all things spiritual as well. Gone is the passion of the flesh that ensnared you for weeks; gone are the lively conversations; gone is the vitality of youth that kept your own youthful spirit kindling. And with these being gone, I cannot live. Nor can I live without the abundance that made me love abundance in the first place.

So, once again I pick up my spirits and dress myself in the most outlandish, original, and sophisticated outfit at my disposal, and go to the Opera. This time, I also add a new item to my attire: a large, splendid white camellia pinned to my décolletage. Men seeking pleasures know what it means. For each courtesan finds unique ways to let these men know when we are available and disposed to take in new protectors. A white flower pinned to my décolletage is my own unique signal. And from the height of my opera box, it is visible to every man who wants to see it.

In no time, the splendid white camellia does its magic and my box fills with new, as well as old, faces. But whether I am indisposed, or my melancholy decided to keep me company tonight, the fact is that I like none of them. Either too old or too ugly or too poor for my liking. By the end of the night, poor Montguyon, accompanied by the General, enter my box. They both kiss one of my hands, to the appalled glares of the ladies downstairs. Then they begin chatting among themselves the same petty trivialities.

This isn't going to be my night. Feigning fatigue, I let the gentlemen enjoy their own treasured company.

THE NEXT MORNING, Rose enters my bedroom, screaming unintelligible things. If not for the news she brings and I discover after making sense of her words, I would have fired her on the spot. She should know better than to wake me up before noon. Such a foolish, boring girl! But her news is not boring, and her hands bursting with hundreds of bank notes, even less so.

"I found a purse full of them in your dressing table!" she exclaims, dangling those beauties before my sleepy eyes.

"This early morning, as I was dusting it! You are saved! We are saved!" she continues to scream as if the sky had just opened up and God himself reached down to save her.

"Agénor..." I whisper for my own ears.

"They were hidden underneath your lace bows!"

"Alright, Rose. Place them there," I say, indicating the corner of the bed. "Now, let me come to my senses."

As she exits, I think of Agénor and his deed. So, he does care for me enough to look after my expenses, no matter how many other ladies he's wooing. I shall not reject him altogether. I grab the bank notes and begin counting them. Thirty thousand francs in all.

This should do for about a month.

But it doesn't.

The spiritual void enveloping me lately gives rise to such an obsessive craving for spending that the first two weeks prove sufficient time to make me part with my last dime. The culmination, an Opera masked ball during the carnival days of January 1844, is spending my last four francs for hire of a velvet mask with satin fringe.

I just turned twenty, and I imagine the ball being given in my honor. Madame Judith accompanies me.

"What have you done to me?" she says, as we step down from my carriage. "Fancy me even considering attending such events before I met you..."

"Not to worry," I reply. "Just keep your mask on your face at all times and your reputation will be preserved."

I smile, looking at her disguise. Besides her oversized lace mask, she is wearing a blond wig, bright red lipstick and a velvet cloak. I wouldn't have recognized her even if she had been swearing on her identity in her most unmistakable voice. My own black-hooded cloak chokes me, but it is the required dress. No woman attending can escape it.

The concierge opens the magnificent door to the grand salon of the Opera to let us in. As he does so, he lets out, like birds from a cage flying desperately and confusedly in all direction, an array of contrasting sounds and impressions.

There are over three thousand men masquerading in the dimly lit place, some dancing, some chatting, some smoking perfumed cigars. Above them, a sea of ladies in black dominoes and assorted masks fill the numerous boxes, laughing, fanning themselves, and throwing fugitive glances downstairs. Enveloping them all is the lively music coming from the orchestra playing in one of the corners of the grand salon.

Shortly after our arrival the *grand galoppe* begins. A gentleman grabs my hand, another grabs Madame Judith's and they haul us about the room, whirling us madly and passionately. The laughter coming from the lips of about five hundred figures dancing the *grand galoppe* intoxicates me, and for a moment, I let go my melancholy. I begin laughing, a laughter that seems to spring from the bottom of a being I thought lost. It is as if I am a child again and all troubles and worries are but distant chimeras I know nothing about.

As I spin, guided by the gentleman's agile hand, my eyes fall on a group of distinguished looking men, who stare at me with inquisitive eyes. They whisper in each other's ears, nodding their heads and smiling.

The *grand galoppe* comes to a sudden end and I guide Madame Judith toward the door to catch our breath. Ever since I gave birth to that unfortunate little soul, my strength seems uncertain and confused, as if not knowing whether to help me in my endeavors or not. A little cough escapes my lips and I reach for my handkerchief to cover my mouth. Almost at the same time, a masculine hand lightly touches mine. The gesture is accompanied by a deep, guttural voice.

"Will the ladies forgive my intrusion?" it says. I raise my eyes to look at the owner of the voice. Another cough escapes my lips, more so a choke. My strength leaves me again, especially from my knees, which seem to have suddenly lost their bones and muscles. The same large blue eyes which are the stuff of poems, the same light chestnut hair, the inspiration of painters.

"Valory..." I whisper through a contracted throat. I have seen the gentleman standing in front of me before or speeding on horseback through the Bois de Boulogne. The resemblance to the one I loved and who abandoned me and kept me despondent for days.

My knees quit me altogether—

"Madame, are you all right?" he asks, rushing to catch me in my fall. His touch is like a thunderbolt spreading throughout my body. The sensation shocks me as much as it pleases me, and I push his arms violently.

"What makes you think you could approach us, Monsieur?" I demand, raising my eyes to glare at him. My own question reverberates in my head and I instantly regret it. Thank God for the mask hiding my face, or else I should have run out the door trying to escape my own embarrassment.

"Forgive my bold intrusion," he says. "But my friends and I thought we should be honored if the ladies would agree to accompany us to supper." He points to the group of men I saw staring at me earlier. They continue to stare, smiling. "I am Edouard. Count Edouard de Perregaux." He bows low to kiss my hand, and the thunderbolt is felt again.

"Under different circumstances I should have been

delighted," Madame Judith intervenes, noticing my restlessness. "But I am afraid I shall retire to my apartments."

The same restlessness forces me to play the unapproachable card, even when my own inner being would actually want to kneel right in front of the man who inspired such passion, if only from afar.

"As shall I," I say. "Unless..."

"Madame?"

"Unless you are able to provide me with the restaurant's guest list." I smile in the corner of my mouth. Surely such thing is impossible. He smiles too and backs up, still looking me in the eyes. Reaching his group, he then returns with a long narrow card which he hands over. I scan the names on it: Alexandre Dumas, the esteemed writer, with his son, Nestor Roqueplan, the theatre director and my friend, Dr. Louis Veron, the most prestigious of them all, a burly, affable, and generous bachelor who became outstandingly rich from selling his invention, a chest ointment—and many more.

"Sir, you proved yourself resourceful," I say, handing back the card. "I shall accompany you and your gentlemen friends to supper."

I hug Madame Judith, as she would not dare show her face in public under such circumstances and climb into my carriage. The men follow on horseback, *the most adventurous way to move on such icy roads*, they say.

Café de Paris is especially pleasant tonight. Designed to look like an aristocratic family house, it has all the elements necessary to make you feel at home, yet in the company of so many brilliant minds and coveted riches. The burning candles and lit oil lamps reflecting their golden light in the grand mirrors persuade you into believing you must have stepped into a different world. A world of illusions, of infinite possibilities. The food at Café de Paris is out of this world, too. The veal casserole—the specialty of the house—is to be savored rather than eaten, for it is nothing short of a culinary masterpiece.

Installed in one of the salons of the restaurant, Edouard holds my chair, then sits on my left. His friends also take their seats one-by-one around the table. I reach for and grab the satin ribbons behind my head to untie and remove my mask. A collective gasp fills the air and I begin laughing. My companion's amazement dispels at the voice of the butler.

"What drink shall please you, my lady?" Edouard asks bringing his face closer to mine.

"Only pink champagne for me."

"Excellent choice."

"And prawns, lobster, and shrimp, please. I am starving!"

He laughs, revealing his beautifully white teeth. The image takes me back in time again, when a similar feeling made me lose my senses. I would gladly skip the pink champagne and lobster just to run my tongue over this stranger's teeth. I watch as he uncorks the bottle of champagne. The ease and gentleness of this gesture, his skillfulness over this simple, yet complicated action, the way his hand muscles contract, and the poised smile on his face, all conspire to pursue my most feminine desires.

"Monsieur," I say, as he pours the pink liquid into a glass in front of me, "I have often seen you on horseback in the Bois de Boulogne, and your mount seems to delight in carrying a cavalier such as you."

The color in his cheeks tells me I stroke a chord. He jerks his head to remove the blond curls from his forehead, and beads of sweat become visible beneath them.

"I, too, have often seen you, Madame, and your attire and beauty did not fail to leave a lasting impression on me."

It is my turn to turn red in the face. My heart swells with joy. But it is not only joy that creeps into it. There is also fear. For the things we most crave in our lives are also the things that hurt us the most. And hurt the most is what I was when I last felt this violent passion within my bosom. But, alas, what can't be cured, must be endured. For I never was able to cure myself of my feeling heart.

"I made no mistake in asking you for supper tonight," he continues, still red in the cheeks.

"You knew who I was then?"

"I've been watching you in your opera box, receiving your... friends. The faraway look in your eyes, your long charcoal curls, and virginal expression kept me awake for many a night. Of course, I knew who you were. Your mask could not keep that faraway look hidden from the one whose dreams have been haunted by it."

A sudden urge to pass my fingers through the curls covering his brow makes me shudder. I have heard these words—or some very similar ones—only too often. I have used these words too often myself. This time however, they manage to pass my inscrutable self to reach for a place I long thought dead within me. A place as starving for affection as my earthly senses for abundance.

"You are a smooth seducer, Monsieur. Any girl would fall prey to such words. You men have learned that the way to a woman's bedroom is through her heart."

"More so through her vanity, Madame. But I am not the man to appeal to such tricks. I speak only from the heart."

"A young heart. What does a young heart know about love? About passion?"

"It is not the age of a man's heart that teaches him about passion. It is something else, something too mysterious for mere mortals to understand. An urge without an apparent cause, intense and deaf to the wisest remonstrances."

"Here we are, Monsieur, having sat for barely a quarter of an hour, and we are already speaking about love."

"Does it make you uncomfortable?"

"It depends."

"On?"

"On what your intentions are, Monsieur."

"My intentions are as pure as that urge without an apparent cause, intense and deaf to the wisest remonstrances." His fingers lightly touch mine and I suddenly feel like a wild wounded forest beast. I resist the urge to pull them from beneath his, but still like a wounded animal, my instincts tell me to attack. To remove the danger.

"Monsieur, I believe you are fooling yourself. The way to a woman's bedroom is neither through her heart, nor her vanity. It is through her stomach, hence through your purse."

His insistent gaze remains unperturbed by my assertion. He squeezes my fingers even tighter, and gently pulls me toward him.

"What is the way to a woman's heart then? For it is your heart I am aiming for, dearest Marie."

I let out a mocking, if not nervous, little laugh. "Forgive my being blunt, Monsieur, but I think I have already answered your question. The way to my heart is through my bedroom; hence, your purse. Have you the means and disposition to reach my heart, you must first prove yourself worthy."

"Very well, then. I accept your conditions, if that is the only way to reach that for which I would cross oceans and climb mountains."

WITH MY CONDITIONS accepted and with the passion which Edouard has attested to the entire night, and I have felt long ago, since first I saw him riding through the Bois de Boulogne, I invite him into my bedroom.

This Count of thirty-two years of age, with the physique of a teenage boy whose features had barely turned into masculine beauties and whose full lips quivered as his gaze sank into mine, becomes my lover on that very same night, in the frosty end of January. It might be the pink champagne dancing through my blood or his words that my heart has been starving for or my wanton nature that brought this coupling about, I do not know. And it does not even matter. It was a night I never knew could exist in the real world. A night that revealed my heart to me. At its end, clutching me in his tender arms, he swore in an impulse of inspiration that I was and would eternally remain the object of his dearest affection.

ROMAIN VIENNE

Marie did not remain indifferent to the transports of this mad tenderness, to that burning declaration of immense love, and the passionate Edouard became the happiest of lovers.

How did he become infatuated so suddenly and violently? It is in vain that one would question the one who suffers the fatigued power of that fascination which Marie exerted over all his senses. There are psychological phenomena whose study is averse to analysis, because, if the effects are appreciable, the causes have their origin in mysterious affinities whence passions spring forth, as lightning comes out of storms, because one's sympathetic propensities occur, develop and extinguish themselves outside our will.

The passion of Edouard de Perregaux was one of those psychological phenomena. That a young man of twenty-five, who has had nothing but passing trinkets, suddenly falls in love with a young pretty girl, well brought up, very sweet, virgin of heart and of body, well, nothing seems to us more rational and in conformity with the laws of our nature.

But here, the case is very different. This is a man of thirty-two years, who had lived a lot and was even libertine. Count Edouard de Perregaux had taken ten or fifteen mistresses, several of whom were in a position to affirm his sincere attachment, his keen tenderness, and his devotion to them. One of them in particular, the last, a woman named Adele Brecourt, had acquired such an empire over him that he had left a portion of his patrimony in her clutches.

Well, that same Count found himself, unexpectedly, from the first encounter, struck by the dizzying passion which Marie inspired in him. He knew she was a well-kept woman but did not care to count her lovers or protectors; and this passion for a pearl immersed in vice had all the sensibilities and the delicacies, and all the freshness of a first feeling.

Subjected to her whims, slave of her wishes, he was absolutely incapable of refusing her anything. With this beautiful girl, whose maintenance required several thousand francs a month, Edouard could not have failed to realize that the rest of his fortune would disappear in a short while without refuge for him, without redemption for her. No, he did not think about it, he had no concern for his interests, neglected his friendships, abandoned his family, renounced all his relations, to be only with Marie and her desires, her actions, her whims. He endeavored to please her by the most gracious attentions and the most pleasant surprises. He showered her with gifts and lavished on her all that the most ingenuous gallantry can suggest to the imagination of a happy lover.

· · ·

MARIE DUPLESSIS

After a couple such nights spent in the company of Edouard, I find myself hopelessly in love. The mere thought of that feeling thought lost is unbearable. Along with it come the other feelings I also thought lost in me: fear and despair. The more Edouard loves me and covers every inch of my body with his affection and money, the more frightened I become. When one loses their heart, one loses everything: mind, common sense, power over actions, independence. And these are what kept me alive and functioning. These attributes made me the woman I am today. Losing these would mean certain death. I am barely twenty, hardly an age where I should be disposed to think about death or loss of the pleasures my age, beauty, and skills have graced me.

The little orphan resurfaces once more to warn me about the danger in which I have fallen.

CHAPTER 14

I find myself eager for the company of the only person who knows my true self, my past and my secrets, who could guide me with sincerity and pull me out of this grievous state. He has jealously stayed away for a while now, as he usually does when I take in a new lover. But at the end of February, spent and emotional, I sent Romain a note, begging him to come and see me.

As he enters my house the following evening, I throw myself around his neck.

"I was very restless," I say as I let go of him. "But now, seeing you here, I suddenly feel some relief."

"What have you done now, my little Marie?"

"I waited for you to dine, and I have sent for all that you need at Voisin. They have the best food in the world."

"That I know. But I should have liked to take you out for once, only you've never allowed me."

"Always childish, aren't you? You push everything to the extreme. I am afraid of embarrassing you. I have no other motive. Besides, I am going to do honor to your wine and your coffee, by smoking one of the good cigars you have brought me the last time. Is not that enough?"

"You have come to be mercenary. Cold."

"I'm sorry. Forgive me. I am not myself these days. I warn you that I must talk at length with you. How long do you have?"

"All night."

"An answer that gives me great pleasure."

I invite him to sit at the dining table. Silence overhangs for about a minute as Romain patiently waits for me to be ready to speak.

"There is so much weight upon my heart that I almost find myself at a loss for words," I say, and without any warning, tears spring from my eyes. Romain grabs my hand.

"I am here to stay. For as long as you need me."

"Have patience, my dearest friend," I say as I dab at my eyes. I urge him to eat his dinner, as I nibble at mine. We talk about everything as people who, having nothing to say to each other, touch all subjects at once. Suddenly, as if this trivial talk was doing me more bad than good, I stand to retrieve something from the mantelpiece.

"Hold out your hand," I ask Romain. As he does so, I place a small miniature cameo in his hand. "I would be happy to have your opinion on this portrait. How do you find it?"

The instant change in his expression almost makes me faint.

So, it is her. In the portrait. It is her!

"But... this is... it is the portrait of Marie Deshayes, of your mother. A bit enhanced, yes, but it's her! Explain, quickly."

"My doubts are dispelled. Your expression revealed the truth. So, this must be it."

"Do tell me fast. You know patience is not my greatest

virtue."

"Very well. You know about the English lady where my mother found shelter and protection, at the instigation of that good Madame du Hays, and through the old English jockey, Father Augustin, who was training horses for the races of Nonant and Paris. This lady had taken my mother and treated her like a relative."

"Very well. I know all that. How did this portrait fall into your hands?"

"Wait, impatient that you are, or you will spoil all the pleasure that the suddenness of your exclamation made me feel."

"How did this miniature come into your possession?" he presses.

"A lady, speaking in a very pronounced British accent, came to see me two days ago. Without any introduction she told me this: *'Marie Deshayes, a woman named Plessis, your mother, entered the service of Madame Baroness Anderson, widow of an English general, and lived in the Rue du Faubourg Saint-Honoree about twelve years ago. Touched by the misfortunes of your mother, by the elevation of her sentiments and her distinguished manner, Madame Anderson did not take long in making your mother her lady-companion, her confidante. To calm her sorrows, to bring about forgetfulness, she surrounded her with affectionate care and lavished on your mother her most ingenuous kindness. But nothing could overcome the terrible evil that was eating away at her life. The affliction, which the privation of her children made her endure, resisted all consolation, and she died of grief after two years on the property which Madame possesses on the shores of Lake Geneva, and where she lives during the summer season.*

'On her dying bed, your mother took the hand of the Baroness, showered her with tears, and made a touching

appeal to her pity for the two orphans she had left in Normandy. Mrs. Anderson promised your mother that she will search for you and your sister and take interest in your fate. As a result of a string of inexplicable errors of name and addresses, she had not been able until recently to obtain the desired information concerning your mother's children. She had resolved, discouraged by her unsuccessful attempts, to give up pursuing her investigations, when a providential chance showed her the way about two months ago, during her stay in Normandy, on her return from England. She now knows that your sister is married, and she decided she will take care of her only secondarily. It proved more difficult to find out your address, because you changed your name. She wanted to see you and get to know you, and she has succeeded in giving me the pleasure of revealing her name to you. An innocent deceit she has used to enter into conversation with you: she knows all about you, knows that you no longer belong to yourself, and she is deeply saddened by it. But this painful discovery has not made her change her mind. Her intentions are the same, she will be glad to report to you the affection which she bore to your mother, and that is why she sent me here.

'She told me I must first of all inform you that Madame Baroness had a single daughter, an angel sent from Heaven, a marvel of beauty, whom death took when she was not yet fifteen years old. This child was her joy, her supreme hope, her only happiness. What this poor mother has suffered is beyond description; it is an inconsolable pain she still feels.

'If you accept her offer, if you give up, for her, your present life, if you wish to replace, in her heart and her benefactions, the child she has lost, she will put an end to her mourning and begin again with you and for you, a new existence; her house will be yours; her maternal love will be reborn for you; you will be the sole object of her tenderness;

she will secure, by an immediate gift, your future against all setbacks of fortune, and before two years had passed she will adopt you, as she promised your mother she would.

'The Baroness having had the opportunity of meeting at the baths of Chamounix a talented painter, commissioned him two portraits of your mother, two miniatures; she keeps one and begs you to accept the other, as the first sign of her affection.'

I look at Romain, who listens with fascination, as well as impatience, his eyes on the miniature he still holds.

"Go on," he urges.

"I listened with astonishment and wondered if these propositions were serious, when the lady added: '*I was going to forget the last recommendation: tell her that I am, from now on, at her disposal for all that she may need.*'"

"What have you answered to such a generous proposal?" Romain asks. "To that maternal urge which dominates a nature animated by the noblest and most philanthropic sentiments?"

"I was deeply moved; my heart more swollen than my eyes. But I have asked for time to think."

"And did you go to the lady's house to meet and thank her?"

"Not yet."

"That's wrong. You should have fulfilled that duty the very next day."

"You're being unfair to me. I wanted to consult you before taking this step."

"I see. What is, in short, the result of your reflections? I expect two days to be enough time for you to think this through."

"I decided not to accept."

"So, you didn't need to consult with me, having already decided not to accept," he blurts. And then, as if propelled by a springboard, he jumps to his feet and rushes to the door.

"Goodbye," he says in a most upset tone. "Before pronouncing myself, I shall wait to hear the reasons for not accepting the offer, after you have paid the visit. You are too intelligent not to go, tomorrow, to meet Baroness Andersen."

Tears are already soaking my cheeks. The desperation I felt before Romain arrived returns with renewed strength and I fall to my knees.

"You cannot leave me in such a state of mind! You judge me with unreasonable rigor and excessiveness. Have I ever judged *you*?"

"I cannot stay longer," he replies. "I would have to fight or even argue, using language you are not used to hearing and will find too severe. I do not have the strength to silence my feelings."

"I allow you to tell me everything you want, just don't leave me yet," I say and picking myself up from the floor, I again throw my arms around his neck. "I know that your severity is only inspired by the interest you have in me, in my well-being. Just like the proverb: *whoever loves, castigates as well*. You are my friend, there is no doubt about it. And our friends are always right. I promise not to be offended by any reproach passing through your honest lips. Just please, don't leave me. Friends should never leave us. Sit down and listen to me."

My tears, my supplicating words, the melancholy in my expression seem to mellow his anger, and dropping his tense shoulders, he finally relents. Turning on his heels, he retakes his place at the table. Still holding the miniature in his hand, he places it on my dining table.

"I shall speak openly then, now that I have your permission. I can see what's going on inside you. Your eyes reveal your tormented thoughts and feelings. It would be marvelous to see you accept the offer from that charitable lady who extends her generous hand to you, offering her home, her friendship, her protection, and perhaps even her fortune, by adopting you. But I remain convinced that you are nothing but the instrument of an illusion, which does not honor your sensibility nor your sensitivity. I see the illusion, but you don't. You let yourself be seduced by the excellence of society and be dazzled with promises that can only be sterile. You see everything in poor light and fail to see the shadows."

My tears continue to fall unbridled, washing down my sorrow, but they do not spring from any offence at my friends' words, but rather from understanding, with my most inner being, that he is right. Yet I cannot escape myself, I cannot escape who I've become.

"My dearest friend, you spoke wisely. But please do me a small favor. Close your eyes and imagine the following scenario: I am at the house of Madame Baroness Anderson, I am her protégé, her maid of honor, her friend, her companion, whatever you wish. After a short while, her entourage discovers who I am and what I was doing for a living before their kind friend took me under her wing. They discover that her companion is none other than the well-known sinner. Soon enough, the baroness notices that her salon is deserted, that the ladies and young girls quit making visits, except for maybe sparse ones out of strict politeness, and that only men appear from time to time. They reproach the benefactress for her indulgence and her kindness for a girl of loose morals, on whose account she has provided, in addition to the sad truth, a thousand repugnant lies.

"You will grant me, I suppose, that this lady is not different from other respectable women of our age; that she has, just like the others, her weaknesses, her self-esteem, and a deep obedience to the others' respect. Do you imagine she would give all of these up to keep me near her? Give up her dear relations, her old friendships? You will say she will seek new ones, in an environment where all will be momentarily ignored, admitting the silence of the servants to whom no wickedness escapes, will be preserved. Do you think she will, for example, settle in London, to breathe in the perfume of the Thames' fog and savor the stiff formalism of English society?

"You, my friend, know better than this. You, dearest Romain, know the failings of the human heart better than anyone I know. It will happen. Infallibly. She will perhaps not regret her good deeds, no. But she will find that the sacrifices are above her moral strength. Then she will become disaffected by a protégé who, instead of being a compensation for the cruel loss of her daughter, only brings her the biggest of inconveniences and instead of adopting her, she will let her return to her old habits."

The feeling of irritation upon Remain's features says he is conquered by my logic. He had come to know me too well to be longer fooled by my mental inferiority as a woman. He knows the ills of the society in which we live all too closely to remain passive to my observations.

"The supposition is admissible, but I am convinced you should go. I am inclined to believe you would take away, along with your farewells, a striking proof of the lady's generosity."

"That would be insulting. And let's say she would give me a very reasonable gift, of twenty or thirty thousand francs. Does this misery seem to you a big deal? If so, you are therefore ignorant of the fact that, by the mere sale of my surplus, I am now able to make ten thousand francs a year, and that, consequently, the probable generosity of Madame Anderson weighs only slightly in my resolutions."

"You should think more about the future. Wouldn't it be wise to prepare for those quiet days?"

"You are quite the financier! You always talk to me about pension schemes."

"That is because they are a solid, effective power; because they are a remarkable force; because money is a certainty that removes the worries of tomorrow. In giving you this advice, I do not think myself a professor of morality. I speak to you as a friend who has only your complete freedom of action in mind. I do not share, in any way, your outlook on things, but I feel I am up against an insurmountable obstacle. So, I limit my task to soothing you on the road that you follow, and I choose to do it blindly."

"But think about it all. If I sold my horses, my carriage, dismissed my staff, took on a modest apartment, reduced my expenditures to a minimum, the following day all my suitors would disappear. It's not our virtues that attract them but our faults, our extravagances, our opulence... and to renounce all this would be to lay down one's arms and serve for nothing. It's only with sumptuous clothes, jewels and horses that we can be assured of conquering the debauched adventurers, and above all, the old men for whom refinement and luxury are essential."

He is silent for a long minute, before speaking again. "Aren't you afraid you might not always be mistress of your wills, and that the time comes when you will do something wrong? Don't you ever feel a sense of human mortality? Do you never see yourself as the victim of a luxury that is costing you so dearly? Your opulence is a lie, since it is ephemeral. It is not even yours alone, it belongs to others. And yet you alone have acquired it, with troubles and misfortunes, and paid with your insomnia and sorrows. Granted, you are young and pretty. But beauty fades. It is your youth that goads you to forget that beauty has the destiny of a rose. So, I tell you, for the last time, you are vain and foolhardy. I prefer to give advice to your present prosperity than a tardy consolation to your regrets."

We both pause to reflect on his words. Romain breaks the silence first.

"Look into your heart, little Marie! What does it tell you? Why is it that you want to see me so often? Certainly not to receive my compliments!"

"I know."

"It is because I alone know your heart. I alone know the needs you have beside those of having abundance and luxury. But you resolve never to pay heed to my suggestions."

"Yet I wouldn't change your presence for the world."

"Hmm. My visits are agreeable to you because my language contrasts very sharply with that of those who only know how to flatter your vanities; because I always appeal to your reason, to what is good in you, to your sensibility; because only with me can you question the memories of your horrendous childhood, of your misery and abandonment; because, alas, while showing myself a severe friend, I am neither a fierce censor nor a brutal rigorist. I know that after I leave, you become pensive and melancholy. When all your senses rest; when your mind is calm; when your heart swells; you admit that I am right. You feel, just like the rest of us, worries and sadness and you feel the void that would be around you if your beauty were to disappear. But then the evenings come and you are besieged with attention, smiles, and adulation. And you no longer remember my friendly remonstrances, the future continues to look bright, you no longer suffer from the chains of this terrible profession to which you have sacrificed your life."

"Your description is not too dark," I say, "and I even think it is not enough. But I do not want to waste my youth in vain recriminations. I take the situation as it is and will analyze the consequences."

"The consequences could always be in your favor, if only you could pay heed to your true nature and relinquish your greed."

"My dear friend, as I told you before, you alone know all I have carefully hidden from the world. You blame my way of seeing things and my actions. Why not try to appreciate my character instead, even in its differences? It seems to me useless to go back to the reasons which prevent me from accepting the generous offer of Mrs. Anderson. I will go to pay homage to her kindness, to express my gratitude, and to thank her bestowal. But I cannot return to honor. Not for you, not for her, not for myself. My existence is forever doomed. It is in vain that I invoke pity, as social conventions are ruthless. When the body has been defiled, what remains in one's heart? Hope! Is it a virtue? Purgatory?"

"I will address the second question that you have posed. I deny it for those who are young and pretty. For those who have aged and are ending a misery to enter another, because they have no choice, and their passions are extinguished. If, among the first, some are capable to redress themselves, I admire them and wish them enough strength and perseverance to resist the new temptations to come. But there are some who have enough power over themselves not to return to the sin of which they have been perniciously influenced. And you, Marie, are one such person. You have enough and are still being offered even more. What remains then? Your greed! Your vanity! Your absolute devotion to vain words!"

"You are wrong. I simply do not feel endowed with enough strength to become a recluse. I loathe hypocrisy. Is it my fault that I lost my mother so young? Is it my fault that I was delivered to the chances of vagrancy? Had my inclinations predisposed me to libertinage? Did I have a will? Should the disorders of my life be attributable to me alone? Was I at twelve, as at fifteen, responsible for my own actions? If society condemns me, then I, in turn, condemn it too. I know that the body wears fast in such a job, that one does not live to become old in this hell. But when one is young, when passions are unleashed, one does not lead one's destiny as one wishes. One suffers its fate. Oh, my friend, how I realize I am making a mistake, and how I wish I could go back. But to me and those like me, there is no way back. There are only ruins left behind us and we perceive nothing but abysses on all sides. I would happily accept the paradise offered me, if I were not certain that it would kill me faster than a prison. I would be exposed to too much physical and moral deprivation. And I would be greeted only by boredom and broken hearts. The calm of such a dwelling would not be a true deliverance, but the peace of the tomb. And I shall not bury myself at age twenty."

"You speak in such exaggerated language. But it is obvious you have reached a resolution beyond any other considerations, and I think it proper not to insist. May this portrait inspire you," he says, placing the miniature in my hand, "and may my sympathy come to the aid of your determination."

"Severe friend, sincere friend...when will you see me again?"

"Next Sunday. I will come to see the results of your visit to Mrs. Anderson."

He shakes my hand and I shake his.

ROMAIN VIENNE
I cried bitterly reading this conversation with Marie

which had been reproduced in detail and with touching sincerity. *I shall not bury myself at age twenty...*

Tears burn my flesh even now as I commit her words to paper. My heart aches at every word written by her delicate, trembling hand.

My poor dear little Alphonsine... her beauty, her charm, her delicate manner, those big expressive eyes looking earnestly into mine, would all be extinguished too soon. Not at twenty, but at twenty-three. Had her resolution been different if she had known this sad truth? Would I have been a more sensitive friend than a severe tyrant? Would I have stayed more often just to hold her in my arms with sincere affection?

I would have. I would have changed myself for her sake.

But this isn't about me and my choices. It is about her and *her* choices. Now that I truly understand her nature—though too late—it would have been unchanged. Just like any orphan thrust on this earth like prey for the beasts, she possessed a free and wild, independent spirit which no pragmatic friend could have contained or made see reason. This was—contrary to any appearances—her beauty. This was her magic and magnetism, the very attraction she held over so many men. Like moths lured by a flame, they too tried to catch her light, only to be destroyed by it—some financially, some emotionally. Herself a metaphorical moth, in the end she'd been destroyed by the light of the world to which she sacrificed her entire life, thoughts, and dreams. The glitz of a society dominated by pleasure, senseless actions, and deceptive dreams, acted on her as it had on so many others like the worst poison of all—that which kills slowly but unmistakably.

Marie Duplessis

After Romain leaves me, I become as he said I would: pensive and melancholy. But I do not remain in a depressive frame of mind for long, as my thoughts and dreams fly to the one that makes me hear the stage music of the heart again. The one that, aside from fulfilling my every material whim, no matter how ridiculous or outrageous, has the power to bring back to the surface of my consciousness the long buried secret dream every merchant of love ever had: the hope for redemption through love.

But the mere allusion to that word — love — has the power to bring my melancholy back faster than it left me. It is as if Romain's sense of logic and futility rubbed onto me, and now my own words ring in my head louder than Sunday church bells.

It's not our virtues that attract our suitors but our faults, our extravagances, our opulence.

The lesson Valory taught me long ago, and which for a while I decided to forget, replays itself before my mind's eye. My spiritual transformation is never in any man's plan. My kindness, romantic streak, sweet words and bending nature never are and never will be incentives for rich young men.

Edouard cannot be any different. It's not possible. No. I cannot go the same path again. I must remain a cold, mercenary woman or else I shall knowingly dig my own grave.

With this last resolution, my melancholy and fear of ever finding myself vulnerable dispel for good. Thus, my thoughts turn to the impromptu, unexpected visit I received yesterday. A visit I purposefully kept hidden from Romain or the flood of his angry words would have depressed me beyond recovery.

The visit announced to me that Count Gustav von Stackelberg resolved to reenter my life.

CHAPTER 15

*A*s I hastily scribble the note to send to Romain, begging that he come visit me as soon as possible, I find I cannot stop my hands from shaking. The visit I just received, which ended in the most pleasant if not startling terms, electrified my entire body; hence, the tremor in my hands.

This Saturday night, at the end of February 1844, proved everything but ordinary. Not to say that any day in my life is ordinary, but when an event proves beyond my ordinary unordinary, the mention is indispensable.

Everything is calm at my home in rue d'Antin, as evenings usually are before I begin the long process of embellishing myself for the adventurous nights to follow.

Ding! The bell rings. This in itself startling, as I was not expecting anyone. A few moments later, Rose enters my bedroom with the expression of one who had just been chased by a wild boar.

"It's the old count!" she screams.

"What?" I scream even louder.

"I told him he should wait outside the door while I check with my mistress on if she is willing to receive him."

"Good! You learned your lesson. Now, quick! Help me dress up!" I demand. With the dress corset laced tightly, I ask Rose to receive the Count in the dining room. I purposefully let him wait another quarter-hour. He deserted me. No man deserting me should think he can return on a whim and find me desperate to receive him.

But a quarter-hour proves quite a long time for my mounting curiosity and I rush to push open the door to my dining room.

The old Count's face looks older than ever. In the few moments before he sees me, I observe his broken physique. It's been only a few months since he, raked with unbearable jealousy, deserted me faster than it took to meet me. He sits in my favorite armchair, head tilted to the side, arms dangling restless on each side of the armchair. The skin of his face hangs even lower than last I saw him, as if invisible weights pull it groundward with shameless obstinacy.

"My old jealous one," I say in the best soothing voice I can muster. He jumps to his feet as if pushed forward by springs. I smile. "To whom should I thank for this considerate visit?"

"Mistress of my heart!" he exclaims, as he bends low to kiss my hand. "I wasn't sure you would agree to receive me. I am very pleased to find you the same delicate, gentle, kind woman as when I left you."

I smile again and try to restrain my sarcasm, but I fail.

"Surely, you meant to say, 'deserted you' rather than 'left you'," I mock, but he doesn't seem to have heard my remark. His eyes are furiously darting all over the walls in my dining room. The sudden gloom in his eyes looks like an autumnal sky.

"Where is it?" he booms.

"Where is what?" I ask, startled, thinking that this man has lost grip of his senses.

"The portrait! The Olivier portrait I commissioned for you! You gave it to one of your many Monsieurs, haven't you?" His eyes now shoot arrows of incandescent light and, for a moment, I believe I should be afraid of him.

"My old jealous one... you haven't changed a bit, have you? You come here with the same demands of old. Have you forgotten you lost your rights the moment you set foot outside this house? Now, now. Let me grab you some hot coffee and we'll discuss your visit."

I trot out of the dining room. "Run to Agénor's house and retrieve my portrait at once!" I demand of Rose, who nods and exits.

In vain, I try to dissuade the Count from looking for the Olivier portrait until Rose arrives, and our conversation leads to nowhere. Fifteen minutes later, Rose returns with the portrait, which she hangs in my bedroom between a framed print of my look-alike — the wistful Matrix — and another unfinished portrait of myself.

"I see that in order to have your trust I must humor you," I say to the count, as I lead him into my bedroom, "or else we shall waste one another's time without any resolution."

The small pinkish lips smiling at us from the Olivier portrait have an opposite effect on each of us. Raising my chin and puffing out my chest, I glare at the Count with disdain. He is suddenly at my feet, encircling them with his arms and wetting them with bitter tears.

"I shall never forgive myself for this unworthy and unjustified suspicion," he sobs as he covers my feet with wet kisses.

"Pull yourself together, my dearest Gustav," I say and

release my feet from his entrapment. "I shall not hold this against you."

He kisses my legs and my entire body on his way up to his feet. I pull back.

"My dear count, you have lost this privilege to which once you had in exclusive terms. You forget I am neither a woman who contents herself with odds and ends, nor one who is predisposed to a decent integrity. In all honesty, I must admit I lacked no material things while you loved me. But I lacked all things pertaining to my soul, which seems to make a habit in showing me it is still very vibrant and demanding. Mind you, I am twenty. So, what do you expect?"

My words roll out of my mouth unrestrained, lest the Count find it suitable to again make a silly demand of fidelity. He is half an hour in my company already and I still don't know why he came. When it comes to this old gentleman, I seem to be at my wits end.

"I shall accept you and your conditions without the slightest of complaints. I have come to the sad realization that I cannot live without you. You, my child, have come to mean more to me than you know. The sadness possessing me every day of my life spent away from you is something I cannot fully fathom. My only concern, more so my deepest fear, is that you might still hold in your heart the resentment produced by my forsaking you. My heart swells with despair at the thought of you rejecting me. Therefore, the question is not whether I accept you in your totality, but whether you, my beautiful child, will be disposed to take back this silly old relic before you, begging you to again love him."

The sadness in his eyes, coupled with his violently aged features, speak of the great sorrow he must have felt in the past months. I remain adamant as to the motive being my absence.

"Why the sudden change in your priorities?" I ask, inviting him to sit, as should I not do so, I fear he may collapse on the floor any moment. He sits at the edge of my bed with a thud, then buries his face in his palms and sobs.

"What is the matter, my dear Gustav?" I ask. Alarmed, I sit next to him.

"It's Elena. My fifth child. The sweetest, most tender one. She too, is dead. Dead!" His sobs become wailings and gliding down my bed, he drops himself to the floor. I lean over to caress his head.

"Oh, my dearest count! I am so truly sorry! How is that possible?"

"The scourge! That's how! The bloody consumption! She died of tuberculosis just like my other two daughters. She was only twenty-three!" he shouts. "Is that an age to die? Is that an age at which one should part with one's dreams and hopes and experiences? She did not even know love! Or marriage! Or the miracle of giving birth! Why did He take her? Why did He make her? Why take all that from her at an age when she was just beginning to truly live? What kind of Maker is this? A cruel, mocking one, I tell you! One playing dice with his offspring!"

My eyes cry with his. There are tears for his loss as well as mine. I remember the loss of my dear mother. And I remember the loss of my own child. A child who never made me question God's actions. A death that didn't even make me question my own actions.

"My words to you are these: there is a reason for it all," I say. "Even though God's doings seem utterly incomprehensible at times, I strongly believe there is a method to his madness."

"I don't believe that! I believe he is just a cruel, sadistic despot with no reasoning. Why didn't he take *me*? Look at me! I am as old as the earth! I lived a thousand lives! I gathered the experience of another thousand! Wouldn't it have been more sensible to take me instead of a child who did not come to fully live?"

"I do not know."

"Everything I ever touch, dies. Even my wife's plants. She forbade me to water her garden. She said I kill all her sprouts only by looking at them. Imagine that!"

I burst out laughing. "My silly old count... you're being a child." I shake my head and in a scolding tone say, "What am I to do with you?"

My words stop his sobbing. "Take me in your arms!" he says libidinously. "Hug me and never let go. Squeeze me until all this melancholy I feel gets out."

"My Lord, dear count! I have my own melancholy to get rid of. I live in a house that no longer suits me. My clothes of past month are worn and obsolete. My servers demand more and more money of me. Not to mention the exorbitant sums I must part with weekly for maintaining the stable of horses, their clothes, accessories, and groomers. And I haven't even mentioned the awful placement of my opera box, which I truly hate and desperately need to change. And you, my dear old count, think you are the only fellow predisposed to melancholy?"

"I am sorry," he says. "I am sorry to have left you. Had I not done so you would not have encountered so much misfortune. It is all my fault. And yes! What is this house? Upon my honor, it's too small! You should get a lease on a bigger one, for you, my dear child, are to have everything your heart desires. Your servants will be handsomely taken care of and your horses will look as if descended from above."

"Your answer pleases me greatly. But I must warn you,

my old jealous one. I am not a woman who can be praised for her virtue of fidelity. You, yourself know this better than anyone."

"Keep your suiters," he says, gesturing with irritation, "and you can keep and take all that you please, as long as you love me again."

"Is the Count decidedly content with his resolution? For I would hate to have to see him bursting out of my home again."

"I have lost three daughters. I will not lose you, too. Not for all my fortune. Elena was the last of my loved ones I buried. This is my resolution. This is my vow."

"Very well then."

And, yes, I *very well* make him happy the very same night. Not as I used to, no. For my old jealous one seems to have taken his farewell not only from his third daughter, but from his erection as well. Am I mean? Maybe not. Just surprised it worked for him for that long. Plus, whoever knows these lions as intimately as I do, knows no amount of harshness is too much if compared to what they really deserve. So, my mimicked explosive end seems sufficient. All the better for me.

ROMAIN VIENNE

She would have been right about my flood of angry words. And then, finding out she has kept this information from me would have hurt me deeply, so now I am glad that she did. For only when you lose someone do things come to your mind that you would have done differently. Only when you watch the last breath being drawn out, as if by merciless claws, of the one you loved so dearly, do you feel an unbearable, if not iniquitous guilt about every unkind word you ever said to that person.

Every deed or less than savory word becomes an unbearable weight you must carry until some distant day of redemption and reconciliation. A day you hope you'll get a chance at having. Why aren't we living our lives as though we are about to lose our loved ones at any moment? And why are we paying so much attention to that ever-gibbering voice in our heads that analyses, judges, and condemns? Ah, how great we are at judging and condemning others! How overbearing, exacting, and imperious!

She never judged me. She never judged any of her friends or acquaintances. She was a whore, yes. But she was also a saint. Her job was of this world, which raised and taught her that to be a whore was the only métier available to a woman who wanted to be free and independent, equal to men. But her soul, her very heart was of a world which we still have to unriddle. A world which bore us, men and women, equal. How behindhand we must be...

Marie Duplessis

One week into Count von Stackelberg's visit, I decide to make a dramatic visit myself. The Sunday I make my appearance in rue du Faubourg-Saint-Honoré is gloomy and suffocating, which doesn't help with my mission.

The warm, instinctive, motherly embrace Mrs. Anderson gives me upon my arrival at her home shakes me to my core. This is not something for which I prepared myself. I prepared myself for an uptight society woman with castigating eyes and reproachful mouth. Having expected that, I have put myself in a defensive state of mind, equipped and ready to smile and ignore. But her warmth, her all-compassionate adoring gaze melts my defensiveness into tears. It is as if I am being embraced by my own long-lost mother. It is as if she at last receives into her arms her long-lost, beloved daughter.

Warring sentiments shake my entire being. My body trembles with joy, then is overwhelmed with distress. My refusal, although in the warmest dismal tone, makes me suffer horribly. The dear woman is sadly affected and when she speaks to me of her daughter, whom she says I resemble, she throws herself into my arms once again and we again shed tears.

How was I able to resist? I don't know. But I know I dare not visit her again... the intensity of my feelings frightened me that much. Our parting is cruel, and when I arrive home my heart feels broken. Pacing my living room, I find it smothering and imprisoning.

I go to the Bois, hoping to rid myself of the somber reflections which have overwhelmed my spirit, but I only see Mrs. Anderson everywhere and hear only her tender appeals.

I go to the theatre, but find I become infuriated by the chatter and intrusive compliments.

And so, finally, I return home and barricade the door. Then wait until daylight for sleep.

It seems that everything frightens me these days. My soul, which I have spent more than a decade hiding from the rest of world, and myself, elbows its way out of me to make itself known again. It feels famished. It feels angry for being kept starving. And the more famished it is, the more frightened I become.

Madame Anderson stirred the memories of a long-lost feeling of being at home, of having a family. A family I never really had. But with the help of my imagination, I created many times the idea of the perfect home, with loving parents and adorable siblings. It supplanted all that I was lacking. And that is what Mrs. Anderson rekindled in me.

Then there is Edouard.

And if Mrs. Anderson's unrestrained warmth frightened me, Edouard's instant devotion, passionate ardor, and declarations of eternal loyalty and love, almost make me go off my head.

My resolution? I begin ignoring him. But I soon find that the more I ignore him, the more infatuated he becomes. Night after night and morning after morning, his dinging at my door makes me writhe in emotional pain.

Rose has been instructed to ignore his visits as stubbornly as I.

"My dear Edouard,

It is impossible to see you. I am a little unwell and shall not leave my bed tonight."

"Impossible to dine with you today. I am still unwell."

"How cross I am, my dear Edouard, not to have received your letter an hour earlier. My friend wrote to ask if I could spend the evening with her; and having nothing better to do, I agreed."

But as I expected and was afraid would happen, a man tormented by the pangs of passion and consumed by his obsession cannot be contained for long.

In mid-April on a rainy spring morning, at about half-past four, and as the old Count leaves my home for his, I am struck by red, almost mad, eyes staring at me from across the road. For a moment I feel I should scream and run to the

Count's carriage, which still lingers. But as the carriage begins to slowly disappear into darkness, the mad eyes begin approaching me. I recognize the broken gaze of the one who brought the sun, as well as the lighting storms, within my soul.

Standing in front of me now, with arms hanging heavy at his sides, with slightly parted lips, and longing gaze, I am reminded again through an ever-lurking fear of why I behaved the way I have in the past weeks.

"I have been searching for you," he almost whispers. "The past week ... it is all I have done. Searching for you." I say nothing, as the lump in my throat, as well as the one in my stomach suddenly rendered me quiet. Subdued.

"In vain have I searched for you on the Champs-Elysées. In vain I wondered on the Bois and through all your favorite theaters and restaurants. Every pretty little raven head would excite me, only to then quickly fill me with despair, as I would, for the hundredth time, realize it wasn't your head or the smile of the one I adore. It has been a week filled with hundreds of smiles that punished and persecuted me. Then, I sank even deeper into my melancholy when I realized that indeed you were punishing me. Not knowing why, took me to the end of my wits and became the reason for my decision to come wait for you outside of your house... for as long as it would have taken me."

The tiny rain droplets clinging to his hair made his sandy curls look as if they were drawn by Olivier. The haunted, conquered expression in his eyes, his wet skin and full lips speaking with a depth of feeling I never knew existed, bring tears to my eyes. But besides my tears, which do release my tormented psyche, I find something else has changed. The fear is gone. It is the man standing in front of me, the man I have held responsible for my fear enveloping me in the first place, who has chased it away. It was not his weakness or vulnerability or love for me that chased it away. It was his courage. The courage to admit his love without the fear of being perceived as weak and vulnerable, and less than the manly man he is. His courage to admit he's been searching for me for over a week. His very courageous determination to stand in the rain outside my door for as long as would have taken for him to find me.

I am coming to the realization that fear nourishes fear, and courage demands courage. And these polarities have finally made a whole. A oneness.

"I ... I was punishing you ... but what I did not know was how much I—"

"I love you, Marie!"

"—how much I ... I truly loved you ..."

Lightning cracks above our wet heads. His parted lips reach close to mine. A moment, which seems an eternity spent in the Garden of Wanton Eden, is enough to mingle our energies and passion and yearning. Cupping my face with his palms, he crushes my lips in the passionate kiss I've been waiting for my entire life. Lifting me in his strong arms, he carries me inside.

What follows would make the most prolific courtesan of Paris blush.

For it is only in the presence of love that whores blush.

CHAPTER 16

The Count's visit hurts Edouard deeply. His moans and heavy breathing, his body sweating profusely while immersed in sleep are signs telling me the depth of my lover's anguish. It does not matter how much I would caress his curls or wipe the sweat from his forehead. His sleep seems to be an unforgiving torment. For only in his sleep does this strange human being allow himself to express his jealousy. Only in his wanderings through Dreamland does he permit himself to reproach me for my conduct or assert himself in the face of the one he is most afraid of losing.

With the light of dawn drawing near and brighter, the city waking also wakes my lover, and his jealousy takes strange forms.

"I have a surprise for you, my dearest Marie," he says, yawning sheepishly.

"You do?"

"Yes, my love, my one and only," he says as he presses another passionate kiss on my lips. "Would you do me the pleasure of coming with me on a short trip?"

"Well... it's barely eight in the morning... could we sleep some more, pray? Or maybe touch me with those masculine hands of—?"

"No, no. These masculine hands are yours forever," he says, stretching his arms toward me. "But this can't wait. I am too excited."

"Very well, then," I grumble, getting off the bed, though doing so before mid-afternoon is like trying to get off the hospital bed after a long, tormenting illness. My head spins and the strange cough returns.

"Are you all right?" Edouard asks, rushing to catch me in his arms.

"This weakness... and this annoying cough. It's probably nothing. We had our clothes soaked to our undergarments this morning," I say dreamily, looking through the window. "The rain has cleared."

"Are you sure you're all right? I wouldn't want you to catch a cold. We can return to bed."

"It's probably nothing, my love. Plus, I wouldn't want to ruin your excitement. You earned this good disposition with so much hardship, and I wouldn't ruin it for the world."

He smiles and I smile, then he goes to prepare the horses. A merciless dizziness possesses me, and I squat, holding myself on my palms. Beads of sweat spring from my forehead and a rush of warmth crosses my entire body. My heart pumps hard, causing me to breathe at an alarming speed. But then, like lightning cracking from a clear sky, the mysterious condition quits my body as suddenly as it possessed it.

I must have imagined it all. I stand up straight to look in the mirror. The beads of sweat still present on my forehead tell me it was not my fancy.

The noise of horses' hooves hitting wet earth puts me at ease. Edouard's arm around my waist, even more so. We travel a few miles, crossing Bois de Boulogne, and then outside Paris.

As soon as we exit the great metropolis the ambiance changes and I realize how much I've been missing the countryside. The green meadows, the clear blue sky teased by wild birds, big and small, the smell of grass, of horses, and burnt wood. It reminds me of my childhood. Of the good memories of my childhood, which were offered to me only by Nature. And I suddenly yearn for a quieter, calmer existence.

Only when man reunites with nature does he rediscover his inherent goodness. Jean Jaques Rousseau was right in his novel, *The New Heloise*: man is born virtuous, in a state of nature; vice comes from living among worldly society and artificial urban pressures.

Two hours into our journey, the carriage comes to a halt, bringing me back to the present.

"Where are we?" I ask.

"Bougival."

"Oh?"

Edouard's hand lightly touches mine. "I was ready to enroll in the army," he says, avoiding my curious gaze. "At the end of last week, after my tormented search for you, I wanted to give it all up and join the Foreign Legion."

"What? But why?" I squeeze his hand tightly.

"Because if I couldn't have you, I wanted to be as far away from you as possible. I felt I was going into a suicidal mission, and strangely, it was the only thought that gave me some hope of escaping my grief..."

His face muscles contract in anguish, no doubt at the memory of his grief. Then, a sunbeam coming through the window reflects on his features, and in turn, his features reflect it further.

"But there was no need anymore," he says with a grin. "I

wandered through the countryside and ended up in this exact same spot. My hope rekindled and my actions took a sudden turn. Come. Let me show you."

He jumps out of the carriage and going around it, comes to open my door.

"Close your eyes," he orders gently, and I comply. Resting my hand in his, I let myself be guided around the carriage.

"My surprise for you, my dearest Marie!"

My eyes open on a small house with red roof.

"A summer house?" I ask, bewildered.

"And it is all yours. Wait till you see the river!" he booms like a child, grabbing my hand and hauling me through the breathtaking backyard, slaloming through the oaks and walnut trees down to the river.

Forgetting about my expensive attire, I allow myself to sit on the bank. Edouard sits next to me. River Seine has never been as quiet and peaceful. Never so beautiful. And to have it right in my own backyard...

Tears gather in my eyes. Why? I do not really know. It is neither the most expensive gift I ever received, nor the most unexpected one. But somehow, the simplicity and naturalness of the countryside, the quiet all-receiving nature, the modesty of my own conduct, suddenly freed by the ever-present need to act and feign and please, have all made way for the vulnerable, soft, uncomplicated part of me.

Edouard reaches to wipe my tears away.

"It is beautiful," I whisper.

"Isn't it? I thought of you the moment I saw it and I knew you must have it."

"Thank you, Edouard. This is so unexpectedly pleasant. It is a gift I never knew I needed but knew I couldn't live without it once I saw it." I rest my head on his shoulder.

"That was my very feeling as I laid eyes on it. But still... it is incomplete."

"How do you mean, my love?"

Edouard pauses and clears his throat, and a feeling of restlessness suddenly churns in my stomach. "It lacks life. It lacks love. It lacks you and me. It lacks us living here, together. The handsomest couple of Bougival!"

My tears dry up at once and I jump to my feet. The restlessness has turned into panic, and now I pace the bank back and forth like a caged lioness. Edouard trots behind me.

"Marie, please. Just think about it for a moment. Don't push the thought out of—"

"Do you wish to do me harm?" I snap, throwing my arms about furiously.

"What? No! I—"

"You are well aware that this could be a disaster for my future, which you seem absolutely determined to make unhappy and unfortunate for me!"

"My greatest wish, my only wish is to make you happy!"

"Make *me* happy? Your only wish is to make yourself happy! You wish to annul my connection to my world, cut me from everybody that could steal me away from you, dissolve my entire existence as I know it! This isn't love! This is selfishness! You are jealous and wish to hide me in here so you could keep me only for yourself!"

"While you work yourself up judging me, you forget that even my jealousy, my wish to have you for my own, springs from the purest of feelings, from the deepest love I've ever been graced to feel."

"You're deluding yourself. Your jealousy does not spring from love. It springs from fear."

"What fear?"

"The fear of losing me."

"Is that so wrong, Marie? That I am afraid of losing you? Is it? Let me ask you this: Isn't fear, in turn, springing from love?"

I pause to reflect on his question. All my recent memories of fear come to replay themselves before my mind's eye. It was out of fear that I rejected him; out of fear that I kept him away from my person the hardest and longest I could; and it was a fear that sprung from the love I felt for him, from a passion that rekindled that blasted vulnerability I've been trying to repress, even annihilate for the entirety of my life.

"Is this idyllic life so terrifying for you? Then, you might ask yourself why."

"I don't have to ask myself that question because I already know the answer."

"Which is?"

"I am capricious, immoral, vain, and depraved. I enjoy carnality, debauchery, my life full of vice as I know it. And I am greedy. My friend said so, and he must be right."

"Nothing that I myself alone wouldn't be able to fulfill. I am rich. So very rich that no caprice of yours will remain unsatisfied. Your greed will be quenched. Your immoral, depraved, and debauched nature will be taken care of by this youthful, passionate, burning body in front of you. And you are wrong. You are not vain. You just think you are because all those ceaseless compliments and attentions made you believe you couldn't live without them. It isn't you who is vain, but those very compliments and attentions. You are smart enough, and sensible enough, to know that what I am saying doesn't come from my need of persuading you to change your life, but from utter realism. I do not want you to merely reconsider your life, I want you to allow yourself to be the person you really are. The woman within you. To be as Nature created you. The sensitive, soft woman always in need of protection from stronger arms."

His words bring tears to my eyes again and I turn away. "I don't need emotional protection, as you say. I am already as strong as I can be and can protect my own self."

Does he really see through me? Could this be? Could he really love me and only me, stripped as I might be from all my glamour and sophistication?

"Upon my honor, Marie! Others would kill for this very moment; had they been given the chance at living it!"

I blot my tears away.

"Well, I am not others. If I were, then your love would have gone out the window. You would have redirected your love toward another Marie, one with glamorous attire and splendid horses and fabulously rich suitors. One who would have laughed in your face with disdain and flaunted her protectors just to spite you. That's the type of women men want! That's the type of woman you, my dearest Edouard, seem to fall in love with. Not some housewife living in a small, red-roofed summer house, patiently waiting for her lover, while busying herself with frivolous household chores. Oh, no, my love! I am not vain enough or conceited enough to think you will love me for myself; a self bare of all the geniality of my attire and conduct and bearing!"

As I turn to look at him, I notice the strangest thing. He's crossed his arms over his chest in a strangely relaxed position, while his features seem to make an effort not to give full vent to a chuckle.

"Are you mocking me?" I snap.

"No, no..." He titters, reaching to grab me in his arms. "Your fears amuse me, that's all."

"I need to be alone," I say, moving out of his reach and retreating under a tall branchy willow tree near the Seine. Edouard is sensitive enough to let me be. Away from his proximity however, I suddenly feel lonely. I want him to stay away, but I wish he would have come after me. I want him to take me back to Paris at once, but I also want him to continue to persuade me to stay.

What is wrong with me?

I toss a pebble into the water of the hungry Seine. The river remains unperturbed. Just a few ripples, then back to its natural course. Through some mysterious mechanism only our brains are aware of, my torment transforms this image into a solution. I am like the river. Strong, indestructible, moving forward with complete determination.

Could I be just as yielding as the Seine, just this once? Could I allow Bougival and this idyllic home to be my pebble?

After all, I can always return to my natural course should something go wrong, should this little pebble be too much to stomach. Just as the Seine opens up to receive, then moves right along, never quite remembering what disturbed it. Then I remember my favorite heroine, the great courtesan, Manon Lascaut. She left Paris for Chaillot, where she and her lover sequestered so that they might live a simple, honest existence.

With the lightheartedness of one who's discovered the treatment to one's illness, I run into Edouard's strong protecting arms.

"Show me inside," I whisper, and we lose ourselves in an endless kiss.

Romain Vienne

Marie and Edouard de Peregaux settled there, or rather they locked themselves in. Their separate lives became only one. Society no longer existed for them. They dreamed of having the ability to manage for themselves without it. Rare visitors were allowed, once or twice a week to bring with them a momentary diversion in the sameness of their lifestyle and break the inevitable monotony that could create weariness, disenchantment and boredom.

I was chosen to be a regular and experienced their life at Bougival in all its detail. Every day, when the weather was mild and the sky beautiful and clear, they made excursions in the neighborhood and further, in the neighborhoods of Paris or in the Bois de Boulogne, Marie's favorite promenade. At other times they would spend their evening at Toulouse, paying their respects at the English Cafe or at the Maison d'Or, only to return the next day to their nest of flowers and grass and willow trees.

They hid as much as possible to be alone, far from the world, far from the noise, safe from the intruders. They gathered enormous bouquets of roses and honeysuckle to give each other and plucked the petals of marguerite daisies while exchanging kisses. They retired early to their bedroom; listened to the last couplets of birdsong in the leaves; hunted for their star in the blue firmament, making the nights longer than the days. They intoxicated themselves with their happiness, burning their blood at the devouring flame of voluptuous ardor.

Marie had until then only experienced frivolous joys and transient satisfactions. The relationships of a few days or weeks she has had, by fancy or idleness, left sweet memories in her heart, but none had loved her like this. I saw her happy and proud of the devoted, fiery and exclusive passion of her lover. Edouard's affection was boundless, without restraint, without moderation. She absorbed all his being. He had completely devoted himself to the worship of his beloved. It was adoration. Madness.

· · ·

Marie Duplessis

The first night spent in the summer house with red roof top teaches me what passion really is. I am standing in the open door to the backyard, wearing nothing but my long white chemise. The soft spring wind blowing through the door lifts the hem of it. I feel I could fly, so lighthearted I am. I feel like a butterfly bathing in the moonlight. The same soft wind sighs through the willow tree branches that bend lazily to touch the river. It is as if the song of the trees wants to mate with the song of the river. As if the lover earth reaches toward his bride, the water.

Edouard's breath on the back of my exposed neck startles me, but I don't move. Closing my eyes, I feel his masculine energy radiating behind me, generously warming my back, my neck, my buttocks. His fingers touching my arms electrify my entire being. They slowly travel up my skin and slide under the braces which glide down my shoulders. A moan escapes my lips as the chemise caresses my body on its way to the floor. I am as naked as Eve, as Nature intended me. My nipples get hard, so hard it is almost painful. I take Edouard's hand and place it on my breast. It is warm and vibrant and yearning, with his fingers squeezing it gently. Another moan exits my mouth, making way through my intensified breathing. I turn around, shove my hand in his hair and look him in the eyes.

"Take me!" I moan. "Take me now!"

But he doesn't take me. He takes his time.

Bending down and taking me in his strong arms, he carries me to the bed. With a swift movement of my hips, I am now on top of him, locking his wrists with my palms.

"No," he whispers, grabbing me by the waist and pulling me underneath him. "Tonight, for once, you will not please. Tonight, *you* will be pleased."

His words and whispers dissolve my judgement. His

fingers and tongue exploring every inch of my body transform me, as if through an alchemic mutation, into a mass of feelings and emotions and senses. My resistance kneels, my mind surrenders under the touch of the man who loves me. Time ceases to exist, as past, present, and future become one. They become Now. The one moment, one body, one spirit. Two separate beings melted together in the explosive oneness of mating.

As our bodies cool off and our sweat dries, the combined sounds of the wind and water reach through the still open door to me. I now understand it. It is the same sound our intertwined spirits produced while in the clutches of lovemaking. Tonight, all God's creations, trees, wind, water, woman, and man, were in perfect harmony. And shortly before sleep comes to fetch me to fly among the stars, I realize one last thing. I finally understood God's greatest secret. It is Love.

Amusements, grand balls, fireworks, and squandering money are the keywords for the second week of June 1844. It is the season of horse races in the little town of Chantilly, which culminates with the Prix du Jockey Club, the grand prize reserved for the winner.

"Do you know who the winner of the Prix was two years ago?" Edouard asks me on a balmy morning at the beginning of June.

"No, my love. Who was it?"

"You are looking at him," Edouard says, proudly puffing out his chest. He looks like a child in search of praise.

"Of course, you were, my love," I say as I approach him, hand extended to touch his red cheek.

"Me and Plover, my horse. He'd love to go."

"*He'd* love to go?"

He grins. "And I, too."

"Is that so?" I ask, slightly mockingly. "And leave your idyllic, magic little spot for the joys of the horse races?"

"Is that so dreadful?"

"By no means."

"Will you join me then?"

"I'd love to."

"How wonderful! I wouldn't have gone without you." He pulls me to his chest to squeeze me in his arms with his unmistakable affection.

But my thoughts darken.

I realize they are never as simple and straightforward as his heartfelt, uncomplicated tenderness. The idea of leaving this secluded place behind for the marvels of a society gathering feels like a hand extended toward a drowning man. A drowning woman. Too enticing not to darken my thoughts. Too seductive not to make me wonder for how long I will be able to continue this charade — for a charade it seems — to pretend that Edouard's love is all I need.

ROMAIN VIENNE

This was the first seed of doubt felt by Marie. Although only twenty, she knew herself with the wisdom of an old woman who had already lived to tell right from wrong. She knew that a life spent in denying love and accepting vain pleasures was what had formed her character and disposition. And she knew that sooner or later she will no longer be disposed to live a life she had invented in the blink of an eye. It took her twenty years to invent herself as she really was: a thunderstorm ever in need of thunders and lightnings; a downpour suddenly finding itself in a place that required only sunshine and warmth and clear skies.

The trip to Chantilly was for Marie a unique opportunity to meet old acquaintances, friendly faces, and probably, future lovers. She never lost sight of these eventualities, for she was always thinking of her protectors, her worshipers. As I knew her, this preoccupation prevailed over all the others.

They left the day before the beginning of the horse races to avoid the fatigue of a hasty journey. When they arrived on the hippodrome in a splendid carriage drawn up at the Daumont, Marie was greeted with murmurs of admiration and flattering exclamations. She was in the full bloom of her astonishing beauty and produced a prodigious sensation. She wore, with charming grace and unrivalled elegance, a dress of unheard-of richness: a trimming of lace worth ten thousand francs adorned the hem of her dress; the rest to match.

Edouard gambled without reflection, without discernment, and won close to one million louis, which he then squandered on Marie, who accepted, without the slightest concern or consideration, as if the offerings had come from an inexhaustible source. Certain in her belief that her lover still possessed the hundred thousand francs a year he had inherited from his family, she let him do so, not suspecting that in doing so she was quickly, yet surely, approaching her ruin.

But then she was, as she always had been, blind and ignorant of the future.

MARIE DUPLESSIS

The joys of Chantilly prove ecstatic. Edouard wins so much money through gambling that we must hire two extra carriages just to transport everything I purchased back to Bougival: dresses, fabrics, rosewood furniture for the summer house, an oak indoor library, and a cedar swing for the backyard.

The joys of Chantilly prove not only ecstatic, but a relief. For I thought myself lost. Now I think myself able to enjoy both worlds: that of amusements, grand balls, fireworks, and squandering money; and that in which the nest of love could be a priority until the next grand ball or trip to Baden or nights spent gambling at the casino. And this thought is indeed a relief. For as greedy as Romain said I was, why should I content myself with only one side of the coin, when I can have an entire one? Purses full of them, bags full of them! And still be loved good at night. Still having breakfast served in bed and feet rubbed near the river, and whims and caprices fulfilled if as much as I open my mouth or throw a suggestive glance.

But it seems purses full of coins and undying love will remain the two things which will always elude me. Our return to Bougival splashes this truth in my face with the force of a tornado. My dream of having the two things I always wished for dissipates like a beautiful dream in the clutches of a merciless dawn.

CHAPTER 17

I do not become immediately aware of the truth that will change my life's trajectory once again. As we reach Bougival, I waste three quarters of an hour imparting orders to the servants as to where all the furniture we bought must be carried and installed. Only when the deed is done, and I declare myself happy with the result, do I allow my tired self a moment's rest.

Dropping into a chair at our magnificent oak dining table, I toss my hand fan onto it. It hits what seems to be a large envelope and knocks it to the floor. As I bend to lift it, I notice the official stamp of a notary on one of its corners.

This doesn't look like my usual correspondence.

Mrs. Anderson comes to mind. Maybe she's died and this is her will, through which she bestows all her fortune on me. My soul cringes and rejoices at the same time, and I hastily push the thought out of my mind.

Opening the envelope, several sheets of stamped official papers are revealed. I hastily gaze over them... *"the amount of money spent by Count Edouard de Perregaux...", "exhausting his inheritance...", "in the name of the Count's family, I bring to your attention...", "family taking legal measure to prevent the Count's complete ruin..."*

A bout of relentless coughing seizes me and I can no longer continue reading. Crumpling the papers in my hand, I raise to my feet and reach for the door to the backyard. Pushing it open I desperately gasp for air.

There he is... I see Edouard gently swinging himself on the newly purchased swing.

How peaceful he is with that stupid content smile on his face.

The sound accompanying this thought is even more frightening. A spent, wheezing puff, as if the breath of life was being taken away from me by an invisible claw, is the last thing I hear before I plunge into complete darkness.

The next time I open my eyes I find myself lying in our bed. Sweat covers my entire body and the cough returns. My thoughts return too, as the peace found in my earlier blackout leaves me in a hurry. I try to sit up, but Edouard's hands gently push me back.

"No, pray. Don't move, my love," he whispers. "You have a fever."

"Where are they? The papers?"

"What papers? You're having a fever, dear. You are delusio—"

"No, no! Don't you dare!" I shout, wriggling to sit up again.

"All right! Just please, stay still," he says, sighing and passing his fingers through his hair. "I've burned them."

I throw my head back and it hits the bed's headboard. "So, it is true, then?"

Edouard remains silent. His expression of desperation, which not long ago moved me into surrendering, is now making my bile rise in disgust.

"Answer me!" I shout again.

"Yes!" he answers quickly. "I have been drawing on the last fragments of my inheritance."

"How much? How much left?" I gasp.

"Less than fifteen thousand francs."

His words feel so painful to my psyche that having no other proper way to release that pain, I begin crying. Edouard mistakes my gesture as feminine weakness and wraps his arms around me. My disgust mounts. Are these the same strong masculine arms that promised protection?

"You've betrayed me," I say as I push him away from me. "You've lied to me about your financial status all along!"

"I've never!" he says, defending himself. "Not one word was said except in complete honesty toward you!"

"Is that so? '*I am rich. So very rich that no caprice of yours will remain unsatisfied. Your greed will be quenched.*' Aren't these your words, Monsieur?"

"Yes, they—"

"*Less than fifteen thousand francs.* Aren't these also your words?"

"They are, but—"

"Then, pray, explain it to me, Monsieur, so that a simple girl like me would understand. Which aren't true? For some of these words mustn't be, as they cannot coexist in a reality of only a few months. *I am so very rich* implies one would do splendidly for a lifetime, and still have fortune left to bestow on one's children. *Less than fifteen thousand francs*, will barely last me, last us, a month. So, which of your words, dear Count, aren't true?"

The anguish on Edouard's face spreads to near panic and he stands up to pace the bedroom. "Maybe I wasn't as rich as I thought I was," he almost whispers.

"Or maybe you knew exactly how rich you were."

"Well...maybe."

"That's better. That's honesty. You've betrayed me!" I shout again.

"I've betrayed *you*? Your very words are now betraying the love I have for you! They betray there was no love *you* had for me!" he roars, pointing his finger at my face.

"This isn't a question about love, but about honesty. You tricked me into this life!"

"You speak about honesty? You, of all people? Why are you here now, Madame? Certainly not for my love."

"You knew who I was. I never hid it from you. And my very honesty proved to be my undoing. For it rendered me vulnerable to your treachery. You knew exactly what I wanted and needed, and that is how you tricked me into relinquishing my perfectly acceptable life for this solitary one. By playing on my greed, by promising the fulfillment of all my needs and desires. By telling me exactly what you knew I wanted to hear!"

Edouard remains silent, while continuing to march the bedroom with his face buried in his palms. When he finally looks at me, I'm startled to see that his expression has changed as swiftly as wind gusts change in mid-winter.

"Is that so condemnable?" he meows, approaching me. "That I did all in my power to have you? And all in the name of love?" The fire in the stove reflects in the tears I see glistening in his eyes. But, along with his words, they produce the opposite effect on me.

"I can see you now for who you truly are. A skillful manipulator. A resourceful schemer. When all your logic and arguments are exhausted, you recoup by making use of that pure feeling on the poet's lips. You're using your love to manipulate me yet once more. To make me feel guilty and ashamed of myself. You're hoping to call up in me the reverence and obedience the word love inspires in people. But haven't I told you, my dear count? I am not like other people. I cannot be the obedient little wife you so wish for. Nor can I be made to feel shame for who I am.

"Haven't I told you I am vain? What was your response to me? *You are wrong. You are not vain. You just think you are because all those ceaseless compliments and attentions made you believe you couldn't live without them.* You were wrong, my dear count, to twist my words into something that suited your needs better. Wrong to see a different meaning in them, when they were speaking the truth louder than the church bells tolling at Sunday mass. And the truth is, once again, this: I cannot live without all those ceaseless compliments and attentions! This was my truth then, and this is my truth now. Yet you insist on recreating me into somebody else, then try to make me feel guilty for not measuring up to your creation!"

My ranting strains my vocal cords and I begin coughing again. Edouard hurries to hand me a handkerchief, which I place over my mouth. He kneels by the bed and pleads with me to send for a doctor. I refuse his plea and resume my crying instead.

"All I ever wanted was for you to love me, tricks or no tricks. And this is still my greatest aspiration," he says taking my hand in his and kissing it fervently.

I look at his gesture with disdain and pity mingled in a queasy emotional brew. The memory of my protectors kissing my hands just as passionately as Edouard does it now, play before my eyes. The words of the great courtesan, Manon Lescaut, from my favorite book also play in my mind's eye. Isn't it startling how strangely similar our destinies proved to be? She too retired with her favorite lover, des Grieux, in the countryside, only to become so destitute that no future together could have saved them from complete ruin. Her reply to her lover could only be my reply to Edouard.

Opening my mouth to speak, I feel the reincarnation of my favorite heroine.

"There is no one in the world whom I could love the way I do you. But you must realize, my poor dear soul, that in the state to which we are reduced, fidelity is a ridiculous virtue. Do you really think that we can still be tender with each other when we don't even have bread to eat? I adore you—you can count on that—but let me have a little time to arrange our fortunes."

But Edouard is no understanding des Grieux. He is already on his feet, shouting and throwing his arms about.

"What? No! A little obstacle and you are already thinking of deceiving me? What do you mean we don't even have bread to eat? Isn't that a shameless exaggeration?"

"Maybe. But I want more than food to eat. I want the luxury that made you and all my protectors love me in the first place."

"Luxury!" he booms. "What a cynical heart you have! And still... I love your cynical heart much more than ever I loved your luxury. I love your curls, your gentle dark eyes, the sound of your voice, even your unwise resolutions. Because they are you! Because all that you are and all that you do make you the unperfected being in front of me; the unwise, unscrupulous, corrupted little woman that enslaved me like no other. If this isn't love, then I don't know what is!"

"Unfortunately, love doesn't make up for everything else. And I am too young to perpetuate a life of want. I must break it off straightaway. I must return to where I can exercise my true power. I must get back to Paris at once!"

I throw the blanket off of me as if my sudden resolution gave me wings to take me where I said I would go. But all I manage to do is be possessed by a dizziness even more obstinate than my will. Edouard catches me in his arms just when I am about to hit the floor.

"Stop! Please, stop!" he begs as he places me back onto the bed. "Just stop and reflect on your decision for a while! You're behaving like a madwoman! Pause for once, for crying out loud! There are always other solutions than returning to that life of yours. It will kill you!"

His last words, as well as my intensifying burning fever make me pause. Holding my palm against my chest to calm the pain produced by the cough, I sigh deeply.

"What other solutions?" I ask.

"I don't know!" he screams, hitting his forehead as if to force his brain to produce a saving idea. "You tell me! Of us two, you are the intransigent, brilliant one. But upon my honor, I'd do anything to keep you by my side!"

His tears are bouts of hysterical sobbing by now. I've never seen a man so desperate, so utterly distraught.

"Anything?" I ask.

His sobbing ceases and he darts at my side. "Absolutely anything. Just name it."

Desperation has been replaced by the starving eager look of a dying man who's just been given another chance at living. It's heartbreaking. But also, pitiless. I smile.

"Marry me, then," I say, in my intransigent, brilliant way.

"I beg your pardon?"

"Marry me. If you cannot afford me, the least you could do is make me a Countess. Give me what every woman of my kind craves for: respectability."

The blank expression in Edouard's eyes forbids me, for the first time, free passage to the ever so open train of his thoughts.

∾

THE NIGHT that follows is a night of new realizations. I remember the first night spent in Monsieur Plantier's home, bed, arms. It was the night that turned a broken child into the mercenary woman of today. A night of firsthand discoveries that snatched naivety out of a motherless waif's heart, and in its stead, placed fear and hate deep within its core. Yet tonight, I realize that no matter how much I've learned since that night, life always has new lessons up its sleeve, which it is ever eager to impart to me.

After Edouard gets into bed, he takes me in his arms. I struggle with my frustration to be able to let him hold me until his heavy breathing tells me he's fallen asleep. Removing myself from his grip, I leave the bed, throw a light smock over my shoulders and exit into the backyard.

The night is silent, only the river can be heard. The stars blink at me from the clear firmament and I find myself envying their brightness and regality. The wind is blowing on this otherwise serene summer night and when it hits the sweat on my body, I shudder. Gathering the sides of the smock about me, I sit on the swing. The wind proves strong enough to make it move me back and forth without any exertion from my part. That relaxes me, and in my tranquil repose, realizations begin to hit my consciousness one by one.

First, I realize that my love, the very passion I experienced for Edouard was merely a mirage. A mirage with roots deeply ingrained into the words he'd whispered, into the promises he'd made, into my very belief in them. Had it not been for these, I most likely never would have experienced more feeling for him than for any other protector. My passion was conditional. Just like the female animal in the wild who chooses her mate after he's proved himself stronger, after he's conquered her through a fierce fight with another animal suitor, I have chosen my mate with the help of the same innate, animalistic, primordial instincts. For we are all animals.

And if men need women strictly for the warmth, sensitivity, and physical pleasure they are able to bring into their lives, women need men for the single reason that they might be able to quiet their fears. This need is one warm, sensitive women have always had and still do: the need of protection, the need of feeling safe and secure, the need that, come hell or high water, he'll always be there to save her from her wants, her fears, her own self.

This is how we choose between ourselves. And, leaving aside the need for perpetuating the species, these are the conditions we impose on the other half in order to love them. And with the discovery that love is always conditional, it ceases to be an ideal, a feeling worth dying for, a reason to relinquish all other pleasures and pursuits and needs. Love isn't, I realize, an altar at which one should prostrate him or herself. It is a mirage deeply hidden in another impenetrable mirage.

Edouard failed to live up to my conditions, just as I failed to live up to his. Ours is not love anymore. What's left could simply be a morganatic existence, and of which fate and end only time will make clear.

My old dictum rings clearly in my head: a man's affection is shorter than a winter's day.

The next realization rings just as clear: my own love and affection were shorter than a winter's day.

As THE NIGHT advances well into the morning, I discover that trauma your mind experiences can swiftly turn into physical pain. Probably a doctor could tell me if this is possible, but I think I need no doctor to tell me something I have experienced on my own, this very day. The shock of

Edouard's betrayal plagued me at once with a fainting fit. Later, in the bed Edouard had carried me to, I was plagued with a fever that ate and still eats at my body, as if an insurmountable fire is crackling and sizzling deep within my insights.

And then, there is the cough. The terrifying dry cough that seems to be wanting to chase the life out of me. No apologies or remorse. Just a sharpening strength and relentlessness that make me feel my lungs are always in my throat. People should never feel their organs. The organs should perform the job they were given by God silently, in the background, never making themselves known to their possessors.

ROMAIN VIENNE

Oh, dearest Marie... she never suspected in that hour just how truly sick she was. And that it wasn't the effect of the news she received, but the effect of her disease that would shortly kill her. It was the onset of the tuberculosis that killed the three daughters of her octogenarian protector. It is perfectly acceptable that the shock of learning that her dream of having love and money at the same time might have triggered the symptoms of the disease earlier than probably ordained by nature, but the undying truth is that the germ, the bacteria had already made itself comfortable in the warmth of her lungs. It was just a matter of time until these symptoms would have showed themselves in all their brutality.

MARIE DUPLESSIS

With the dawn scaring my insomnia into surrendering, and with the cough returning, I quit the swing for the more comfortable bed inside. Lying next to the one I used to love, but now see only as a stranger, I make a pathetic attempt to order my thoughts so as to forget everything through sleep, to cease their torment. My efforts fail though, so I squeeze the handkerchief I still hold in my hand even tighter. When the quacks, clucks, oinks, and baas from the neighboring farms reach my ears, my anger gets the best of me. I sit up and throw the handkerchief to the floor. And right then, my last discovery reveals itself to me. The pure white silk handkerchief looks dirty. It has been tainted by droplets of blood spewed from my lungs. Dark red. The ugliest, most baleful color I have ever seen.

CHAPTER 18

*E*douard's hand on my forehead wakes me when I thought I had just fallen asleep.

"Your fever dropped," he says with a grin.

Through barely opened eyes I see he is dressed and freshly shaved.

"And yes," comes his next utterance, "I would very much love to make you my wife."

My eyes open wide now, and I prop myself in one elbow.

"Are you leaving?" I say, trying to retain a full-faced smile.

"Yes. You look better, so there is no need for me to postpone my visit. I am going to see my aunt. I need to put an end to this charade and communicate my desire and resolution to her."

"Your aunt?"

"Yes. My aunt, the Duchess of Raguse, must be the one producing this commotion, since I am an orphan and my brother couldn't care less about my inheritance."

With these last words he kisses my forehead and exits the bedroom.

The first few days of Edouard's absence, I give myself over to understanding my condition. After he leaves, the image of the stained handkerchief returns to haunt me.

Blood doesn't just spill out of you for no reason.

With this truth ringing louder and louder in my head, I write a letter to Dr. Pierre Louis, begging him to come see me at Bougival. I promise to pay for his trip, as well as a handsome reward for his consultation. In less than a week, I receive him in our dining room.

I show to him the stained handkerchief. He looks at it in silence, examining it, then takes it near his nose to smell it. I find his action repulsive, but I keep my thoughts to myself. He examines my eyes, ears and skin, then proceeds to listen to my heart and breathing. I silently pray. I pray it is just a violent flu. I pray his words would be congratulatory on my speedy recovery, and I pray all he needs prescribing is just a gargle solution or some mysterious powder that would make it, whatever that was, go away forever.

"Madame, I am afraid you are suffering from consumption."

My reply is as strange as the condition the doctor says I have. I burst loudly into laughter. My next action is stranger still. I see him to the door and rush to my writing desk to formulate another letter to yet another doctor.

Only a fool would take one doctor's opinion as law.

The second doctor, Pierre Manec, arrives sooner than the first. His words are just the same, and I invite yet a third to visit me. A German doctor, Ferdinand Koreff. Surely his German expertise is superior to the French. But when he, too, opens his mouth to speak that blasted word— consumption, I fall wheezing into an armchair. Fastening my gaze to the ground, I let the doctor speak without interruption. He prescribes what the other two had: rest, country air, nutritious diet, Bordeaux wine, and meals at regular intervals. He then proceeds to give me a drug to which he gives some diabolic name, probably so that I won't know what it really is. In a few days however, based on its side-effects, I suspect it is poison.

My DAYS BECOME nights and nights become days. The insomnia which I thought to be a temporary annoyance, due to the mental shock I suffered, becomes now a constant. The doctors say it is linked with my consumption, as there are other things as well: poor appetite, night sweats, weakness, fever, chest pain, dry cough, weight loss, and an assortment of other symptoms, which I proceed to forget.

By day I sleep, or when sleep refuses to visit, I lie in bed, face-up, thinking about my future, if there will be any future at all. The doctors say if I follow their advice to the bone, I'll recover. So, I try my best. Except that I no longer know what gives me more insufferable symptoms, the disease or the poisonous pills the German prescribed. As soon as I swallow the daily dose, I have again poor appetite, night sweats, weakness, fever, chest pain, dry cough...

By night, I walk about the river despondently, rereading by candlelight the many missives Edouard routinely sends.

"The news I brought to my aunt produced shock and unhappiness. She appealed to my honor, to my righteousness, and to the affection I have for those close to me. All I said was that the person I feel close to me most is waiting for me at Bougival. E. P."

"Today, my aunt made all sorts of promises and even went as far as to propose an alliance—a most exceptional

advantageous alliance—but I turned it down. All her promises and alliances I have turned down. For you, holder of my heart. E. P."

"My aunt decided today to send my guardian, Mr. Delisle, to Nonant, your place of birth, to make inquiries about you under the pretext that they were made with a view to your marriage. But what she's truly hoping to uncover is some shameful truth about you, my love, that would make my marriage to you impossible. So, I decided to accompany my guardian to Nonant. E. P."

"Not much we could find in Nonant, and we are next guided to the town of Ginai and that of Exmes. We are leaving today for Nonant again. Yours in heart, and mind, and spirit. E.P."

This last missive sends an icy shiver up and down my spine. For what if they find out about father and his atrocious deeds? What if Edouard discovers about my Father's initiation, as well as that of Monsieur Plantier?

I shall be ruined.

Romain Vienne

Marie's concern proved to be unfounded. The two gentlemen's latest appearance in Nonant was practically an event, with everyone wondering about the significance of these mysterious trips. It was well known what they wanted, but why these subsequent visits when it would take twenty-four hours to find out all there was to know?

The lover was received with a certain sympathy mixed with a strong dose of feminine curiosity. Mr. Delisle, on the other hand, was viewed with cold reserve. The information in Nonant and Saint-Germain-de-Clairefeuille was as favorable as could be hoped: no one, in effect, felt hostile toward this unhappy young girl, who could not be blamed for her background. People had sympathetic memories of her well-loved mother and almost nothing was known of Marie's Paris life. The old nun, Francoise Huzet, who had taught her to read and prepared her for her First Communion, was full of touching praise for her dear little Alphonsine and asked the two gentlemen to pass on her affectionate memories.

But the real damage was of a different tinge altogether. A good girl, very impressionable, but positive and resistant, she knew the romantic affair was over. She felt more despair than regret, more spite than sadness. She was not a woman to let her imagination wander through the clouds. She was happy only when she bathed in a shower of gold.

It was then that she noticed, by the sudden cooling of her sentiments, that she had loved him only superficially, in the intoxication of deceitful hopes and that she had been the dupe of lying appearances, building her projects on shifting sands.

She already felt embarrassment and was in no mood to endure what she called privations. With Edouard's love ruined, she had nothing to take away but the gift of a memory. Her long stay in Bougival was becoming unbearable. Already annoyed with the assonant monotony, now the beautiful summer season was coming to an end and the noisy, eventful life which she had given up to please Edouard, now appeared even more seductive.

Her resolution was soon taken.

MARIE DUPLESSIS
By mid-August I am already at the end of my tether.

With Edouard still away to reason with his aunt and rummage through my past, I am left with the birds and their songs to fill my days and chase away what has become unspeakable boredom.

And if that wasn't enough, Edouard's guardian, Mr. Delisle, decides to pay me a visit.

Although I am visibly annoyed by his audacity, he nonetheless invites himself in.

"Forgive me, Madame, for my unexpected visit," he says, as he points at a chair, mutely asking if he can sit. I nod. "There is quite a commotion in Monsieur de Perregaux's family and I am afraid you are the cause of it."

I remain stationary and smile at the gentleman. Except, he isn't a gentleman, but a fat, perspiring swine with a red face and presumptuous gaze.

"Monsieur Delisle, I am afraid I don't care. Neither about the commotion you mentioned, nor that I might be the cause of it. Although, pray, allow me to contradict you. The cause of the commotion, Monsieur, is not me. It is the greed of Count de Perregaux's family."

"Not yours?"

I clench my teeth, then force the smile back upon my lips.

"Monsieur, I doubt that you have come all this way just to insult me. You ought to know that your insults neither bother me, nor touch me in any way. I suggest you move on to the reason behind your visit, else I shall be compelled to show you the exit."

"You're quite smart with words, aren't you? Smart and cunning. Now I understand ... I understand the reason behind the Count's stupid action to part with his inheritance."

"Monsieur, you, on the other hand, seem to be neither smart, nor quick to grasp. Shall I repeat myself, then?"

He grunts and pulls out a handkerchief to wipe off his sweat.

"I have come to appeal to your sensibility, provided you have one," he says in what I now take to be his customary language used with women like me. "The Count is financially incapacitated, but not only that. He has acquired a staggering amount of debt. He borrowed money from all his friends. He owes them fabulous sums, an amount he doesn't even know, so childish he has acted. And all of this to keep you happy, Madame. Isn't it only right you should now think about the Count's well-being in return?"

I give a scoffing little laugh. "My dear Monsieur, let me once again correct you. The Count was no child when he met me; hence, he's always been in complete charge of his faculties. His spending was of his resolution. It is not my fault that the Count decided—for his own happiness and contentment, I may add—to make the woman he loved happy with the help of his purse. Moreover, he is no child now either, so I don't see why it should be me that must make decisions for his future, and not the gentleman himself."

"I see," Mr. Delisle says, shaking his head. "I should have appealed to your sensitivity instead."

"You wouldn't have succeeded in gaining much more from me. My reply would have been the same."

Mr. Delisle suddenly jumps to his feet. "You shameless, corrupt woman! Have you no remorse? Have you no bloody sympathy in your heart for the one who gave you all? You've ruined him!"

"If the Count is already ruined, I don't see what more I could do for him."

"Give up this outrageous marriage project of yours and I will not hesitate in granting the necessary authorization for the full liquidation of the Count's liabilities! I will also guarantee the Count an annuity of eight thousand francs, paid quarterly."

"Shouldn't you take it up with the Count then? He is no child, have you already forgotten that fact? Maybe he will find your offer so appealing he will leave me at once. Your chances are with him, not me. Occupy yourself with M. De Perregaux and do not bother me. I believe I have the right to hope, Monsieur, that you will cease these visits, which are useless for you and disagreeable for me."

The wrath on his face makes me think I should be afraid of him. A bout of cough grasps me again, and I ask the gentleman to leave.

Insensitive and steeped in his own will and ideals, he pays me another visit the next day. This time, his arms are full of official papers as proof of Edouard's financial ruin. I find it difficult to understand his insistence, and again invite him to leave.

He returns a third time but is not received.

Sick and tired of the guardian's importunity and Edouard's prolonged absence, as well as my own weariness and monotony, I resolve to commence packing my belongings.

On my way back to Paris, gazing through my carriage's little window, I am suddenly reminded of the poet's words: *absence makes the heart grow fonder*. Accompanying this thought, my last realization of this whole Bougival affair comes as a revelation. I am no romantic muse, just a sexual one. My heart shall never be inspiration for poets.

CHAPTER 19

*M*y return to Paris feels like a rebirth. The rebirth of Marie who drives and walks through the Bois de Boulogne's magnificent park, and along the rue de Champs-Elysées. The Marie who nourishes herself with the homage she is paid in her drawing-room. The Marie who cannot wait for a first performance by Madame Judith or other great actress, old and new; who cannot do without the procession of worshipers to her Opera box; who can again have as much English coffee as she pleases. And finally, the Marie who can freely resume her fine suppers at Maison D'Or and Cafe de Paris, as well as her passionate nights in the arms of the worthy.

But I am not the only one who's happy about rediscovering myself. Count von Stackelberg turns a decade younger on hearing of my return. So great is his happiness that he decides a new, more splendid home is required in which to lodge his private obsession. The ground floor apartment at 11 boulevard de la Madeleine is the count's choice. Overlooking the resplendent boulevard, seen through five enormous windows, it also has a courtyard at the back. My own courtyard, right in the heart of Paris. There is no private river anymore, but who needs it when the Seine is just a breath away?

The first time I enter the magnificent apartment, tears invade my eyes. They aren't tears of gratitude or those springing up from quenching some vile sense of greed, but tears forming at a memory. The sad memory about the orphan girl who roamed barefoot about her village, wondering if she'll ever have a place of her own. The bitter memory of the day in which the waif realized men and their coins can buy her freedom and chase away her only permanent companion: hunger.

FOR A FEW MONTHS, I give myself over to redecorating the new place. I cover the length of the entrance hall with an unheard-of trellis of gold wood interlaced with flowering plants. I commission handmade lace curtains that permit the daylight to pass through, and flank them with cerise damask curtains. I cover the walls in gold and red silk wallpaper and Venetian mirrors that reflect the light coming from the gilt-metal and rock crystal, antique chandelier. Sofas covered in Beauvais tapestries, small rosewood tables displaying Clodion pottery, and Riesener trinkets with copperware chiseled by Gouthiere ... all give the impression of an interior as grandiose as the king's palace.

In consequence, it is only natural that such a home should become the gathering place of the most brilliant minds of Paris. My own salon animated three times a week with the most sophisticated chatter. To that end, I redecorate the dining room to reflect men's tastes: dark walls of Cordoba leather, plain Henri II cabinets, sculpted oak bookshelves with folding glass doors so my guests can peek at my delectable library. The cost of it all, including the feasts ordered from Chez Voisin and La Maison d'Od, are supported by the Count, who is never invited to enjoy them. For only a fool would believe jealousy could be cured.

I relinquish my old maid and hire a new, smarter one, Clotilde. She is instructed never to receive anyone without my express permission. Her quick wit and complete devotion to my instructions prove worthy when every evening, at about the same hour, Edouard rings the bell to my door. When the door fails to open, he quits ringing and starts pounding it with his fists. Through a slightly open window I hear his pleas and sobs and renewed promises. But all fail to reach that place in me that in the old days would have compromised. Between Edouard's tears and that place, grows a thick wall of selfishness, covered in poison ivy and adorned with the toughest thorns.

Dozens of letters, couched in the most dramatic tones reach me every week, but I refuse to open and reply to them. Rather, I resolve to continue doing what I have always done: ignore him altogether. It is only through a mutual acquaintance that word of his renewed attempt to join the Foreign Legion reaches my ears. Then I shed a few tears, but not for the gentleman's utter distress, rather for my inability to feel what I ought to feel for a man who loves me. I admit there is sympathy left, but the love is gone. Perished. Dissolved. Like dew drops evaporating in the heat of the sun.

And if the heat of the sun dissolves dew drops, I discover that it does wonders for my health. I scoff at the old ways in which people considered the sun, indeed the very air they breathed, to be poisonous to a convalescent and would barricade themselves in lightless rooms, windows nailed shut, curtains closed. Light and air and sun could have chased away the afflictions that plagued them.

So, even though the first months of 1845 prove

unexpectedly cold, I keep all the windows in my home wide open, even at this below zero temperature.

My spending habit changes, too. Less shopping for opera gowns, cashmere shawls, and lace gloves and more for nightwear, a dozen cashmere nightdresses and an equal number of night caps to be changed hourly to keep the wind drafts away from my profuse sweating.

I resume the visits to my three doctors, who all prescribe further poisons: laudanum, belladonna ointment, ether, leeches, opium patches, and some elixir of life, which tastes and smells like stale, bitter, cheap wine.

Of them all, laudanum is the only acceptable one. Instead of reminding me of pain and death like all the other prescribed treatments, it makes me forget I am even ill. Twenty drops in a glass of water should alleviate my diarrhea, the doctors say. And even though it is also bitter, the effect is so sweet that it makes me forget not only about my diarrhea, but about my whole self as well. Once the magical twenty drops mercifully cross into my blood, my melancholy is generously replaced with the experience of pleasure, excitement and an intense feeling of well-being and happiness.

One thing hasn't changed though, laudanum or no laudanum ... my insomnia. It continues to linger, as would some insufferable protector I cannot stand. Unyielding and insistent, with slobber forming at the corners of his mouth.

Ah, sarcasm! My only dependable weapon in times of need. For I do need it now, more often than not, if I want to believe all will be well. And what better way to chase away melancholy than with sarcasm and humor? Humor is what I need in order to believe my doctors when they say I might get well. Humor and compulsion. Yes, compulsion. For the illness did not come alone. It carries a compulsory need to live as fully as ever. To live as one should, when knowing that death may come before one's time.

With my newly acquired zest for living, I decide not to tell a soul about my illness. It might go away anyway, so why create a fuss and risking losing prospective protectors, when I could just as well live by my own precept for once: *be as silent as a grave and as cold as a stone.*

Ahh!! The mere allusion to the silence of the grave brings back my stomach cramps and throws me in an almost fainting fit.

"Quick!" I shout at Clotilde, who jumps up, startled, from her chaise-lounge. "Dress me up! I wish to attend the theater tonight."

"How I wish I could attend it, too! But long gone is my time," a high-pitched voice pipes up, and it isn't Clotilde's. I look at her and she indicates the dressing room window with her chin. I approach it and find that it looks directly into the dressing room of my neighbor, the lady with the high-pitched voice. With her elbows resting on the windowsill and looking straight into my curious eyes, she throws me a slick, effortless smile.

"Bonjour," I say, part curious, part shy.

"Well hello my dear. Long time I wanted to meet my famous neighbor," she says in a most unassuming voice.

"So, you know me then?" I get even closer to the window and adopt my neighbor's position.

She laughs. "Who doesn't, my dear Marie Duplessis? You're as famous as the King. I am Clémence. Clémence Prat." She raises a bushy eyebrow at me, seeming to expect that pronouncing her name will ring a bell.

"I am sorry," I say, embarrassed. "I am afraid—"

"Not to worry, my dear, I am accustomed with people's ignorance nowadays."

Not sure what to make of her words, I continue to

simply smile, and she continues with her strange introduction.

"I've been like you; once one of the most beautiful courtesans. Well, maybe not as beautiful and famous as you are, but I had my fair share of ridiculously rich visitors. But then, I didn't have these..." She shakes her arms, which sends her plentiful fat tissue jiggling. "Or these..." She laughs, pinching the rolls of flesh resting on her belly. "And most definitely not these..." She continues with her self-mockery, pointing at her freckles.

"I find you quite beautiful, Madame Prat," I say, for lack of anything better. "You mustn't be so hard on yourself."

"Nah!" she boasts, making a quick gesture with her hand as if to dismiss my kind words. "More cunning than beautiful. In my job, one has to be."

"Cunning in a millinery business?" I ask almost mockingly, referring to the shop she runs from her apartment, and of which I have heard about only casually.

"That's just a cover."

It is my time to arch an eyebrow, as she calls me nearer with her finger. I stretch myself halfway through the window and she does the same. Almost near my ear she whispers: "I'm a procuress. A very well-known one."

"Procuress?"

"Of rich men, of course. For beauties like yourself." She draws back and winks.

My first thought flies to the Count. Had he known what neighbor lived in the house next to the one he'd rented for me; he would have balked and run away with all the speed an octogenarian could muster. I make a mental note to tell him about Madame Prat and her métier, just to tease that jealousy of his. What can I say? I am young and ill; and as such, must amuse myself at all costs.

My second thought is of a milder disposition. I think of

how nice it is to have an acquaintance who knows all there is to know about my job, without me having to utter one word. What's more, unlike Madame Judith, Madame Prat would not be ashamed to be seen with me.

"My box, my treat," I say.

"Pardon me?"

"You said you wished you could go to the theatre. I say, 'why not'? I could use you as company, and you could use me as your entrance ticket. What do you say, Madame Prat?"

Her lively eyes turn into burning coals. "I say you're not only very beautiful, Madame Duplessis, but very smart as well."

We both laugh and retire to our dressing rooms to turn ourselves into resplendent beauties.

THIS END of February evening is extremely cold. Inside the theater though, the heaters suffocate the atmosphere with their exquisitely pleasant warmth. The hall is bursting at the seams. All of Paris seems to be here: lots of journalists, artists, authors, stockbrokers, theater-lovers, society men and women, courtesans, students, and even schoolchildren. They scramble through the doors to occupy their seats. Those already seated do what theatergoers usually do while waiting: fan themselves, cast glances over the hustle and bustle, peer through opera-glasses, acknowledge each other with waves and nods.

"I like it," Madame Prat says, as we take our seats in my theatre box.

"Pardon?"

"The flower." She points at the red camellia pinned to my chest.

"Ah, this," I whisper, gliding my fingers over the velvety petals. Madame Prat bends forward and buries her nose into the flower, sniffing profusely.

"It has no scent," I say. "Camellias don't have a fragrance. That is why I keep and wear only them. Any other flower would make me empty the contents of my stomach right on the society ladies in the stalls." I start laughing and grab the opera-glasses to scan the hall downstairs.

But it seems Madame Prat can't leave it alone.

"Why would that be?" she inquires, her question charged with suspicion, even more so than her gaze.

"For no particular reason," I reply, averting my look. Uncomfortable silence hangs between us for a few moments, then she says, "I rarely sleep at night either. Business to take care of. But I've heard you cough, you know..."

"Oh?" I keep my face averted. *Does she know?*

"...and your maid's encouraging words. She always says you won't die of it, for you are strong as well as young. I wish I had such a sympathetic maid."

Resigned, I turn to look Madame Prat in the eyes, but now *her* face is averted, no doubt embarrassed for insisting on snatching my secret out of me. I cast away my irritation and smile.

"Then I shall have a companion on my endless insomniac nights."

She turns to face me and returns my smile. "Red," she says pointing at the camellia again, to dispel the embarrassing clouds. "Hard to come by."

"Indeed. But I use it only a few days a month."

"How so?"

"Well, you know, those...uncomfortable days of the month. It lets the protectors know I am being...indisposed."

Madame Prat squeezes my arm. "Mon Dieu, my dear, you are very clever, aren't you? Why haven't I thought of that before?"

Her words get swallowed by the loud gong announcing the beginning of the play. The vaudeville *Premieres armes de Richelieu* give us back actress Virginie Dejazet, after an absence of a few years.

Ten minutes into the play, Madame Prat whispers in my ear:

"I know her. I know Virginie Dejazet very well."

"Do you now?"

She nods with quick movements, then proceeds on relaying before my mind's eye tens of incredible secrets from the actress' life. My ear starts to burn, as well as my patience. Apparently, the play isn't to the Madame's taste. Taken aback by my indifference to her gossip, she grabs her opera-glasses and begins scanning the people in the theater hall downstairs.

"And that's her son, Eugene. There!" she cries out, nudging me in the ribs.

This callous woman with no manners is something to behold. But not in the good way. That she was a courtesan at one time is beyond my comprehension.

My thought process seems to have taken too long for Madame Prat, as she nudges me again. Infuriated, I grab my own opera-glasses and look in the direction she's pointed. I acknowledge the man she wanted me to acknowledge, a youth displaying Madame Prat's present disposition: callousness, nerve, and the insufferable disposition toward fidgeting. He is talking in the ear of a companion sitting on his right, a companion that seems to possess my own present disposition: bored and irritated. He picks up his opera-glasses and raises them toward me. My opera-glass lens meet his and I almost jump from my seat. I set them aside.

"Who is that?" I ask my fidgeting friend.

"Who's who, my dear?"

"Your friend's companion."

She eagerly glides her binoculars to her left. "Oh!" she chuckles. "That, my dear, is none other than Alexandre Dumas Fils. The famed author's son."

Her words succeed in dispelling my irritation and replace it with enthusiasm. But her own enthusiasm seems to have turned into madness, as she now waves the two gentlemen over.

"What are you doing?" I ask through clenched teeth.

"My job. I am introducing you to the worthy." The satisfaction sprawled on her face reclaims my irritability.

"I don't need you to procure men for me! Worthy or unworthy!" I blurt. "I can find my own men!"

"Now, now, dear, why don't you let me help you? You are not as well as you used to be. You are ill, and a little help never hurt anyo—"

Her reasoning is stopped short by the gentlemen's arrival into my box. She begins introducing them to me, but the damage has already been done.

"Enjoy the play," I say to Madame Prat and standing, I head for the exit.

"Can I accompany you?" I hear Alexandre ask in a most timid voice.

"If you will," I retort indifferently.

Once into the street, I breathe in greedily. The cold does wonder for my psyche and I relax. I wave at the valet to bring over my carriage.

"My lady?" I hear Alexandre behind me. "Would it please you to walk for a bit?"

His proposal is very seductive, but if I were to walk through the cold for no more than a few minutes, I would be sent to bed for weeks.

"It would please me, but perhaps some other time." My reply must have gotten across as even colder than the weather, for the desperation in his eyes seems boundless. His cheeks redden, no doubt, my rejection hurts him deeply. "But, should you wish, you could accompany me on my drive home," I hurry to add, pointing at my carriage slowly nearing us. His expression enlivens, the flush is gone.

"I'm Alexandre Dumas Fils," he says as we speed into darkness.

"I know who you are. I'm—"

"I know who you are." We both laugh.

"Well, since we already know each other, we must definitely become good friends," I say. "I'd love having a friend who possesses such an admirable quality."

He blushes again. "And what quality would that be?"

"That!" I say, pointing at his face. "Modesty, my dearest Alexandre. Shyness. In my circle of friends, not many men have it."

"Thank you," he says, turning bright crimson.

"You don't need to thank me, but God. He was in a happy mood when he made you."

"I meant, thank you for not saying what every other woman that first meets me says," he lets out with a smirk.

"Oh?"

"Well, as soon as a woman takes my arm, the first thing she does is lift her skirt to stop it from getting dirty, and the second is to ask me when she can meet my father."

Mon Dieu. That would have been my next question. It is my turn to flush bright crimson, and I fake a cough to escape my embarrassment. It is one of the few times my cough comes out as a hoax. Most of the time it comes when I least want it. When I need it, it stays away. It seems my cough is as capricious as its owner.

"Oh no," I finally say. "Why would they do that? I

mean, yes, your father is well worth knowing, famous and rich as he is, but you, my dearest friend, cut a striking figure yourself. I mean, look at you, the way you dress, your creole complexion, even the way you wear that golden knob cane... a true dandy, a person anyone would love calling friend."

"Yes, but I am neither rich nor famous as my old man..." Desperation comes into his eyes again and I think of what a sensitive man accompanies me home. A rare being, indeed, which makes me want to comfort him.

"One day you will be both. Do you also write?"

"Not to the extent I wish. I only write articles for *Sylphide* and *Paris Elegant*."

"Well, elegant as you are, I think no other would do a better job writing those articles. And trust me, my dear friend, one day you will write books, too, just like your father. You will know your subject once you see it. And then no one would be able to part you from pen and paper."

Romain Vienne

I cannot but be astounded by Marie's prediction. Maybe her words were just trying to soothe the young man, having felt his frustration with himself for not living up to his father's image. But what she didn't know and never would was that her words would one day come true. Also unknown to her, or him for that matter, was the fact that the subject he was looking for in order to write his ardently desired masterpiece was sitting in the carriage across from him. Yet she would have to die first. That's the thing with writers, I suppose. They thrive on drama. Or perhaps that's what the public needs: to read about other's misfortune so they wouldn't feel alone in wrestling with life's struggles.

The book Alexandre Dumas Fils would write —*The Lady with the Camellias* — would make them both famous.

But, Marie had to die. Marie's death was in a sense the sacrifice all writers are known of needing to produce enduring works of art.

Marie Duplessis

"Your words, my lady, are music to my ears."

"Well, then, I am not just a woman of loose morals, but a nightingale as well." We laugh some more, while the carriage comes to a halt. "I guess this is it. My home. You can take the carriage with you and bring it back tomorrow," I say, looking out the carriage's small window.

"It is greatly appreciated. I cannot even say how pleased I am for making your acquaintance, my lady, and for having allowed me to—"

But I no longer hear his words. The red, almost mad, eyes of the man standing motionless on the street across from my house, paralyses me.

"Edouard..." I whisper, as an invisible claw closes in around my throat.

"Pardon me, my lady?"

I grab Alexandre's hand. "I said that, on a second thought, I would very much like us to continue our pleasant conversation inside."

And thus, once again, I escape.

CHAPTER 20

*E*scaping Edouard's love, I soon discover, is no easy
task. For with a man willing to join the Foreign
Legion and hoping he would perish in that service, there is
nothing left to lose. And for a man who feels he has nothing
left to lose, opposition, no matter how resolute, is a faint
obstacle. In consequence, everywhere I look I see Edouard's
searching eyes, unkempt hair, and frailer physique. A
diaphanous shadow, permanently chasing my own. A
wondering ghost who can neither stay nor depart. If I am
promenading or shopping, there he is, walking behind me at
a safe distance or waiting outside some store like a punished
dog. If I am attending some play or opera, there he sits,
downstairs in the stalls looking up at my private box for
hours on end, eyes teary, from either fatigue or his
tormenting sadness.

And then, when I am too tired or too ill to go out, there
he stands in the alley across from my house, holding a
bouquet of white camellias. At those times, I throw even
bigger soirees at my house, lest he suddenly find it
acceptable to approach me. By now, I am even a bit afraid of

him and of the actions one who has nothing to lose might resolve to take.

A week after my attendance at the theatre, I throw one such soiree. The entire Parisian cream attends it. There is my newest friend, Alexandre Dumas, as well as my oldest one, Nestor Roqueplan, accompanied by a grissette of no more than fifteen. Louis Veron, who had requested the table next to Ernestine's and is chatting with her spiritedly. And Albert Vandam, the famed journalist, as well as my German doctor, who's quite a controversial character, but always requested at my soirees by my lady friends. Madame Prat is also present and sees fit to apologize for her behavior at the theatre by bringing me a stuffed peacock. Her apologies are accepted. As for the peacock...well, let's say it will not be seen in my house ever again.

And of course, my loyal friend Romain Vienne is also present, though always being teased by Lola Montez, a courtesan friend, for his shyness. Just now, Lola enters the room singing an opera tune and places one of her dainty feet on the arm of Romain's chair. Lifting her dress to expose her thigh, she asks him to slide the ribbon from it. My poor friend, in an attempt to show her he isn't shy at all, does just what he's been asked, only to be slapped by Lola, who turns her back and runs off laughing.

"Please excuse her," I tell a bewildered Romain, "she behaves like this with all men—it's her way of amusing herself." The flushed Romain just nods, and then plays with his meal, head down, in an effort to conceal the color in his cheeks.

The food from Chez Voisin is splendid: pigeon with peas, trout with prawns, partridges, mashed potatoes, salads, desserts of vanilla bavaroises, glazed fruits, biscuits, macaroons, and lots and lots of Bordeaux wine. But by the third course, my cough, light at first, becomes troubling enough that I instinctively clasp my chest with both my hands, as my head gets pushed against the back of my chair. I close my eyes in pain and pray it would go away.

In the background, I hear Alexandre say, "My God, she's turning purple. Is she okay?"

"This happens every day," Madame Prat retorts.

Taking my handkerchief to my mouth I continue to cough until the stains of blood soiling its white force me to stand and retire.

"Let her be," I hear Madame Prat say on my way out of the dining room. "She will soon be back."

But my newest friend ignores my neighbor's advice and follows me into my bedroom. Only a candle lights it and I thank God for that. As of late, I hate seeing myself in the mirror while in the clutches of one of my merciless coughing fits.

Alexandre approaches me from behind and places a hand on my shoulder. "My dearest friend, you are not well," he says in a broken voice. Turning to look up at him, tears gather in my eyes.

"You know, Alexandre, you are the only one showing concern for my indisposition. Have you seen the others? Going about their conversation without the slightest acknowledgement of my distress..." A tear appears in my friend's eye and I feel remorse for allowing free rein to my self-pity.

"But let them be," I continue. "I wouldn't want to spoil my guests' good-humor and ease. Could you please help me unlace this dress? It suffocates me terribly."

He approaches to do my bidding. "You look deadly pale..." he whispers, his voice as dead as my complexion. "Here, rest on the sofa..." he continues while carrying me there and helping me lie down. Struggling to get my breath back, I press my heart with my hand.

"Please bring that bowl with water near me," I ask. He does so and I ask him to leave. "I need to spit. It isn't a view I would want a sensitive friend such as you to be subjected to." But he resolves to turn a deaf ear on my plea and sits on the sofa next to me. As I begin to spit blood mixed with saliva into the small silver bowl, my friend takes my hand and squeezes it between his. Then, like a small child, he cries as he kisses it.

"How dear you are," I say, raising my fingers to wipe away his tears. "You just met me, and here you are, already loving me."

"You're so tiny and frail... and now, weakened further by this cursed illness... how can I not love you?"

I give a short little laugh. "Be warned, my dearest friend, that others have seen me the way you now do and ended up either brokenhearted or bankrupt. At times, even both."

"I need no warnings, for I have but debts; hence, I am in no danger of becoming bankrupt. I already am bankrupt. As for my heart... let's say I prefer it being broken by you than killed by the privation of feelings. I wouldn't be an artist if I were able to live in the absence of dreams, hopes, and ideals."

"Ah, ideals!" I mock. "And dreams and hopes... I had them, too, once. But my ideals were taken from me by old, wrinkled, trembling hands. My dreams...oh, my dreams I still have, as well my hopes, but they are so different from yours, my darling friend. I am no artist, mind you, although I can turn into one while behind the pink muslin hanging from my bed frame."

His look has shifted to the window, his gaze staring dejectedly into an unknown distance.

"What happened?" I ask him. "Is someone there?" My thoughts run to Edouard standing stationary outside my house, and I prop myself in one elbow.

"Yes," Alexandre replies. "My past. I was staring into my past. I had my fair share of misfortunes and ill health." My muscles relax, and I fall on my back again.

"How so? Was it your sensitive heart?"

"Literally. I suffered from heart palpitations and nervous crises well into my adolescence and young adulthood."

"Poor you..." I whisper, raising my arm to caress his short curls.

"I shall never forget the words my mother uttered when I was but a small child: *'Son, you do not have a father. That doesn't mean your father is dead. It means that a lot of people will despise and insult you.'* And she was right. That cursed private school I attended, Pension Saint-Victor, was a prison. A torture house, with my peers as torturers. Monsters, devils who bullied me relentlessly. They would interrupt my sleep at night so they could attack me in the worst possible ways. They would call me "bastard" until I almost forgot my real name. They would draw lewd pictures of my mother all over my exercise books...I became sick...so very sick. It was then that this sensibility of mine was born."

We both cry, with his tears coming in floods of sadness, mine in the floods of an even more violent coughing fit. Alexandre pushes the silver bowl away, takes me into his arms and carries me to my bed. I again tell him to go and join the rest of the guests, but he won't have it. With a bravery I knew not to exist in sensitive, bashful people, he lies next to me in bed, with one hand pressing a wet cold towel on my forehead, while the other caresses my disheveled damp hair. And right there and then, with my guests still chatting and laughing in the adjoining room, I make love to Alexandre.

To the heart of the bashful artist my sudden outburst of passion might have meant something. To me, alas, it meant little. It was my way of seizing the moment, of living as unburdened by worries and fears as I once used to, it meant paying back to a dear friend the kindness and consideration he's shown me. To me, it was mercy lovemaking. For the man I just let explore my wet burning insights is poorer than the young, orphaned Alphonsine. And in addition to being as poor as a waif, he has no title either. His only excellency, if one can call it that, is having a famous wealthy father, to whom I am not to be introduced.

Poor ordinary Alexandre wants to keep me only to himself. Alas, merciful, friendly copulation is all he'll ever accomplish.

I awake with a startle shortly before dawn. Slowly quitting my bed, I realize Alexandre is gone, as well as all the other guests. I jump into my slippers and instinctively approach the window. And then, I realize someone else is gone as well. Edouard has deserted the alley in front of my house for some happier place known only to himself.

Four months will pass before I will see him again.

To Count von Stackelberg's disparagement and teeth-clenching jealousy, Alexandre becomes my indefatigable companion. Nonetheless, the Count continues to bolster my increasingly extravagant life-style, including my regular visits to my many doctors, and those to the alpine retreats renowned for the beneficial effects of the thermal waters. In exchange, I reserve him a spot at my side twice a week: one time to accompany me to the theater or the opera, the other time to visit me in my bedroom. But I am no heartless woman and knowing the pain the Count has suffered at the loss of his three daughters by the hand of consumption, I offer him my best two days of the week. The days in which the same merciless disease bothers me less. For he must not know that I, his soul's very lifeboat, have contracted the scourge. His age renders him too weak to stand such news; yet not as feeble as to stop monitoring my every move. The remaining days of the week I impart between Alexander and my protectors.

ONE SUCH ASPIRANT protector first makes his existence known through his groom on New Year's Day 1845. Solemn in his grand livery, he silently hands me a key upon his admission into my dining room.

"And this is for...?" I ask, but the groom just smiles, nods, and momentarily exits the room, only to return a few moments later carrying a box in his hands. He places it on the floor at my feet, bows and exits again, this time for good. My curiosity mounts and inserting the key I've been given into the box's keyhole, I rotate it and lift the lid. A fruity smell hits my nostrils. Inside the box, I find twelve oranges, arranged in the shape of a heart, each wrapped in a thousand-franc note. My eyes, glistening with enthusiasm, pause next on the card laying among the oranges.

"Homage from Monsieur le Baron de Ponval to Madame Marie Duplessis."

Great, I tell myself, overwhelmed with intrigue.

But for a fortnight I hear nothing more from Monsieur de Ponval. Then, two weeks down the road, the groom reappears in his same grand livery, wearing the same quiet disposition, yet carrying a slightly different gift and note. Another box, but this one overflows not with oranges or other fruits, but with splendid eye-blinding jewels. I honestly don't know what glows more... the jewels or my eyes upon seeing them.

*"Should Madame Marie Duplessis decide she would like
to meet me, I request the small favor, and honor, of being
received by her the following evening,"* the new note says.

I decide I should do him the honor. A tall, somewhat
awkward youth with reddish-blond hair and bushy
sideburns enters my dining room the following evening.

"Ma-ma-madame," he says, bowing low. "You you loo-
look very tem-tem-tempting." My first reaction is to close
my mouth. My second is to sit down.

"Do you know, Monsieur, what is very tempting now?"

"What is tha-that?"

"Throwing you out in the street."

It is his turn to open, then close, his mouth. "Have I-I
said some-something wrong?"

Everything about you is wrong. I am half-furious, half-
amused. *You are an idiot; a stammering idiot. And your title
is worthless since it didn't help at all in teaching you
manners.*

"Let me say that your choice of gifts is far more
endearing than your civilities," I say, unable to recall my
feminine delicacy.

"Please do-do forgive me, Madame. I am afraid I made a
fo-fo-fool of myself. May I sit ne-ne-next to you?"

"You may not, for your visit will be very short. You can
come at another time, provided you will behave more like a
gentleman and less like a gauche schoolboy."

"I-I must say wh-what I want, shouldn't I?"

I purposefully let the baron stammer out his wishes,
only to amuse myself. His choice of words, his stuttering,
indeed his reddish peasant-like hair, make me break up on
the inside.

"Monsieur le baron," I say, raising my hand to signal
him to stop talking, "I realize that mine is a sordid

profession, but I must not leave you ignorant of the fact that my favors are very expensive. I spend, on average, five hundred francs a day, and sometimes I indulge in even more extravagant expenditure which doubles this figure. My protector must be extremely wealthy to cover my household expenses and satisfy my many, varied and strange caprices. At present, I am approximately thirty thousand francs in debt, which is very reasonable for me. I find nothing alarming about this figure." My declaration is a desperate attempt to put the Baron to flight. "What can I say... I am capricious and do not mind admitting that my debts are sometimes even higher. There it is, it's an obsession I have, along with plenty more. It is not my fault, after all; it is not I who dance too fast, it is the violins who can't keep up. When my current debts have been paid, I hurry to contract new ones to justify the old, and so as not to get out of the habit. Alas, it is stronger than I."

But it seems that nothing I say deters him, so I continue with my intimidation monologue.

"In addition, I must point out to you that, in my lover's company, I wear only those outfits which his generosity has provided. As for the old ones, I either make them into relics, or give them as presents to those less fortunate than myself. I think these confidences are sufficient to explain to you why I always have new outfits; they do honor to those who love me. I am always frank: I intend to remain, at all times, absolutely free in my movements and mistress of my fancies; I give the orders, I do not receive them; I have no desire at all to be compelled to receive a lover whenever he expresses the wish to see me. I have also the misfortune to believe neither in promises nor in fidelity; it is enough to tell you that I acknowledge sincerity only when it has been proven to me."

I look at the Baron, expecting to see him doff his hat and

turn on his heels. But he just stands there, nodding and smiling like a cretin. It seems that the more obstinate I become, the more his chasing instincts arouse. Such prodigalities can only be seen in the tales of the *Thousand and One Nights*. Every evening the monsieur rings the bell to my door. I begin to develop a sort of antagonism toward the bell noise, and desperately think up a way to see the last of the lacking Baron, before I erupt with hives.

The following evening, I turn Clotilde into a splendid courtesan, equipped with all the courtesan's accoutrements. The transformation is so convincing that I take a moment to congratulate myself for both my marvelous idea and ensuing artistry. I instruct Clotilde to tell the Baron that I am indisposed and cannot receive him. While his disparagement might infuriate my uptight maid, she is to be polite nonetheless, as any woman of her newly acquired reputation would be.

And polite she is, so much so that the imbecilic Baron finds himself at once enamored with the poor girl, never suspecting she is just a servant playing the role of her life. The meeting results in all sorts of uncouth wanton propositions and my maid ends the encounter in a near fainting fit. She resolves never to become a courtesan and jumps back into her maid clothes. The Baron, on the other hand, resolves to remain undeterred in his seducement of us both, but he is never again received.

THE FOLLOWING MONTHS, to Count von Stackelberg's annoyance, I spend most of my quiet time in the company of Alexandre. He accompanies me to the theater and the opera, sharing my box, as well as my mockery, directed at the lustful worshipers who enter my box to pay homage to me. Being the same age, we discover to have many things in common and like two youths apparently unburdened by worries or anxieties, we roam the dark alleys of the Champs-Elysées, bathing the magnificent street in our childish laughter. On warm windless days, we make excursions outside Paris, sometimes to the stables of Ravelet, the only place that owns cast-off horses that kick, rear, and bolt, and we both test our riding proficiency by mounting these wild untamed marvels of nature and riding them at top speed.

DURING THE CALM of the long nights, in which sleep insists not to fetch me, I recount to him the Monsieur le Baron episode and we both roll in the aisles, interrupted only now and then by my merciless coughing.

But then, I make another mistake.

I indulge in details about my new protector, an extremely wealthy Englishman who, in return for the kindness I showed him by hosting a dinner in his honor, saw appropriate to send me a most marvelous gift: an enormous rosewood trunk one meter high by two meters long full of chocolates, each wrapped in a hundred-franc note.

Right in the midst of my detailed outpouring, something changes in Alexandre's expression. I cannot tell what with any certainty, but the outcome became apparent soon enough. He vanishes from my life faster than he entered it. Just like Romain, who'd stay away each time I take in a new protector, Alexandre, too, makes himself invisible. The only difference is that unlike Romain, Alexandre never returns.

Dear Alexandre,

Why have you not let me know how you are? And why are you not talking frankly to me? I believe that you should regard me as a friend, so I am hoping for a word from you, and I kiss you tenderly as a mistress, or as a friend. It's your choice... Whatever the case, I will always be your devoted... Marie.

In vain I try to explain that the Englishman was of no consequence. That friends should remain friends to their graves. I even hint at my past warnings and hold him responsible for his infantile action. It is to no purpose. Only at the end of summer do I receive a letter from my dearest friend. But as soon as I open it, my enthusiasm flies right out the window.

My very dear Marie,

I am neither rich enough to love you as I would like, nor poor enough to be loved as you would like. So, let's both forget, you a name which must be a little indifferent to you, me a happiness which has become impossible. It is useless to tell you how sad this makes me, because you already know how much I love you. So farewell. You have too much heart not to understand the motive of my letter and too much spirit to not pardon me for it. A thousand memories.

A. D.

30 August, midnight

And thus, another friend falls victim to the merciless claws of jealousy and possessiveness. Why do our companions mistake friendship for love? Or is it I who mistakes love for friendship? I do not know. What I do know, alas, is that here I am alone and empty again, forsaken by another soul who I thought would be there to the end. But as the proverb says, all good things must come to an end.

And so, I resolve to raise up my chin.

CHAPTER 21

My brooding over Alexandre's cold-blooded desertion does not last long. I even try to ignore the frosty words in his last missive and continue to write letters to him in the most friendly terms. Toward the end of October, I write one such letter, in which I ask him to secure me a good seat at his father's premiere of *The Three Musketeers*. He does not reply, and I can't help but feel slightly resentful. However, the motive behind his purposeful disregard becomes clear soon enough.

On October 27th, the evening of the premiere, the Theatre L'Ambigu-Comique is bursting at the seams with all sorts of people. They are not the kind of people I am accustomed to, mind you, but those that attend cheap comedies, dressed in equally cheap clothing.

As I walk among them to reach my seat in the stalls, I become aware of my callous observations. I berate myself for my lack of affinity, and in my head, picture myself as the waif wearing wooden clogs. Yet for some reason I feel slightly vexed this night. Perhaps it is because I find myself having to return to the cheaper seats in the stalls or because

Count von Stackelberg bothers me with his simple presence. I am not completely sure. Maybe both reasons in equal measure.

The Count is especially attentive and proud looking. At my side, he seems self-consciously aware of his hunchback and tries to stand taller than everyone else, with tough-as-nails determination and on-demand availability. His compliments of my person intensify on this rather boring evening, but I would rather not hear them, considering how libidinously they are uttered.

Romain Vienne

Of course, the Count was libidinous. How could he have not been? Marie was an apparition, a marvel in a gathering of bourgeoisies. She walked on the muddy floor as though she was traversing the boulevards on a rainy day, raising her dress intuitively. The whole of her appearance was in keeping with her young, lithesome form and her face, a beautiful oval shape and rather pale, corresponded with the charm she diffused around her, like an indescribable perfume.

She wore a muslin dress with full panels, a cashmere shawl embroidered at the corners with gold thread and silk flowers and a bracelet, one of those thick gold chains which were then just beginning to be fashionable. The curls of her black hair and her gloved hand, which made you think you were looking at a painting. Plus her handkerchief marvelously trimmed with costly lace, while in her ears shone two pearls from the East that a queen would envy. All those beautiful objects were as natural to her as if she had been born amid silks and velvet, beneath some gilded ceiling of the grand faubourgs with a crown upon her head and a crowd of flatterers at her feet.

You would have looked in vain in the very highest circles for a woman who was more beautiful and in more complete harmony with her jewelry, dress, and conversation.

MARIE DUPLESSIS

Ah, there he is... As the Count and I take our seats in the stalls, I casually lift my eyes to scan the opera boxes upstairs. Sitting in a box near the stage with his almighty father, is Alexandre, and at his arm is what appears to be a new conquest. Anaïs Lievenne, the Vaudeville actress, has taken my place in Alexandre's affections. I soon learn he has rented an apartment for her in his name. A deep red color stains his cheeks as he notices me looking. Then, an acknowledging nod from both sides puts an end to a friendship I never thought had reason to die.

The adventurous, somewhat comical, play bores me. It seems these days that I have a growing fondness for drama and everything dissimilar bores me to death. During the first interval, I consider if that is the only reason for my fidgeting or does the fact that the play is based on Alexandre's father's novel have something to do with it. There they are, looking proud and smug in their expensive box, drooling at the attention coming from the chaff of bourgeoisie. I feel resentful, as any orphan would at being relinquished again and again. But I do suppose this resentment, as I call it, is nothing but fear. The ever lurking fear of being abandoned even if one has nothing but flatterers and worshipers at one's disposal.

At the second interval, I discover I can no longer sit still in my seat. I command the Count to stay behind as I make my way toward the foyer. And right there, among the uncultivated people in the stalls, I see him. The man who had inspired such awe and admiration within my bosom when I attended one of his concerts the past May. A regal face among the proletariat. A long thick mane of dark hair frames his beautiful face while in repose, then turning mad with movement while his fingers hit the piano keys he masters with such brilliance. The man who can bewitch with his music a hall full of people, an entire city, the whole of the world. Franz Liszt— Hungarian composer and pianist.

I slow my walk as I reach his seat and stare intently in his eyes. He stares back with the same intent and I suddenly get the strange vision that our looks, the admiration read in them, are making love right there in the air between our gazes. A strange thought that cannot be avoided secures my mind. This man is going to be my next conquest.

As I walk past him, I hear his companion speak.

"She has taken a fancy to you."

"What an idea!" Liszt replies.

"Do you know her?"

"No. Who is she?"

"That is Madame Duplessis. She'll take possession of you—mark my words."

AT THE THIRD INTERVAL, I again make my way to the foyer. The noisy crowd gathered there feels like a relief from the hubbub of the play. I scan the foyer in search of the long dark locks and spot them near the greenroom's fire.

It is my turn to feel the deep red color staining my cheeks, but this is no determent. On the contrary, most men adore blushing, timorous damsels seemingly in need of their protection. That's how I became wealthy in the first place.

I pinch my cheeks further still and make my way to where the gentleman sits talking to his companion.

"Good evening, Monsieurs," I say, bowing my head slightly. "I hope I am not disturbing your conversation, but could I approach the fire? I feel terribly cold."

The men look slightly puzzled, Liszt even more so than his friend. Being approached by a woman with such boldness is not a usual thing. But I am no usual woman.

"The choice of my petticoat for this evening was very uninspired," I continue, allowing the men time to snap out of their inertia. "Could I approach the fire, then?"

"By all means!" Liszt finally says, standing halfway up from his chair and indicating the chimney with his hand. I approach it and waver my fingers about the sizzling flame. As I sit on a chair near the fire, I again turn my gaze toward the master.

"I don't think we've been properly introduced. I am Marie Duplessis."

"My friend told me who you were. He was puzzled by your presence in such a place. I am Franz Liszt."

"I know." A hint of pride as well as surprise teases his features.

"Yes, yes," the friend booms in a rather annoying voice. "There are more caps than hats with feathers here and more threadbare overcoats than new suits. Seeing you in your splendid attire, one couldn't but be surprised by your presence."

Liszt turns to his friend. "This is Jules Janin, the drama critic of the Journal des Débats. And, my friend."

"Delighted," I say, as the friend, a husky, white-haired gentleman bends slightly forward to kiss my hand. But my gaze can't pause on him for longer than a moment.

"Monsieur Liszt," I say, reverting my gaze to him, "your playing had set me dreaming."

"Are you acquainted with my music then?" he asks.

I let out a little laugh. "I am more than acquainted. I was

so moved by your performance of last May that I rented myself a piano in an attempt to learn to play it. You are a muse, Monsieur Liszt."

He flushes. *Great. Sensitive to flattery.*

"Last May? I was here, in Paris," he mumbles.

"Yes. After your concert, you accidentally dropped your gloves. I shall never forget how the women in the audience seized and tore them into pieces. They were like women in love, women obsessed. I have never seen anything quite like it."

"Yes, I shall never understand it...why people do that... why humiliate oneself to that extent? As you can see, I am flesh and bones, just like everyone else."

"But not everyone is inhabited by the ghost of genius." The blush in his cheeks renews and I relish every second of it.

"Will you be staying in Paris long?" I ask.

"Well, I arrived two days ago and shall be here for a week at the most. Monsieur Janin and I are working on a cantata, which he then promised to translate into French, for as you can see, my command of your language is not too commendable."

"Well, maybe not as commendable as the command of your fingers, but delightful nonetheless," I say piercing his gaze again. Our eyes make love once more in a suddenly quiet room. Only our breathing is heard and the sizzling embers. The spell is broken by the solemn knocks of the prompter calling the audience back into the auditorium.

"I shall like to hear you play the piano you rented," Liszt says.

I look at his exotic face and smile. "How about tomorrow evening?"

∾

Tomorrow evening it is, and when Clotilde opens the entrance door upon the ring of the bell, I know something has changed. Liszt arrives accompanied by my doctor, the German, a mutual acquaintance, it seems. The look in Liszt's eyes worries me. Whereas last night it was overflowing with lust and passion and longing, now it reserves space only for compassion. For pity. I feel my entire blood rising to my head.

"He told you, hasn't he?" I ask Liszt as soon as he approaches me.

"In disturbing detail." He reaches to take my hands. "I am so sorry to—"

But I can hardly hear him anymore. My glare reverts to Dr. Koreff, who understands at once he is no longer welcome. He mumbles a few unintelligible yet obviously embarrassed words, then exits my house.

As if a great danger has just passed me, I drop my shoulders and let myself fall upon the sofa. I begin to cry tears of resentment, pain, and helplessness.

"I shall not live..." I finally say.

"Mariette..."

"Only God knows how much I have left," I whisper, as my tears turn to sobs. Liszt's pity turns to tears, and we both let them fall unbridled, while embracing each other for the first time. And yet it feels as like the last.

Also, for the first time, I make love to a man through tears. It serves to connect me to another human being on a level I never knew existed before, and this is further reason for my unwillingness to suppress those tears. It feels as if I am a witness to a lot of things for the first, as well as the last, time.

As we lay in bed facing the ceiling, the menacing melancholy I know too well, nestles in my bosom.

"You will be leaving Paris soon, won't you?"

"Right after the premiere of my cantata. That should be in a few days, I suppose," he whispers the harsh truth.

"But then, you can always return, can't you? For my birthday, perhaps? It's not too long in the future, just a couple of months from now, and then I could play the piano for you. Wouldn't that be wonderful?"

He turns on his side to look me in the eyes and I again see pity in them. *When did I turn into a pitiful woman, begging for affection?* I sink into in complete dismay. *Does brewing death do that to people?*

"Mariette, ah, lovely Mariette..." Liszt wails, piercing me with his compassionate eyes. "You are the most perfect incarnation of Woman who has ever existed. I feel strangely attached to you, delightful creature that you are—"

"And I to you," I say, my heart swelling with hope.

"That is why you will understand how painfully difficult it is for me to refuse you. But, nonetheless, I must. For in January I am to embark on one of the most exhausting tours that could last for as long as a year and a half."

The feeling of impending abandonment grasps me again. I might not have a year and a half.

"But then I want to be done with this," he continues. "I want it over with touring and concerting. Alas, it is too exhausting. My greatest wish, nay, my greatest dream, is to settle in Weimar, right in the heart of Germany. I have been appointed as director of court music there."

"Planning..." I sigh. "A luxury I no longer have...I shan't be able to hold onto this life I know not how to lead and which I can equally no longer endure..."

"Nonsense," Liszt says as he props himself on one elbow. "Planning for the future is the best way to keep anyone sane. Plus, who says you don't have a future? Your doctors? Do you really believe them? I'd say you shouldn't.

Never was a creature more alive and more filled with child abandon than your beautiful self, lovely Mariette." He reaches to caress my face.

This man's positiveness and complete confidence in his words rub onto me and I suddenly brim with enthusiasm. Sitting up, I smile ear to ear.

"Then take me, take me anywhere you like! I shan't bother you. I sleep all day. In the evening you can let me go to the theater, and at night you can do with me what you will. Take me, take me to Weimar, then! Yes!"

He sits up, too. But his look ceases to be enthusiastic.

"Mariette, dearest... you are a Paris woman and shall find Weimar too boring and provincial. You will resent your decision soon enough, and then what?"

I push from the bed and begin pacing around the bed. "I will be an embarrassment to you, is that it? Of course! For what would a woman like me do by your side, except always remind you of how low you've sunk in the scale?"

"No, it's not like that..."

"I could never possibly be introduced to the court, of course. And the townspeople will never welcome me. I shall forever be a thistle in your bottom."

My tears renew and Liszt jumps from the bed to embrace me. "You are a silly little thing, aren't you?" he says in the warmest masculine voice I've ever heard. "I have another idea. Meet me in Pest the next summer, and we shall travel together to Constantinople. We will breathe in perfume, exchange coal smoke for the gentle whiff of the narghile. What do you say?"

I dab at my tears and smile. "Surely, any kind of smoke will alleviate my condition," I muse.

"You're right. I am sorry," he says, realizing his gaffe.

"I shall be there."

With the idea of that exotic place entering my head, I

feel alive again. Longing for the East seems like planning to me. Liszt is right. Planning feels good. It keeps you sane.

And yet my enthusiasm does not last long. My suspicions prove accurate, as a few days into our liaison, Liszt premiers his cantata. Not at the Opera, as was expected, and where everyone could have freely attended, but at his companion, Jules Janin's house. I, of course, am not invited. For what would a whore like me, a woman with a reputation beyond rehabilitation, be doing mingling with those cultivated minds? It would put them all in the most unfavorable light, sully their high-breeding status, defile them if I would as much as ring the bell to the house.

Liszt's action hurts me deeply. For he could finally have been the man I have always looked for and needed. The exotic man with feminine features bound together by purely masculine bindings. The man with a self-created reputation who, above all, is not afraid to show kindness and romanticism and attention. The man who could take me away from the hell I have created and see me through my darkest moments lying ahead. A man who could restore and rejuvenate my entire being.

And I, I embarrass him? I, the most famous woman in Paris? The woman who has created her own reputation all by herself, which by the by, is a task so much harder to accomplish than ever is for a man? But what am I saying? Our reputations couldn't be more antagonistic. How much easier it all would have been, had I been the pianist and he the seducer... for a man is forgiven such impulses, even more so, he is commended for having what can only be envied: power over women, a bed never empty, and plenty of stories to go with all of that. Ay, how he would be held in awe!

But I... women...

Alas! They are not only the most disgraceful harlots; they are dogs with mange!

. . .

Right after his cantata premiere, my exotic lover with the long brown mane leaves Paris.

I cannot say with complete certainty what possesses me for the remaining winter months, but possessed I become... one of his many possessed women.

Never in my life have I written so many letters, and never shall I do so again.

My dearest Franz,

You have no way of knowing how greatly your departure affected me. I, myself, had no way of knowing how I would long for your kind eyes, and masculine jaw, and the lovely words you so kindly whispered in my ears.

Do you remember what my first words to you were? How I told you you had set me dreaming? My dear noble artist, dreaming is all that I do ever since I met you, and am dreaming even more now, ever since you left.

Will you still take me to Constantinople next summer? I am dreaming of that, too, and of the many and wonderful memories we will create together.

But let us talk about the present, for it is the only time we have. The past, as well as the future—and this you have taught me—are only in our heads; psychological time we cannot alter.

Do you know who visited me yesterday? Had you been here, I would have let you guess, easy thing for that quick brilliant mind of yours. It was our mutual friend, Lola Montez. I usually take pride in keeping myself informed to all things pertaining to my friends, but this time I was overcome. Lola told me all about how she met you; how she ambushed you, I should rather say, by claiming to be a guest at the unveiling of Beethoven monument event that you, my dearest, were coordinating. She was laughing when she told me you completely ignored her, and she was left with no other means but to spring up onto your festive table, knocking off the bottles and glasses laying on it. But at least she's got your attention, hasn't she? I would expect no less of our scandalous friend.

You know what else is humorous, my darling composer? My own little harmless decoy. There was no piano at my house when I met you. Tired by endless notes hit poorly and frustrated by my own inconsistency with learning to play your compositions, I had returned the wooden monster that created so much misery for me. I just had to have you, my love, and just like Lola, any means would have done it if the result would have been the expected one.

Do you love me still? Please tell me that you do and more than ever. I seem to need to hear it ever so often.

A thousand kisses on your full lips, and eyes, and soul.

Eternally yours,

Mariette Duplessis

For two months there is no reply to my endless letters. And because obsession has already claimed me, it does to me what it would do to any other obsessed woman in the absence of the affection and acknowledgement from her object of obsession: spin me in a dark endless vortex of emotional instability.

One thing leads to another and I become ill, so very ill, I can hardly quit my bed anymore.

The nights are the worst. There too, one thing leads to another. Resting tightly clutched in the arms of Sleep is but a beautiful distant memory. It's counterpart, Insomnia, has made it its mission to claim me, too. And when I cannot sleep, I cough. Blood. Increasing amounts of dark red blood. Of it all, the shortness of breath is the worst. It reminds me, with every breath I take that does not reach my lungs, that the end is near. It tells me I should have loved myself more, quit the life I was leading long ago. Then, guilt sets in. And it never comes alone, but with endless tormenting thoughts that feed my insomnia further ... and too, my cough.

It is a vortex that surrounds me all around, a vicious circle that almost drives me mad.

And yet it seems that God hasn't forsaken me. Perhaps He was softened by my torment and sorrow. Or maybe my late-night shouting and screaming at a black starless sky have reached His merciful ears. Whichever it was, in January He extends his hand to caress my head. On the 15th, my 22nd birthday, a box is dropped at my front door. Together with Clotilde and Madame Prat, we struggle to get the monster in. That sets me coughing some more and I fall wheezing onto the sofa.

"My God, what is it?" Madame Prat asks, in her usual poke-and-pry manner.

"Open it, and you shall see," I whisper, trying to catch my breath. As she does so, I sit up to look at what she unravels.

"My God!" she exclaims again. "But it's a vertical piano!" Her hands go to her mouth, and then fly to the envelope laying on the piano. I extend my arm, palm open. A reluctant Madame Prat places it in my hand. My hands shake with anticipation as I open the envelope and pull out the letter inside.

My Dearest Mariette,

My wonderful creature, I hope my gift pleases you. Your harmless ploy had me rolling on the floor with laughter. Only your mischievous pretty little head could have mustered such amusing, innocent deed. Or perhaps, Lola's, too. But you, my dearest child, are no Lola. Your winsome nature could only surround you with glee and happiness, while her impetuous one could only breed scandal.

I am so happy to have met you, little being, and am looking forward to meeting you, as planned, this next summer. Meanwhile, please enjoy my gift for your birthday, and I expect to hear you play my composition to perfection.

I am in Budapest now, and will soon depart for Romania. The tour is taking a toll on my health. How I wish I could rest in your arms, my darling little angel!

But do learn to play! I shall be a tough critic!

Happy Birthday, my dearest one, and many more to come,

Ever yours,
Franz Liszt

Tears spring from my eyes unrestrained. *So, he was thinking of me all this time,* I am smiling ear to ear. Through my tears, I stare at the piano. I don't think I've ever seen anything more beautiful. Through my tears, I also notice Clotilde peeking out through the lace curtains.

"Is there something wrong?" I ask.

She turns to look at me. "Yes, Madame. There is."

I rise from the sofa and approach the window. There, in the alley across the street, I see Edouard, camellias in hand, staring in my direction. My instincts tell me I should lock myself in the house, but my logic disapproves, whispering that a man who did nothing but love me for so many years could not possibly hurt me.

I throw a light gown over my shoulders and walk out into the street. Edouard's eyes are no longer possessed by harrowing sadness, but by a fiery incandescent light. The months he's been away have turned him into the man I met: unspeakably handsome, utterly self-confident, and deliciously tanned. He smiles a bewitching smile.

"Marry me!" he says.

CHAPTER 22

The image unfolding before my eyes seems plucked from *A Thousand and One Nights*, with Scheherazade herself whispering the story in my ear. Yesterday, I was brooding over nobody loving me. Today, I am asked in marriage. But my thoughts fly to my pianist, and to how much I wished it was him proposing.

Edouard falls upon his knees. I wince as I hear his bones hit the concrete sidewalk. But he doesn't seem to acknowledge his pain.

"Let this be your wedding bouquet," he says, as he extends his arms to hand me the camellias.

More relieved of my fears of him than happy by his proposition, I too, sink upon my knees and clasp his face between my palms. I kiss his eyes. This is the man who loves me unconditionally. This is the man who has thrown at my feet his entire fortune. This is the only man who, in an age dedicated solely to the pleasures of the flesh, has seen and loved Alphonsine. And this is the man who has only one thing left to give—his title—and he offers it to me while on his knees.

"My dearest Edouard, you are not a man either of or for this world," I gently whisper to his face. "You were born in the wrong place at the wrong time."

"Marry me!" he continues, ignoring my words, my hints. "Marry me, Marie!"

For what seems like an eternity, I ponder Edouard's proposition in my mind. I feel my mind is acting as a sort of scales, the load of my thoughts switching between the two pendulums. Should I answer with my heart then? If I do, then I will turn down the only human being in this world that truly loves me. Should I listen to my judgement, then? But that would mean stepping over dead bodies to advance my goal. Who should decide? Alphonsine or Marie?

"I will hurt you further," Alphonsine finally says. "Let me, at last, do a pious act toward you and refuse you, even though in doing so I am renouncing one of my greatest dreams; that of becoming a countess, of finally acquiring the long lost respectability through your title."

"I need neither your pious acts, Marie, nor your pity. Marry me!"

I cover my eyes with my palms. What am I to do? The thoughts that keep crossing my mind are cataclysmal. If I act on them, then I shall be damned forever. And I shall damn him, too... this soul...this man who all he ever did was to...

"Marry me!" Edouard booms for the seventh time.

His insistence fills me with turmoil. "Our marriage would be null in France," I say quickly, and pray to God it would dissuade him from his ruin.

"Then we shall marry in England!" he says resolutely, and raising from his knees, he lifts me up in his arms and carries me into the house.

.   .   .

AFTER A NIGHT SPENT in Edouard's company, the pendulum scale has decided. This man's drilling insistence made Alphonsine seem like a distant shadow from the past, a paling ghost chased away by the stronger, calculating mercenary, Marie. The same drilling insistence inflamed in Marie her two worst attributes: capriciousness and impetuosity. For you cannot offer a capricious, impetuous woman the very thing she wants and needs most, without making her forget about integrity, decency, and rectitude. Alas! Her morality is at once strangled to death by her recklessness.

It takes me several months to obtain a passport from the Prefecture of Police, but finally, on 25 January 1846, only ten days after my twenty-second birthday, I am holding the coveted document in my hands. Shaking with anticipation, I open it and read:

Mlle Alphonsine Plessis, person of private means, living in Paris at 11, boulevard de la Madeleine, 22 years old, height one metre 65 centimetres, brown hair, low forehead, light brown eyebrows, brown eyes, well-made nose, medium-sized mouth, round chin, oval face, ordinary complexion.

To acquire the necessary money for our journey, Edouard sells the summer house in Bougival. And while the parting with it breeds sadness in his soul, it breeds no feeling of remorse or melancholy in mine. He even sheds a few tears over "the unforgettable moments we spent there", but all I can do is smile at him, feigning my best possible compassionate facial expression.

On 3 February, I obtain a visa from the Ministry for Foreign Affairs and we set off for England at once. And there, almost three weeks later, on 21 February 1846, in a small room at Kensington registry office in London, with two witnesses flanking each of us, Edouard and I finally become man and wife. The entry in the marriage register deems Father as "gentleman", and that alone makes me forget I just became a Countess and sends me into a fit of laughter.

Poles apart, more tears gather in my new husband's eyes. He even takes me to the new opera of *Don Quixote* at the Theatre Royal, Drury Lane, as half of his wedding gift. The night of passion that follows the opera is to be considered the other half. So much for expensive jewelry, fur coats, and Bougival houses. But at least, and at last, I now am a Countess. At age twenty-two, I can finally call myself Countess Marie de Perregaux. I have come a long way. Longer than the orphan wearing wooden clogs ever thought possible.

THE TRIP back to Paris is disturbingly quiet, interrupted only now and then by my cough. Edouard shows himself utterly concerned, but I am no good actress for nothing.

"Monsieur Alexandre Dumas was a heavy smoker," I say. "Thank goodness he is no longer part of my life or he would have weakened my lungs for good."

Edouard's distraught expression doesn't quite reveal if his concern is still for my health or has now shifted to the startling thought that his new wife still speaks freely about her lovers.

He looks me in the eyes, as I wonder what his next words will be.

"You were coughing at Bougival, too, dearest. And there, no one was smoking."

Now it is me who is slightly concerned, for Edouard is no fool. Only his love for me turns him at times into one.

"Ah, that! You forget then, my dearest husband, how you kept me in the rain as you professed your eternal love?"

"Of course not. And, pray, do forgive me," he says, color flushing his cheeks.

"I am but a fragile woman."

"You are my fragile woman now, and I shall protect you," he says gravely.

"It passed, by the by. As it will this time. Pray, be not concerned," I say, as I reach over to kiss his forehead.

"You are my only concern," he says and grins.

Perfect. The smile is back on his lips.

Yet his loving words, as well as my own dreadful thoughts, turn my stomach into a burning pit. I fasten my gaze on some faraway distance beyond the carriage window and we continue our journey in the same uncomfortable silence.

Once arrived at my home, in Rue de la Madeleine, I fall exhausted upon the living room sofa. The cough returns and I go out of my way to conceal it. He must not know. Edouard must not discover I am ill. Clotilde rushes to hand me with a glass of warm honey-sweetened ass's milk, which always subsides my coughing.

"I shall bring some of my garments in the evening," Edouard says, as he enters the living room. "For now, I should like to rest in your arms, wife." He chuckles like a small child handed sweets.

But his chuckle, his calling me 'wife' in my own home, and the...the threat of bringing his clothes here, send me reeling. I lurch from the sofa and begin pacing my living room. *I must tell him. And I must do it now. I must not prolong neither his suffering, nor the inevitable.* The frightening thoughts go over and over in my head with alarming speed.

"Is there something the matter?" Edouard asks, as he takes my place on the sofa.

"Alas, there is!" I burst out. His expression turns grave

again and I hate it. It will not make it any easier for me, I realize.

"Edouard... you are not to move in here. That is the matter," I commence, speaking in fast short sentences, lest the pity I feel prevent me from continuing to say what needs to be said.

He smiles with incredulity, and I resume my pacing.

"Should you like to move someplace else, we could..." he says.

"No."

"Perhaps a new neighborhood?"

"No."

"Don't tell me you have second thoughts about Bougival?" he continues, expectant hope rekindling in his eyes.

"No!" I shout.

My reaction startles him into jumping from the sofa.

"What is going on, my love?" he asks, approaching me to take me in his arms.

"You are not to move here. We are not to move someplace else. We are not to live together as husband and wife."

He pauses to sink in my words. "Have I done something wrong? Have I offended you in some way? Because if I have—"

"Offended me? No. Have you done something wrong? Yes! A thousand times *Yes!* I told you, you shouldn't have married me!" I continue shouting. I don't even know why I do it, but the shame I feel, the embarrassment and the pain at what I am about to tell him, need a way out. Like those river ducks that ruffle their feathers and wag their tails after they've attacked each other. Perhaps, just like them, I need to let the negative feelings out.

I resolve to erase the mystified expression from his face.

"Edouard, I married you for your title."

He sighs. "I know that."

"I know you know. And perhaps you wonder what good there is in having a title except for acquiring a hypocritical respectability? And here comes the part you do not know."

"What part? What don't I know?" he puffs. "Marie, this talk makes me nervous!"

I pause briefly to look at him. Then, I decide to end his torment quick.

"Edouard, I am in love with another. This is the truth. I am telling you I love another man."

Tears would pass his lids if only the blow would have been more sluggish.

"But unlike you, my dear Edouard, this man feels upon his heart the heavy burden of shame. Shame to marry a woman of disrepute, the incarnation of debauchery. But now, that shouldn't be a problem, should it? Now, he can be seen with a countess, can't he? And now, he can take me to Weimar and make me his companion. Introduce me to the court."

"What have you done?" he asks in a voice as cold as death.

"I have told you, haven't I? That I would hurt you? Haven't I begged you to let me make a pious act towards you and refuse you? Haven't I?"

No reply comes and I again pause. Looking at Edouard, who is now standing motionless in the middle of my living room, I almost faint at the image unfolding before my eyes. He has shoved his hands in his hair and is pulling. Pulling and pulling until his fists overflow with his beautiful strands. A little scream escapes my lips and I throw myself at his feet.

"Pray stop!" I plead, as I encircle his ankles with my arms. "Pray, forgive me! I beg you!" I beseech, as tears burst from my eyes. "What I did was wrong! So wrong!" I continue to lament, distraught by Edouard's sobs, by the terrifying image of his hairs falling to the floor near me, by my monstrous deed.

"Will you ever forgive me? Edouard? Pray, say something!" I scream, as I pull at his pants with my fingers.

But Edouard says nothing. He just glides his look from an unknown spot in the room and straight into mine. The look in his eyes...it...it isn't hate as I expected it would be, it is not even sadness anymore, nor anger at the only woman he has given everything to, just to be betrayed and abandoned like a dog. It is pity.

The shock of seeing that feeling in Edouard's eyes paralyses me. My tears freeze, my heart stops throbbing. All I can feel is the painful lump in my throat. I open my mouth to again ask him for forgiveness, but no sound comes out. Releasing his feet from my grasp, my beguiled husband silently exits the room, my house, and my life.

Should I resolve now to longer dwell on the rupture, I shall be killed faster than would the merciless illness that so obstinately insists on claiming my life. But I can still hear his words, his last words to me, mercilessly unreeling in my mind: *What have you done? What have you done? What have you done?*

A memory surrounding the same question, at that time spoken from my own mouth, as Father sold me to the satyr, proceeds to unreel next, over and over, until the pain, the guilt, and the harrowing shame I feel, succumb me into haziness, then shroud me in complete nothingness.

Betraying the only man who ever loved me unconditionally proves to be a turning point in my young life. For the first time since Father's frightening visits, I feel fear. It is not the type of fear that keeps you from promenading unchaperoned after darkness settles on rooftops. It is the kind that paralyses all your senses, clouds your judgement, and turns you into a psychotic wreck for most of your waking hours. It is the one and only feeling governing your actions, thoughts, and plans for the future. The feeling that convinces you there is *no* future, apart from the one in which you are an eternally lost soul persecuted by God's wrath.

The terror I feel, which I intuitively understand is fed by relentless guilt, makes me behave like an old woman. An old woman who senses her final departure drawing nearer and thus, spends her waking hours in prayer and contemplation. And as an old woman would, I notice, for the first time since moving into this home, the church across the street. Facing my apartment almost directly the Church of La Madeleine has been there for centuries. It would have taken me another century to become aware of its presence if the guilt and panic now possessing me wouldn't have insisted so fiercely on becoming my intimate companions.

My insomnia worsen as well, and when I do succeed in falling asleep, at the latest possible hour of the morning, it feels as if I have closed my eyes just a moment, just to reopen them for fear of some superstition crossing my half-sleeping mind or a cold chill or the terrifying thought that I wouldn't wake up at all. This begins to act like a sort of ritual, so it is no surprise that my early mornings are all spent kneeling at the base of the Marochetti's High Altar— the marble statue of Mary Magdalene being borne heavenwards by three all-powerful angels.

Now, with my spirituality awakened from its blissful sleep, I start to believe that moving across from this church is no coincidence. Maybe God has been aware of the course of my destiny all along. Maybe it was Him who guided me here, knowing that at one point, a point in my life I am now living, I would need the solace of His saints. And the saint across the street being Mary Magdalene, the patron saint of lost women, couldn't have been a coincidence either. If she, a prostitute, had been meritorious enough to receive God's forgiveness, then I, the whore of all whores, might be shown the same mercy.

These thoughts bring an unexpected real sense of relief, and I redouble my visits to the church. When my illness prevents me from attending the Mass, I spread the tapestry-covered prie-dieu on the floor of my bedroom, and holding the rosary blessed by Pope Leo XII himself between my fingers, I kneel and pray in the quietness of my own home.

For several months, I take in no new protectors. The mere idea of raising from the prie-dieu to receive some horny gentleman makes my bile rise in rebellion. As a result, my debts increase to an alarming amount. By the spring of 1846, I owe over forty thousand francs, most of which was spent on linen, laundry bills, doctors' visits and prescriptions, and acts of charity. It comes as no surprise when my creditors' lawsuits come pouring in. My lingerie merchant sues me, as well as the owner of the horse stables, for failure to pay my rent.

But for all my spiritual transformation, my remorse, my allowing myself to become molested by my finances, for my cold-blooded betrayal, and for all my other efforts to become a redeemed woman, I seem to be incapable of gaining the thing I long for the most. My composer's love seems to be fleeing further and further from me. His letters become fewer and farther in between. And their contents, which up until now were overflowing with affectionate words, burning passion, and heart-warming kindness, are now resumed to short sentences chronicling the weather in the many cities his touring takes him or the details of some meaningful event, or as less as a few jokes about the people he encounters, jokes that, according to him, are meant to "lift up my spirits".

If this is nothing but God's punishment for betraying Edouard in such ruthless self-serving manner, I am not in the least surprised. But "lifting up my spirits" my pianist— doesn't. Instead, he succeeds in crushing my spirits; his cold, heartless ignorance succeeds in ruining what I have accumulated with so much pain and suffering over the past few months. My spiritual transformation, my fears, and my redemption, switch places with a renewed appetite for living. And if I am now going to end up in Hell, I might as well arrive there in splendor.

By the end of May, I resolve to accept the insistent attentions of a new millionaire protector.

Count Olympe Aguado de las Marismas, an eighteen-year-old possessor of a staggering wealth of over sixty-million francs, becomes my new lover. Another spoiled youth whose fortune had been inherited upon the death of his father less than two years prior. Not to say he isn't one of the clever ones, but having so many coins at one's disposal from such a young age shapes one's character in the direction of a less orthodox disposition, whether one becomes aware of it or not. Not particularly handsome, with his Spanish black beard, hair combed forward, and a physiognomy that lacks expression, Olympe is nevertheless an enjoyable creature. His heart seems to be in the right place, and his sweet nature and outstanding generosity quickly elevate him in my affections.

. . .

OUR FIRST ENCOUNTER proves less romantic than businesslike. I enumerate my demands and so does he. Encountering a protector who has demands feels strangely appealing. It makes me regard him with friendship, somehow seeing him as an equal partner with equal rights. He is not to be exclusive, he says, grounding himself in a long, complicated relationship, but that will not diminish his complete attention and affection, he assures me. Our bond is that which unites two caprices, for both of us feel bored or are in search of new distractions to help us forget someone or something.

"A trip would save us both," Olympe says to me, one fine June evening. "A tour of the German spas!" I couldn't agree more. Certainly, the Rhine, with its shores lush with flowers and waters lost in the sands, would prove a sweet river of oblivion.

In mid-June, we board a train to the German village of Spa. Concerned with my declining health, Olympe resolves to bring his doctor, Casimir Davaine, on the tour with us. A firm believer in nature being a crucial element of restoring one's health, the doctor advises I should use this trip to reconnect with nature and the healing capabilities it provides.

For the first several days after our arrival in the beautiful village, I resolve to pay heed to the doctor's advice. I go for long walks, pausing now and then to read under some branchy tree that honors me with its shadow. And yet, as good as my intentions prove, it is all in vain. The high fever, which has now became a constant presence, as well as a constant reminder of the grim prospects of my curing, not only goes against the burning sunlight, but it also intensifies during my sleepless nights. Thus, I resolve, once and for all, to pay less heed to my doctor's words and more to those of a dear friend, who once told me: "In Spa, no other fever is known than the ball fever, no other remedies but those of talking, dancing, music, and the excitement of gambling."

Replacing my physical fever with the fever of living, I toss my books into the fire, and mounting a pure-bred stallion, I spend my days galloping, senselessly clearing high hedges. During the nights, in spite of Olympe and his doctor's vehement objections, I overwork my insomnia at the casino. Should throwing huge piles of money on the green baize be my last living action, then so be it.

ROMAIN VIENNE

Our fair friend was welcomed with an eagerness somewhat rare in this rather prudish village. Soon, she became the lioness of this beautiful spot, and the life and spirit of every party and ball. She made the orchestra play her favorite tunes, and when night came, when a little sleep would have done her so much good, she terrified the most intrepid gamblers by the heaps of gold she piled up before her and lost at a single stake, as indifferent to gain as she was to loss.

The Count, however, was not happy. He would have preferred they would enjoy the tranquility of the holiday resort, get lost together in the midst of rural wild sites or peacefully observe the grandiose spectacle offered by the mountains and the vast panoramas. However, his companion was thinking of everything but the magnificence of nature, the splendor of creation. She was, alas, in the grip of an incessant and fatal concern. *What will tomorrow hold?* was the only question burning out Marie's spirit, as well as her last physical resources.

MARIE DUPLESSIS

One week or so into our vacation, on a splendidly sunny afternoon, after I manage half an hour of sleep and am getting myself ready for the casino, Olympe takes my hand and sits me at the corner of the hotel bed.

"I have two hundred thousand francs in savings," he says to me, "and I put them all at your disposal for this trip. I want this vacation to be as enjoyable as possible for you, dearest Marie, far from Paris and from all its troublesome and indiscreet people."

"But you know how I shall spend it, don't you?" I inquire.

"Only too well, my dearest. And you have my approval to spend it as you please."

"Very well then," I say, preparing to stand up and leave the room. Olympe grabs me by the waist and asks me to linger. I sit again, curious to what he'll say next.

"Marie, you have come to mean very much to me," he begins. "And I value you too greatly not to be straightforward. You deserve that much, and God knows, so much more. So, Marie...we will love each other as much as we can for these two or three months; but when we return, I will cease to be your lover. This noise, this compulsory agitation, this nervous existence of yours only serves to irritate me. I am more sensible, I suppose. I also love my complete freedom, as I already told you, wish to form only transient relationships. But one thing I promise you, Marie, for you deserve that much. I promise to you that I will remain your faithful and devoted friend."

"I thought you were bored," I manage to say, as his blunt confession startles the peace out of me. "I thought you, too, were looking for distractions."

"I was bored. And I do look out for distractions. But my kind of distraction seems to be so very different from yours."

"I see."

"Marie," he says as he squats and takes my hands in his, "I am in no way judgmental of your behavior. I understand it more than you can guess. The reason behind it is deeply disturbing to me, and no man has ever loved life so much as I do, hence no man could ever better understand you. But to me, fun is gazing at an orange sunset, not at the green baize or at the light reflecting from the piles of gold and silver on it. And what am I, if I can't bring myself to be next to you, cheering at your enthusiasm while you watch the ivory ball spinning into the bottom of the roulette wheel?"

"A mere friend?"

"That's right. All I can be is a mere friend. And I promise you: I will never abandon you as friend."

The sudden burst of laughter exiting my mouth throws my head backwards.

"*Promise you...never abandon you...*" I mock, while releasing my hands from his clasp. "I shall forgive you for these casual words, for you do not know the weight they should carry nor the hurt they produce. I shall put it on your young age and advise you not to ever again use them so lightly."

"Well, dearest Marie, we shall live and see."

"*Live...*" I mock again and stand up. "My dearest Olympe, you will not, I suppose, be terribly upset if I shall continue the tour alone. I am in need of even more action and watching an orange sunset simply isn't my perception of action."

"By all means. Will you be safe?"

I smile. "What possible harm could be out there to eclipse tuberculosis?"

Olympe smiles, too. A sad smile. "I should allow you to pack then," he says as he heads for the door.

"Olympe?"

"Yes?"

"Thank you for the money."

He bows. "I'll see you back in the city of iniquity," he says and exits.

MY LONELY TRIP takes me first to Baden-Baden. I again rent the best suite at the Hôtel de l'Europe, the one facing the river and the Conversation House. But I soon discover that the memories here are too much for me to bear. The tall fir trees, the masked balls and the casino, all serve to remind me of a time, not long ago, when my youth and health goaded me to behave as if the sun shone out of my backside: presumptuous, proud, and demanding, all too conscious of my youth and beauty. Now they further serve to remind me that those attributes are no longer of any meaningful use. What were my thoughts on my last visit here? I recall the fir trees above my head reminded me of a long-lost world, a world in which nature and simplicity were enough to mankind. A world in which neither the brilliance of one's attire nor the refulgence of one's finery mattered. Then, I resolved to believe that simplicity would be my doom.

Another mistake, I suppose.

As my thoughts serve to bring back my loyal despondency, I again begin to pack my gowns. Then I once again change my mind and decide I don't need them. Renouncing my carriage, I travel to Wiesbaden on horseback. Mounting my horse again, I gallop to Carlsbad, then Hamburg, then finally to Ems. And it is here that, suddenly, living in the present with every ounce of my being, proves too much. My body decides it no longer can keep up with the idiosyncrasies of a dying woman.

Spent to the point of dropping dead on the floor of my hotel room, I struggle to reach for pen and paper, then struggle some more to scribble the following:

Pardon me, my dear Edouard, I kneel to you in begging your forgiveness. If you love me enough for this, I ask of you only two words, my pardon and your friendship. Write to me, poste restante at Ems, duchy of Nassau. I am alone here and very ill. So, dear Edouard, quickly, your forgiveness.

    Adieu.

CHAPTER 23

The return to 'the city of iniquity', as Olympe described Paris, I make by train, where I rent a one-bed sleeping berth. Not that sleeping is an option for me, as it hasn't been in months, but standing on my own two little feet proves to be more and more of a challenge.

Paris greets me with new entertainments: lying in bed, receiving my doctors' visits, and brooding over my splendid past. Going over my bills, I realize that from October through November, Doctor Salpetriere and Davaine have together visited me one hundred and twenty-three times. And each time they try to encourage me by announcing, with great emphasis, the discovery of a new remedy that could restore my health. But their eyes speak another story. The narrative in their look is as grim as is this November's sky.

Doctor Davaine is the kindest of the two. He even goes as far as seeking advice from Auguste-Francois Chomel, personal consultant to the king. Their combined prescriptions sound like one of Balzac's knotty novels.

Massage your armpits with a pomade of potassium iodide one part to ten. Continue with the solution of Fucus crispus. Drink ass's milk sweetened with syrup of fern. To moderate sweating every day in the first spoonful of soup put 2 grams of soft extract of cinchona wrapped in a piece of wafer. To be drunk with meals, eau de Bussang mixed with a 6th of wine. Lie on horsehair in preference to wool. Take an enema prepared with a solution of starch in which is dissolved a little vinegar, 30 grams of sulphate of quinine and hold it in for as long as possible. Try using Icelandic lichen.

Each time I read this, I rub my eyes and ask Doctor Davaine to increase my daily dose of morphine.

In the month of November, word about my illness begins to circulate outside of my close circle. This turns my bedroom into a sort of final destination for the pilgrims, while I begin to feel like a fossilized relic at the museum.

Count von Stackelberg is the first to visit. The gentleman lingers for several hours without exchanging a word. Only now and then do I notice tears rolling from his eyes. As he parts, he says he will stay true to his vow; that of not burying another loved one. It's too much for him to bear, he says. He asks nothing about my finances, which he could have helped increase a little, now that all the money Olympe has given me is gone, spent either at the casino or on medical bills. But alas! I have always said that old men assume odd habits. It is a dictum I shall never be graced to experience in practice, but to take to my grave.

Ernestine comes next. Her magnificent gown, her carefree chatter, and her pinkish cheeks serve only to depress me further; to remind me of Romain's words, that health and beauty in this métier have the destiny of a rose. And while I am able, through some act of divine indulgence, to retain my beauty, I am forced to experience the fate of a fallen rose trampled underfoot. In her chatter, Ernestine lets out, perhaps by mistake or maybe on purpose, that she's seen Count von Stackelberg walking by the sea in the company of an elegant young beauty.

Nestor Roqueplan and Dr. Louis Veron come together, and their visit is by far the most entertaining. They bring the latest gossip and jokes with them as well as a case full of green apples to celebrate my first encounter with Monsieur Pont-Neuf on the bridge of the same name. Or is it a departure gift? Whatever the kind man's intention, it only reminds me of Eve, apple in hand, luring Adam into discovering shame, evil, and sin. More disturbing memories invade me, but as the morphine conquers my bloodstream, I realize I can barely make sense of them or of the gentlemen's words anymore.

Laden with flowers, as well as positive wishes, Madame Judith comes, too. Then, busy with conducting a healthy plentiful life, like everyone else around me, proceeds to send in her stead a small bouquet of camellias every day of the week. "Until you're up on your feet again", she writes every time. And each time I believe her, but then the nights come, with their disgusting sweats and intestinal inferno, and I proceed to again forget her words.

Also, every day, I receive the visitor I least expected would come. Olympe, the youngest of them all, has kept his promise of friendship. The gifts he brings are the most thoughtful and practical, and so are his words. Each time he leaves, he leaves me in tears, for I have come to love this kind, generous creature without his knowing it. I might not have felt so in the past, when an entire world of highborn testosterone was prostrating at my feet, but who is to weigh and condemn the caprices of the dying?

Then suddenly, all becomes quiet. Not even Madame Prat comes by anymore. Even though she has her quarters next to my own and an insomnia as persistent as mine, I am no longer of any use to her. For when I ceased walking, hence attending every social event there was, I ceased reminding her of the life she's spent in the clutches of a worshipping society. To her, as to everyone else, I must come across as Death itself; we all know it is coming, but none of us wants to think about it; let alone look it in the eyes or keep it company.

My only solace, during endless nights of sweating, hallucinations, and coughing up blood, comes from my household staff and my pets. I believe there never was a creature imparting so many indecent details to dogs and parrots, nor will there ever be. But loneliness is an unforgiving foe. Couple it with several pain-relieving drugs and your actions turn as bizarre as the hieroglyphs of ancient Egypt.

To Clotilde, my maid, I promise to leave all my possessions, in gratitude for her concern and loyalty. I even tell her to summon a notary so I can make it official in my will. But she always dissuades me with reassuring words.

"Why, Madame?" she asks. "You're going to get better. If it was the end, and if you were really dying, I would obey you. But I am going to stay by your side. Then I will hear you say that you made a mistake and that in a few days you will be saved."

I cry and proceed to believe her, for what is left to me, a paling beauty, if not hope? And hope is what makes me see reason again and start planning for the future. I ask Clotilde instead to pawn some jewels and with the money to rent a place where I could hide my most precious belongings, thus saving them from the mounting bailiffs.

"Because they'll return in a few days to seize more, and

this time they'll succeed. I can't be allowed to die hungry, and I want to keep something for starting again, when I will be healed," I tell Clotilde and she agrees. She leaves to do my bidding and for the next two months I take recourse to pawnshops at least twenty times. I rent several apartments in the passage of Tivoli, the rue de la Chaussée d'Antin and the rue des Dames, where Clotilde and my staff carry furniture, jewelry, and ornaments.

And yet somewhere at the back of my mind, in some secluded, dark corner of my brain, the possibility of my actions' futility lingers. It not only lingers but proceeds to regularly come out in the light of consciousness to mock me.

What are you saving for? Who are you saving for? I doubt a corpse will be in need of furniture. Perhaps the jewelry will adorn your beautiful dead body, and maybe some ornaments, your casket. But furniture? You won't need that. After all, you're not some Egyptian pharaoh, to be buried alongside your belongings.

At these moments, when it appears that I have become one of my enemies, I ask my concierge, Pierre Privé, to go out and buy a two-franc bottle of champagne and a camphor cigar. In fact, by the end of January, I make it a habit to drink only champagne. The thought of having to drink one more glass of ass's milk or another bottle of eau de Bussang is even more distressing than the thought of having to perform my daily enemas, which I cross out from the prescription as well. Whether it is this new self-prescribed treatment or the last struggle of a wasting body, the truth is that in the last month of 1846, I am graced with better kinder days.

However, they aren't going to last.

❧

THE WEATHER in January 1847 proves mild, on this otherwise freezing month, and on the 27th I feel able enough to quit my bed. I spend the morning receiving my protégées, orphans, beggars, and destitute women who, poor as I once was, had fallen into the same trap as I. Girls who got caught in the snares of rich men with plenty of coins to buy beautiful youthful bodies. Having not much money at my disposal anymore, I impart to them personal items that are of no use to me anymore.

In the evening, I call for Dezoutter, my hairdresser, as I would like to attend the theater one last time. He fits the crown of six white camellias in my hair, as well as shiny little diamonds around them. The contrast with my raven hair is simply dazzling. Staring at the image reflected by the mirror is like gaining at least another six full months of life.

Despite the devouring fever burning my flesh, I ask Clotilde to dress me. White satin and lace, of course. I also demand she apply perfume, ignoring her objections that the smell would make me nauseous. And she applies red stain to my lips and cheeks, without which I should have looked like a cadaver.

"The carriage is ready," booms Etienne, my coachman. He stands in the doorway, looking sympathetically at my image in the mirror. "And you, Madame, look ravishing," he continues. I see tears gleaming in his eyes. He looks as if he is already mourning me.

"My sweet, loyal Etienne..." I say, turning to face him. "Look at you! The gold braided uniform never looked better."

"Ah, this," he says as he runs his palms over his uniformed chest. "I thank you for this. It is a marvelous gift."

"I hope it won't grow on you now. Next time I hear, you've abandoned me to join the Foreign Legion," I say, and at once remember Edouard. Rumors of him having again applied for admission into the Foreign Legion reached my ears the other day.

"Never! I will never abandon you, Madame," says Etienne, and I suddenly feel sick to my stomach. Clutching my belly with my hand I desperately search for air.

"I told you, haven't I?" I hear Clotilde. "Haven't I told you the perfume will make you nauseous?"

"The rascal!" I shout. "He took his revenge! Only one thing I asked of him: forgiveness! What kind of human being doesn't forgive a dying woman? The scoundrel! I hate him! I hate him more than I ever loved him!" I continue screaming, maddened by grief.

Clotilde hurries to my side. "Madame? Are you all right??"

"I don't want him ever to set foot in here! If you open the door to him, I order you to chase him away! Do you hear me?"

"Chase away who?" Clotilde asks meekly, obviously distraught by my behavior. "Madame, you are not well. Maybe going out wasn't such a good idea. How about I'll take you to bed for a little rest?" She looks at Etienne, who nods.

"I am fine, Clotilde. Please open the window a bit. Let some air in."

The cold air reaching the sweat on my body serves to bring me back to the present. I breathe it in greedily, as I look at the confounded expressions of my servants' faces. Then I laugh. So loudly and heartily that they must truly believe I took leave of my senses. Then, my laughter ceases as abruptly as it started.

Looking gravely at my servants, I say, "Thank you for your kindness, dearest souls. Thank you for paying off the bailiffs with your own money." Etienne and Clotilde look embarrassed and confused, and I smile.

"You think I don't know? How Pierre's wife cleans the house for free every day? How her husband spent hundreds of francs from his own money on our food? How, you, Etienne, got rid of that locksmith and his lawyer, by paying the sum I owed them? You, dearest souls, are the only people in my life who have proved the most humane. I wish I could say I will repay you, but..."

"Don't concern yourself with that now, Madame," Etienne says as he squats near my seat. I look at him for the longest time. I wish I could erase the sympathy in his eyes and replace it with the joyous look of old. But, alas, you can't command people to stop caring for you, to quit loving you, to cease to suffer knowing they would soon lose you. It simply can't be done.

"Captain Etienne," I burst out, "let's go to the theater!" He complies, and lifting me up in his arms, he carries me to the carriage.

THE PALAIS-ROYAL THEATER looks just as it has on the many other occasions I attended it. Yet tonight, for some unknown reason, I perceive it differently. Tonight, the humongous concrete monster seems to be alight. The gas lamps adorning its edges and dropping from the rooftop like burning icicles baptize the building in a magnificent golden light, giving birth here and there to little shadows that make its outstanding architecture all the more impressive. I have never looked at its details before, somehow believing it will be there for me to admire for many decades to come. But decades to come for me there are not, hence I am looking at the theater building as if seeing it for the first and last time.

I enter the magnificent place, carried in the arms of

Etienne and his son. By the heavy silence in the foyer, I gather the first act of the play has already started. The two men open the door to my box and carefully place me in my seat. *La Poudre de Coton* is playing tonight, a revue of the satirical roundup of the inventions, plays, and personalities of 1846. A light comedy, it is the perfect genre for tonight. I want to hear laughter, to hear people's loud cheers in my ears long after the play is finished, and I am home struggling with my insomnia.

As I look down in the stalls, it seems as if the play has stopped, and now all its spectators are looking up at me. I smile shyly and bow my head. The different emotions emanating from the people's faces are an intricate play all on its own. Some send up sympathy and admiration. Others —women especially—smiles that betray contentment mingled with smugness. It is as if they would rather stand up and scream at me what they had been holding back for so many years. *You, whore, yes you! You're finally getting what you deserve! Stealing our husbands and fortunes! Whore! Whore!* At those, I smile back or bury my nose in the big white camellias bouquet I hold in my hands.

The faces sending up sadness and sorrow and pity are the faces of those that, whether they knew me in person or not, loved me or not, still have their hearts in their right places. Some are whispering to their companions and, now and then, I can read their words on their lips... *a shadow of a woman... white and diaphanous... consumptive pallor... burning fever ...any day now...*

As the play ends, I ask Etienne to linger in the foyer, so I could look at the people a little bit longer. "I am not ready to go home yet," I tell him. He nods and places me on a red velvet sofa, a huge mirror behind it. The people's chatter enlivens me and so does the music. There is music being played, a melodious waltz that reminds me of Franz Liszt. I smile and let the memory of him desert me, for there is no time left for sorrow and recriminations.

ROMAIN VIENNE

At the beginning of February, the inevitable had already produced itself, but my shock wasn't yet past and Marie's coachman, Etienne, invited me for drinks. And what he told me of that night, the way he described it and Marie, is something I will never be able to forget.

"One believed, on seeing this beautiful specter with inflamed eyes, covered with diamonds and enveloped in a flood of white satin and lace, that Marie had risen from the grave to come and reproach this brilliant society of young fools for their abandon and their unfeeling forgetfulness. She appeared that way for she was already mortally ill. The pure whiteness of her skin had been melted like snow by the fire of her fever; the flush of exhaustion wasted her thin cheek, the light had extinguished in the huge black eyes, and there were circles beneath them...

And yet, she had dressed herself that evening with a wild brilliance. She was wearing all the necklaces and diamonds from her jewel box, like the Roman empresses who envelop themselves in purple robes before they die. Sitting drowsily on a small sofa she fixed on the crowd her eyes, opaque with disgrace and boredom, until a waltz tune brusquely revived her from this dismal slumber. It was one of those Viennese airs of a sentimental gaiety whose ethereal, distant melody strikes you as supernatural—like music from the spheres commanding you to follow it in the whirling intoxication of an embrace.

The stirring sound raised her from her seat and, as regal as a princess, she went over and put her hand on the arm of a young man, who was overwhelmed by this good fortune. She danced for a long time with passion, with rapture, with a giddy and vertiginous ardor which caused a shudder in anyone who knew how little breath she had left."

The words so gracefully combined with one another, by a man from whom you would never expect to hear such words, produced in me a feeling of nauseating emptiness. I was in complete muteness.

MARIE DUPLESSIS

The waltz demands I stand up and dance. It is as if it is played for me, a last tune chasing away my devouring fever. The notes produced by the violins, the piano, the clarinets, and the flutes, sound more like words... heartening words that goad me to pause the lurking death for one more dance, one more embrace, one more kiss. I approach a young man and, placing my hand on his arm, we begin waltzing right there in the foyer full of noisy people, cutting through the cigar smoke hovering in the air. The exhaustion I feel at the end makes me lose my equilibrium for a moment. But the young man is faster than my consumption and catches me in his arms. Looking up at him with feverish eyes, I press my lips upon his.

Grabbing my coachman by the arm, I bow low, and then make my way to the exit. As I walk, a path is cleared to let me pass and more than two hundred people, their eyes lowered, bow in front of me. Tears glisten in my eyes, for at long last death made them accept me.

After he places me in the carriage and takes his seat on the high-bench, Etienne turns toward me.

"Where to, Madame?" he asks, reins in hand.

I smile. "Home, my dear Etienne. Where else? Take me home to die."

He looks at me for the longest time, then urges the

horses forward and the carriage jolts, speeding away into darkness, taking me toward my last journey. A journey for which no carriage is needed. Still smiling, I look through the little window.

"Farewell, Paris."

EPILOGUE

BY ROMAIN VIENNE

I had not seen Marie for two months when I was required to leave unexpectedly for Normandy, following the death of my mother. I pondered as to Marie's motive for not recording my visit, for upon my return to Paris on October 20th, I had visited her. It was a month before everyone else had discovered the truth about her illness or her *little secret* as she used to call it. Most likely she did not remember me being there, as the strong drugs she was taking made her forget things and behave bizarrely.

When I had gone to see her the evening after my return, without having warned her, I found her lying in bed, leaning back on her pillows, looking very frail and bored. My visit was very agreeable to her, for as soon as she saw me some color came into her cheeks. Her sudden animation made me believe that she suffered only from a slight and momentary indisposition. I let her reproach me for my absence and, in return, I lectured her. She spoke to me with volubility, saying she was well enough to get up and go out with me. I could stop her only by promising to stay with her for a couple of hours.

Then suddenly, her mood darkened. She began complaining about her lovers and how every one of them, including her friends, had abandoned her. She spoke wildly about her German doctor, who she accused of poisoning her. Then without transition, she jumped to detail her plans for the future, then again cursed her lovers, especially Edouard de Perregaux, who she said she hated more than ever. When I asked why she hated him that much, she only said it was a matter of the past now and she should hate to think more about him. On the other hand, she continued cursing him...

I told her that it was the morphine talking through her mouth and she should give herself a moment's rest. But my words produced the opposite effect I was hoping for, and she ranted even more. Her harangue embarrassed me, for I have never seen Marie like this—she who was so sweet and good, who never had a bad word for anyone. So, I raised from my chair, pretending to leave, and that brought about a swift change in her conduct. She became sweet and cheerful, and now wanted me to talk about her sister. She commissioned me to ask Delphine for forgiveness in her name and to tell her that she had been wise in choosing a modest, respectable life for herself.

"She has done a thousand times better by staying in the village," she said, with an awful expression of melancholy in her swollen eyes. "How much happier she is... and how misguided I was to have tried to persuade her to live a life like mine."

As she uttered these last words, I looked at my watch and saw it was already ten o'clock. She began to laugh at my astonishment. I told her I had to leave for Normandy the next day.

"Now, I'll be able to sleep, our conversation revived me," she had said. "It seems to me that I am no longer sick. Will you come tomorrow morning to say good-bye, while I take my bath at eleven o'clock?"

"Impossible, I have an important lunch meeting," I replied.

"When will you come back?"

"In two months – three at the most."

"Will you promise to visit me first thing?"

"I promise you, Marie, from my heart." And shaking her hand with the conviction that I would see her again in January, I took my leave.

I had not returned to Paris until February, that is to say, four months after our last meeting. Some of my friends were waiting for my arrival, and after dinner we took a stroll on the Boulevard de la Madeleine. On the way, I placed on the table of Marie's concierge, who unfortunately was absent at that moment, a letter thus conceived:

Tuesday, February 1, 1847
Please tell Madame Duplessis to reserve me an hour
for the evening of Thursday; I will arrive at eight o'clock.
Romain Vienne

At the specified hour, on February 3, I rang the bell to Marie's door. I had barely entered, when Clotilde coldly announced, "Monsieur, Madame is dead."

I glared at the stupid maid. "Come now, Clotilde, why this morbid joke?"

"Unfortunately, Monsieur, it's the sad truth. Follow me."

I found myself following Clotilde through the dining room, still asking myself if what she said was true. She opened the bedroom door, which was draped in black and lit by candles. A young priest was praying by the fireplace; the coffin was placed on the right under the window, raised on two trestles. *So, it is true*, I thought, shaken by one of those horrible sensations the memory can never quite forget.

"I knew you were coming, Monsieur," said the priest, "and I thought you'd like to see her one last time; that is why I did not screw the lid."

But I could not reply. I just stood there as if struck by a bolt from above. Clotilde removed the cloth and lifted the lid. I am not superstitious, but there's nothing more hideous than the sight of death. I pulled the shroud aside and when I saw that poor girl of only twenty-three years, whom I thought of as very much alive, lying in that coffin, I was overwhelmed by a fit of indescribable anguish.

Her hands held a bouquet of camellias in the midst of which was a crucifix... her coffin was filled with camellias. With both hands I gently lifted her head and after stroking her forehead and temples, I opened her lips and half-closed eyelids. Her hair was loose and uncombed. I divided the long tresses into two and placed one on each side of her body, along her arms. Then I took her icy hands in mine, which were burning, and examined them with such minute attention that Clotilde could not stop herself from shuddering. None of my actions escaped her.

The priest, moved by an instinctive curiosity, got up to see what I was doing. Motionless and silent, they both looked at me with bewildered surprise. I asked Clotilde to fetch me a pair of scissors and continued my examination. A cloud suddenly passed in front of my eyes; a cold sweat broke out on my forehead; a terrified emotion strangled me, and I felt I was going to faint. Barely managing to lower the lid, I rushed into the dining room, where I fell into an armchair.

When I regained my composure, Clotilde was standing in front of me holding a pair of scissors.

"I brought you, Monsieur, what you asked me."

"Oh no, I do not have the strength to do it. Please, Clotilde, cut a lock of her hair in my stead."

Two minutes later, the maid returned holding what I had asked for.

"Here, Monsieur," she said.

"That's good. Thank you," I said, taking the lock and placing it in my coat's pocket. "Clotilde, when did Marie die?"

"This morning, a little before three o'clock."

"And it did not cross your mind, since three o'clock, to report it to me?"

"No Monsieur."

My sadness was now replaced by anger. "You received my letter on Tuesday evening; what is the reason that prevented you from telling me?"

"I did not receive your letter; it is Monsieur R., the bailiffs' representative, to whom all documents must be handed over."

"Is that so?"

"Yes, Monsieur."

I could not look at her face one moment longer without saying something I would have later regretted, so I made my way out of the house.

I had scarcely set foot on the pavement, when I was greeted very politely by Marie's coachman, Etienne.

"Good evening, Monsieur Vienne," he started. "I knew you were coming, and I've been here since seven o'clock."

"Ah, it is you, Monsieur Etienne. Did you wish to speak to me?"

"Yes, and at length. Would you allow me to accompany you a hundred paces from here?"

"By all means," I said.

We entered a café and sat at a table near the window.

"You can speak freely, Monsieur Etienne," I said. He

nodded, and looking through the window into a faraway distance, he said, "I am deeply sorry that I was not given your address...you could have consoled the dear lady in her last moments, and she could have confided her last wishes to you. But Clotilde did not want this. I believe I will not be telling you something you don't know if I say that she does not like you."

"Nothing truer. She thought I should have visited Marie more often. And when I did, it was always as a friend, not a protector, so I never tipped her maid. That's why she hates me."

"That's it, Monsieur Vienne, that's exactly it."

We both paused, lost in thoughts. It felt as if talking about Marie, still fresh in her coffin, made her presence felt right there at our table.

"They all have abandoned her," Etienne says, breaking the silence. "All but that poor Monsieur Edouard. And yet, he was the only one banned from the bedroom of her for whom he wept. From September, the time the poor man returned to Paris from the countryside, he came almost every day and rang her doorbell, but each time was forbidden entrance. I never understood why. He loved her, despite everything, as much as in the beginning. In utter distress and desperate to learn how much time she had left, he had begged Clotilde to smuggle out for him one of Marie's flannel vests, so he could take to a psychic to interpret."

"My God, how sad...how desperate..." I whispered.

"*Go quickly to her*, the psychic had said to Monsieur Edouard. *She has no more than a few hours to live*. Actually, she had two days left. But still she forbade his entrance."

"And Olympe?" I asked.

"Beside Edouard, Olympe was the only one who had stayed with her 'til the end. He helped her as he could, but she was beyond all help. On Madame's twenty-third birthday, January 15, the bailiffs stormed into her apartment. Madame was in bed, frail and indisposed, to put it mildly. I looked at her as she listened to the bailiffs' voices making an inventory of contents. The furniture was being moved, and it made a terrible sound. Count Olympe was with her. He wrote a check for a thousand francs and sent the bailiffs on their way. But several days later they returned like hungry ravens and started moving the furniture again.

The Count wanted to help again, but this time Madame had told him: *There's no point, my friend. I am crushed by debts and my creditors are pursuing me relentlessly, which means that my end is near. Let them ruin me to the point of destitution. If I don't die, then I will learn from this lesson.*

The poor young man left in tears. He went home and asked his mother for help, for he was still a minor. His mother listened to him, and every other thought disappeared in the face of death. She told her lawyers to see to it and paid the dying girl's debts. Then, forty-eight hours before she died, Monsieur Olympe came again. She still recognized him. She took his hand and said: *You've come to see me. Adieu, I'm going away now.* So distraught the poor man was that he said he will never again celebrate his birthday. You see, Madame died right on his birthday."

I was shaken by what I was hearing. My throat contracted with bitter tears. But I was too proud to show them and tried to avert Etienne's attention away at all costs.

"What about the Count?" I asked.

"Count von Stackelberg?"

"Him, indeed."

"A miserable old screw. When you're as old as the medieval plague, what's the point of economizing? As soon as he realized that she was dying, he completely abandoned her."

The guilt I felt at not having had come earlier, forced me again into silence. I was in Paris two days before Marie died. Why hadn't I come then?

"She was alone during her last hours. And very frightened. Only I was there, with Clotilde and the priest," Etienne continued as if having heard my thoughts. "*Oh, I'm dying!* Madame cried, grabbing Clotilde's hand. *I want you to bury me yourself. Do not declare my death straight away so that I can stay here longer in my house. And what if I'll come back to life? I want you to put a very weak bolt on my coffin. This is the most important thing of all,* she begged her maid. And her cries...Monsieur Vienne...her cries were the worst. And then it all became worse. When the death-rattle began, she made the strangest exclamations. The poor Madame, who had never spoken of affairs of state, cried out three times, an hour before her death, a pronouncement so very baffling for this era..."

"What was it?" I asked, perplexed.

"I will not reproduce because it is impossible even if certified as true... Then it was all over. She was still squeezing Clotilde's hand when she passed, so hard that it was almost impossible to disengage the hand of the living from that of the dead. The maid closed her eyes and kissed her on the forehead. Then she dressed her as she had asked her to, and put her in her shroud..."

Tears filled Etienne's eyes, and I was happy to see how much he loved his mistress.

"This morning," he continued, "an hour after her death, three men came into her bedroom. One of them was Edouard. He knelt by her bed and began praying. His sobs were as heart-wrenching as were Madame's. The two others searched through all the drawers in all the chests. Clotilde helped them. They took letters and papers, but they did not find the important one they were looking for, a document in English..."

"Their marriage certificate..." I whispered.

"It was then that I managed to take this and hide it," he said, placing his hand in his coat's pocket and retrieving a letter-bound notebook. "I thought you should have it, Monsieur Vienne, since you were her oldest friend."

"What is it?" I asked, looking at the object the coachman placed on the table in front of me.

"Madame's diary," he replied. "She liked to write down her thoughts and reminiscences. I couldn't bring myself to read but a few pages. Alas, it is too sad for me."

My astonishment at this surprising revelation made me stare unblinkingly at the notebook. With a trembling hand, I opened its cover and read the first words Marie committed to paper.

"I have loved sincerely, but no one ever returned my love. That is the real horror of my life."

My astonishment made way for a harrowing sadness and I could no longer retain my tears. I thanked Etienne for imparting with me Marie's last moments, as well as her treasured diary, and went on my way.

TWO DAYS LATER, on February 5, the funeral carriage carried the coffin covered with several white wreaths to the church of the Madeleine, which was across from Marie's house. She wanted to be taken there, as it was her consolation place in her last months. A gathering of mournful people awaited our arrival and it was a sad image to see.

The same gathering followed the catafalque to Montmartre cemetery. I was right behind it, with Edouard next to me, and Count Olympe at a close distance behind us. Aside from the incredulous happening I was part of, I could not help but be saddened further by Monsieur Edouard's bitter tears. I could hear him sob and see his swollen, blood-shot eyes. Never in my life had I been witness to such display of hopelessness and anguish.

Other people were waiting at the cemetery and after the coffin had been lowered into the pit, I saw women crying on the tomb. They had come to say goodbye to the one who had been so good to them. These were the destitute or fallen women for whom Marie went out of her way to help with either money or good advice. But I saw someone else there, and it shook me. It was the Vital couple, the distant cousins with whom Marie stayed upon her arrival in Paris. The people who had thrown the poor young woman into the street, and thus into the hands of her first protector. They were responsible for Marie's fate as much as she was.

I was happy to see them there, that is until Madame Vital spoke. "I have come to pardon her," she said. I had turned away, just in time for my words to remain contained. *I should chase you away like the vermin you are,* escaped my lips only in my imagination.

Kneeling at the gravesite Edouard looked more and more pale. The priest saw him, and being afraid that he will faint, handed him the holy water sprinkle. One by one, we retired, leaving the grieving lover alone by the grave.

A WEEK LATER, Marie's sister Delphine, arrived in Paris with her husband. I myself took them to the cemetery, but as we reached the place where Marie was buried a week before, we were greeted by an astonishing sight. The grave had disappeared, leaving behind only a pile of dirt. Flabbergasted, I went to search for the concierge, but ran into the cemetery gardener, who guided us to Marie's new resting place. Pressed by my further inquiries, the gardener let out that some Monsieur Count de Perregaux had bought the vault we were now standing near.

"It was the strangest thing, Monsieur," the gardener had said. "The Count lifted the casket's lid and talked to the dead for several hours before surrendering her again to the sepulchral worms."

I looked at Delphine, who had begun crying, staring at the engraving on her sister's tomb.

Alphonsine Plessis
Born 15 January 1824
Died 3 February 1847
De Profundis

Two weeks after Marie's death, her house opened for auction. All of Marie's belongings, including her furniture, paintings, books, dresses, jewels, even her enema apparatus, were to be auctioned. Marie's debts, still accumulating during her last weeks of life had now to be paid. The amount of 21.000 francs still owed was easily covered from the total profit of 89.017 francs. The rest went to her sister, Delphine.

In the four-day sale, almost all of Paris had crossed the door to Marie's former dwelling. Some were collectors with an eye for rare things. Others, society ladies especially, were there out of simple curiosity. They went through the poor girl's stuff with the disdain of those who would place themselves above those of Marie's kind. Even though embarrassed to be in such a place, the ladies nonetheless snooped around with greed, then made the sign of the cross upon exiting. It was a show of mockery, cant, and deepest hypocrisy.

Some were admirers, eager to acquire some item that once belonged to the famous courtesan; while others, those who knew her, were drawn by personal memories, by the melancholy of loss.

One such person was Alexandre Dumas. I saw him sitting at Marie's dining table, lost in thoughts. No doubt memories of the departed, once sitting at that very same table across from him, replayed in his mind. Later that night, he wrote an elegy, which he then published in the paper for which he worked. "I cried when I wrote it, and I cried on reading it," he said. But it was a different work that he wrote, and which was to make Marie, as well as himself, immortal. *The Lady of the Camellias* became an instant success. Just as it was with the interest the auction raised among Parisians, the novel too, was a further glimpse into the life of one of the most fascinating beings our era had seen. Later, Dumas turned his novel into a play and it became a theatrical phenomenon, turning both the author and his heroine into legends.

Later still, after attending the play of *The Lady of the Camellias*, Giuseppe Verdi gave birth to *La Traviata*. Six years later, at the premiere of the opera in Venice, thousands fell in love with a girl so wild yet so kind, so capricious yet so generous, a girl I knew and had the honor of calling *friend*.

All of this was somewhat strange to me. I had shared so many hours, as well as secrets, with the one that was now being turned into a myth. The memories of her incessant talk and laughter and exquisitely elegant gait, still so very vivid in my mind, could never have made me picture her as a character in a book or play or opera.

But the most startling thing, perhaps the strangest thing of all, was yet to come.

One late afternoon in 1869, twenty-two years after

Marie's death, I was visited by her sister. Filled with curiosity upon seeing her distraught expression, I pressed her for the cause of her torment.

"A young man in his late twenties just left my house. I ran here to see you, for you are the only one who might know," she said breathlessly, tears already forming in her big dark eyes. I pressed her further, for by now I was almost mad with curiosity. "He asked to see a portrait of my sister. I gave what he had asked, and he looked at it for a long time in silence, with visible emotion and not managing to hide his tears. He then thanked me and greeting me graciously, went on his way. Good God, Monsieur Vienne, how like my sister he was!"

Only rarely have I been so utterly reduced to silence.

"Who was he?" Delphine pressed. "Could he be? Is it possible? You knew Marie best. Please tell me, even if it were the last thing you ever said to me."

My eyes fixed the ground, while my thoughts began searching through memories. I remembered asking Marie if she had requested the proof of her son's death certificate from his father, Monsieur Viscount de Méril. She said she had not. Taking Delphine's hands in mine and asking her to sit, I resolved to tell her everything.

As for myself? Exactly one year after Marie died, the government of Louis-Philippe d'Orléans fell. France was swollen by revolution and Paris became unrecognizable. I have always wondered if Marie's political prediction upon her death had been about this. To satisfy my curiosity, I even went to search for Etienne, but he never could be found.

As our country plunged into economic crisis, rumors of the discovery of gold in California became more and more believable. Thousands of French emigrants left their country for the dream of the New World.

I was one of them. My meandering across America kept me away from my beloved home for almost a decade. At one point, I was even reported missing by my peers, when rumors of cholera among the French emigrants reached their ears. But my roots proved stronger and finally, in 1858, I returned home. Settling in my hometown of Nonant, I had become a local racing journalist. Four years later, a short while after I turned forty-six years old, I finally decided I should enter the world of matrimony. My wife, a tall young beauty of twenty-three, with long raven hair and dark charcoal eyes, had proved a solace to the end.

Her name? Alphonsine.

BIBLIOGRAPHY

Primary Sources:
- Julie Kavanagh, (2014). *The Girl Who Loved Camellias: The Life and Legend of Marie Duplessis.* Vintage; Reprint edition
- Romain Vienne, (1888) *La vérité sur la Dame aux Camélias, Marie Duplessis*, 2nd edition, Paris, Paul Ollendorff, Editeur

Secondary Sources:
- Rounding Virginia, (2003). *Grandes Horizontales, The lives and Legends of Four Nineteen-Century Courtesans*, Bloomsbury Publishing Plc., London
- René Weis, (2019). *The Real Traviata: The Song of Marie Duplessis.* Oxford University Press; Reprint edition
- Baedeker, Karl (1884). *Paris and environs: with routes from London to Paris and from Paris to the Rhine and Switzerland*, Eighth revised edition, Leipzig
- Ballon, Hilary (1991). *The Paris of Henri IV: Architecture and Urbanism.* Cambridge, Massachusetts: The MIT Press

- Cotolendi, Charles (1701). *Saint-Evremoniana: Ou Receuil de diverses piéces curieuses*. Amsterdam: Pierre Mortier

- Evans, Henry Ridgely (1909). *The Old and the New Magic*. Chicago: The Open Court Publishing Co

- Fournier Édouard (1862). *Histoire du Pont-Neuf*. Paris: E. Dentu. Vol. 1 and vol. 2

- Lacroix, Paul (1858). *Curiosités de l'histoire du vieux Paris*. Paris: Adolphe Delahays

- *Lasteyrie, R. de* (1882). *Mémoires de la Société de l'Histoire de Paris et de l'Ile de France, vol. 9*

- Metman, Yves, editor (1987). *Le Registre ou plumitif de la construction du Pont Neuf: archives nationales Z1f 1065*. Paris: Service des travaux historiques de la Ville de Paris

- Strohmayer, Ulf (2007) *The City and the Senses: Urban Culture since 1500*, edited by A. Cowan and J. Steward. Basingstoke: Ashgate

- Whitney, Charles S. ([1929]; reprint 2003). *Bridges of the World: Their Design and Construction*. Mineola, New York: Dover Publications.

ABOUT THE AUTHOR

A. G. MOGAN has always loved history and the personalities that were born of bygone eras. Her interest for the world and its people fueled her passion for human analytics. She's used her knowledge to analyze people and their behavior throughout her adult career, including using her in-depth research to craft poignant biographical novels that readers eagerly devour.

When not studying great historical figures or long-lost stories from the past, she can be found at her home in Europe, enjoying the spoils of a wonderfully ordinary family life.

To learn more, please visit the author's website at
www.AGMogan.com

ALSO BY A. G. MOGAN

HISTORICAL/BIOGRAPHICAL FICTION:

- *The Secret Journals of Adolf Hitler*

  The Anointed - Volume 1

  The Struggle - Volume 2

- Stalin's Sniper: *The War Diary of Roza Shanina*

NONFICTION:

- *Love on Triple W: A Heartbreaking True Story About Love, Betrayal, and Survival*
- *Humorous History: An Illustrated Collection of Wit and Irony from the Past*
- *Tragic History: A Collection of Some of the Most Catastrophic Events in Human History*

THANK YOU!

Thank you for purchasing this book! It means the world to me. If you enjoyed reading it, or otherwise found it entertaining, kindly leave a short review on Amazon. That helps me tremendously.

A. G. Mogan